CAN LOVE SURVIVE ANYTHING?

Thomas is torn between saving a past love and protecting the woman in his present. Traveling to Africa to save his wife's life, he leaves his ménage unprotected against political forces that will stop at nothing to destroy the black ops organization he works for—even if it means attacking women and children.

On the day she thought her greatest challenge was going to be interviewing nannies, Celia finds herself chased by thugs. In order to survive she must evolve from Kitten to Tigress to protect not only her unborn, but also Thomas's four young children.

On the run and without either Master or Lord Fyre to protect her, the question is where Celia's journey will end.

Content Warning: BDSM during pregnancy, lactation play, MMF

CRIES OF PENANCE

The Chronicles of Surrender Book Five

By
Roxy Harte

Lyrical Press, Inc.
New York

Lyrical Press, Incorporated

Cries of Penance
13 Digit ISBN: 9781616502478
Copyright © 2010, Roxy Harte
Edited by Pamela Tyner
Book design by Renee Rocco
Cover Art by Renee Rocco

Lyrical Press, Incorporated
337 Katan Avenue
Staten Island, New York 10308
http://www.lyricalpress.com

All Rights Are Reserved. No part of this book may be used or reproduced in any manner whatsoever without written permission, except in the case of brief quotations embodied in critical articles and reviews. The unauthorized reproduction or distribution of this copyrighted work is illegal. No part of this book may be scanned, uploaded or distributed via the Internet or any other means, electronic or print, without the publisher's permission.

PUBLISHER'S NOTE:
This book is a work of fiction. The names, characters, places, and incidents are products of the writer's imagination or have been used fictitiously and are not to be construed as real. Any resemblance to persons, living or dead, actual events, locale or organizations is entirely coincidental.

The publisher does not have any control over and does not assume any responsibility for author or third-party Web sites or their content.

Published in the United States of America by Lyrical Press, Incorporated

First Lyrical Press, Inc electronic publication: September 2010
First Lyrical Press, Inc print publication: December 2010

DEDICATION

To Blackie

My beautiful black cat walked into my life fifteen years ago, no bigger than the palm of my hand...and while I was editing this book he walked away.

Always independent.

I will never forget our late night walks.

I will miss you.

"Faith is the strength by which a shattered world shall emerge into the light."

Helen Keller

CHAPTER 1

KITTEN

San Francisco

The air is warm and seems to shimmer with expectancy as Master climbs from the limo. I follow, exiting gracefully, well-practiced, hands first, long stretch onto the pavement, stepping, hand, hand, knee, knee, making sure that each long-armed stretch is provocative, each knee forward wiggles my ass just so.

A plastic banner ripples in the cool night air: *LEWD LARRY'S SLAVE AUCTION TONIGHT.* It's the seventh annual charity event that my Master, Garrett Lawrence, has orchestrated. Of course, he is dressed to the nines—tux, bow tie, white silk shirt—and dazzling. He turns every head as he makes his way past the line, which wraps around the block. I know it certainly isn't the naked and painted feline, trailing on hands and knees at his heel that draws the attention, though I hear plenty of gasps as I make my way to the front doors.

"My God, she's pregnant!"

"Do you think that's why Lord Fyre went away?"

Lord Fyre, Lord Fyre, Lord Fyre. God, I miss him. A foghorn rises above the night sounds, traffic, people, and a sad saxophone, and I am comforted by its sound, remembering another evening I heard it, the night I was purchased by the boss and made headlines. That night I'd felt alone on this sidewalk, the only person in the world to ever stand in my shoes, making a commitment to be auctioned. Boy, was I wrong!

Lewd Larry's Slave Auction is a big deal, then and now. Slaves from a dozen different states, not just the small burg of San Francisco, are here to be auctioned. As far as the BDSM world goes, this is *the event* of the year.

I shouldn't admit that I'd have rather stayed home tonight…especially after Master tried so hard to make this a special night. I wanted to camouflage the fact I'm expecting, but there's no hope in that. Pregnant with twins, it seems my girth gets greater by the minute. I wanted to be sexy, but I suppose there's no hope in that either.

It took hours for the body paint artist to work his magic, painting me from head to toe to resemble a calico cat, complete with long, gracefully soft whiskers shooting out from my upper lip.

"See! She's still wearing both Master's collars. I'm telling you, Lord Fyre will be back."

"You didn't see the blonde he was here with. Oo-la-la. Hot does not begin to describe that one."

He is not with Eva!

I want to yell and scream and shout it to the rooftops that my other Master did not leave me for another woman. He's coming back. I know he is. I just can't tell anyone anything about what is going on because the truth could get him killed. No one needs to know that he is a secret agent. No one needs to know that he's on assignment. As long as I know the truth, that's all that matters—right?

I focus on my crawl. *Hand, hand, knee, knee.* Master holds open the door for me and it's better when we get inside. Not because it's quieter, just the opposite. The music is eardrum shattering loud. Perfect. I can't hear what anyone is saying as I crawl the long length of the dance club to the glass elevator in the back.

We ride to the third floor, leaving the noise behind the closed doors. Our gazes meet in the intimate enclosure. Master asks, "Are you okay?"

"Meow-meow." *Yes.*

"I know this is hard on you. Every night. I hear them too, Kitten. I don't want you to think I don't. But we know the truth. It's going to be okay, we're going to be okay until he returns to us."

I nod, fighting back tears. I try to be strong in front of Master. I don't ever want him to think he's not Master enough for me, but that doesn't mean I miss my other Master less.

As the elevator opens onto The Oasis, our member's only level, I am relieved. *I'm home.* My kitty pillow is here and my bowl and my litter box. Here I can be myself more than anywhere else in the world. This is my domain. This is where Kitten belongs.

"Will you be all right alone?" Master asks.

"Meow-meow." I don't know why he's so worried. I only know it's a relief when he descends again, back to the public arena, leaving me alone. I crawl—hand, hand, knee, knee—to my cushion, placed front row and center to the stage below for tonight's event.

As the soundproof glass slides back to open up The Oasis to the full sensory overload of the lower level, the sounds of an impatient crowd floods our normally serene room. The music is too loud and the crowd rampant. Stomping, clapping, chanting, "Lewd Larry, Lewd Larry,

Lewd Larry!"

It is obvious when they have him in their sight. The magnitude of sound doubles. They are screaming for *my* Master. Male and female alike squeal, because gender isn't an issue. It only matters that he is beloved by the masses, the most notorious Dominant west of the Mississippi. My Master.

With theatrical flare, the lights dim suddenly and a spotlight points center stage. Master strides into view, his broad smile and easygoing nature drawing the crowd closer. Hoots and hollers follow his every move.

I don't yell or shriek. He's mine. I get to go home with him, and that truth makes me lift my chin a little smugly. Whereas the crowd can only imagine if the bulge in his tightly tailored slacks is all man or a wad of socks, I know for a fact he is well-endowed. And yes, the muscles in his thighs and ass really are *all that*.

"Well, aren't you just looking like the pussy who licked up all the cream?"

I smile broadly, turning to face Master's best friend, Jackie, the one and only person on the planet who gets to call me pussy. I bounce excitedly, looking up at her. It's a long way *up*. She is well over six-and-a-half feet tall, probably closer to seven feet in her platform stilettos, and it's fairly obvious by her overall size that once upon a time she was a man. She has very real cleavage now, though. It puts me to shame at any rate. Although with my pregnancy, for the first time in my life I can actually say I have boobs.

I'm not nearly as excited about that fact as I thought I'd be.

Probably because of the job breasts perform: nursing infants. I know that Master and Jackie, and the support group I have at the Primal Birth Center, are trying to be helpful, reassuring even, but their thoughts and feelings and suggested reading material about breast feeding is not appreciated. I'm really not interested in nursing my babies…and that makes me feel guilty. I guess I was hoping my breasts wouldn't grow, wouldn't *work*, and then I wouldn't have to consider doing it.

Jackie pats her knees for me to climb into her lap.

"Meow." *No, as in this is such a bad idea.* I point at the paint covering my body.

"I don't think it will rub off, child, and so what if it does? You climb up here and give Jackie some pregnant kitty love."

I smile, unable to help myself. Jackie is more excited about these babies than anyone.

She helps me to get comfortable, and we both watch transfixed as Master takes charge of the auction. *This* is a big deal. Men and women are auctioned at this annual event that is attended by the wealthy and famous. The event supports many charities near and dear to the hearts of Hollywood's biggest and brightest, lending to rock-concert level pandemonium and paparazzi everywhere.

The large stage is brightly lit and a theater-size screen behind televises in close-up every reaction larger than life, every smile, every frown, every tear magnified so that the crowd doesn't miss a thing. The slaves come from every walk of life, some experienced, some with no experience at all. On the big screen the personalities are the focal point whether shy or outgoing, embarrassed or proud. And their physical attributes…some a little sexier because of the wide-angled close-ups and some…not so pretty.

They all get bought, and not for spare change. Thousands of dollars. Tens of thousands of dollars. No one has ever sold for more than my purchase price though—a quarter of a million dollars—unheard of before or since. Sitting here, watching, is a different perspective for me and one that never gets boring. From my position I can see the bidding as it happens. I have seen sheiks, celebrities, and politicians place bids. I have also seen some fairly average Joe's walk out with beautiful property. I always worry a little when the bidder is overly old and the slave bid on overly young. Something inside me shrieks a little, I couldn't imagine going home with someone's grandfather...or great-grandfather. I feel a little guilty, knowing I got the cream of the crop. I got *Master*.

Between slaves, the stage darkens and a spotlight flies over the crowd.

Looking at Jackie's program I see that a hundred slaves will be auctioned tonight. It's going to be a *long* evening.

Thankfully, the night becomes punctuated by *moments*.

Slave number twenty is Bernard, the pudgy, slightly balding ex-pet of Jackie. I see that she's trying to not pay attention as he crawls the semi-circular stage, shaking his tail. He pauses center stage and barks playfully. Jackie sighs heavily but doesn't bid, not a single penny, though I think she might have wanted to.

Slave number forty-three is dragged center stage by her leash and there is much simpering and crying before it is determined that she has chickened out. Her Master isn't pleased but *oh, well*. The slave really does have all the power on that stage. "I don't want to do it" doesn't require a safe word.

It is slave number sixty-eight that makes my breath catch. I lean forward in Jackie's lap, watching intently. She is tall, thin, and not even an A-cup on a good day. Her hair is cut short, her eyes are as big as saucers, and she looks scared shitless, but when she is asked to make the semi-circle walk she lifts her chin bravely and walks. She could be me two years ago. I watch her, holding my breath. I sneak a peek at Master to see his reaction to her, but he barely takes a second glance at her. My heart pounds so hard against my chest, it is painful. The bidding is fast and furious but never goes over seventy thousand. I suck in a deep breath, wondering what I expected. Did I think Master would bid on her? Did I think her going price would reach two hundred and fifty grand?

Chuckling with an odd relief, I settle back against Jackie. I hope she didn't notice my interest, but knowing her as well as I do, she didn't miss it. She says, "She was pretty."

"Not *that* pretty." Too late I remember I'm in The Oasis and I spoke. I climb out of her lap and settle into the middle of my cushion.

"Are you okay?"

"Meow-meow."

"She isn't as pretty as you."

"Meow-mee-ooow." I hope my tone lets her know I think she is. I blink at her, wanting to ask something, but not knowing exactly what it is I want to know.

"No one will ever get as high a bid as you, Kitten."

I sigh, unable to fit *why* into meows. *Why would anyone keep bidding to get the bid so high? Who was bidding against Master?* To this day I don't know the answer.

I watch him commanding the stage and know the second he searches the upper levels for me. I crawl forward and press my face against the glass. Seeing me, he flashes me a thousand-watt smile and blows me a kiss. Ducking, I blush.

"I wish I had a camera so I could show you just how beautiful you are. God, Kitten. *You are stunning.*" Jackie ruffles my hair.

I don't take my eyes off Master. So many numbers later, he *finally* leaves the stage. I lick my lips when I lose sight of him, waiting, waiting, until seconds later I see him again as he crosses the back of the dance floor and enters the elevator. Turning, he meets my gaze. I smile, crawling as I keep watching him, as he keeps watching me.

I'm waiting at the elevator doors when they slide open. He doesn't step out so I crawl in to join him. The elevator doors close. "I'd really like to take you home right this minute."

I crawl around his legs, pressing against his trousers. "Meow-meow."

"It's the busiest night of the whole damn year. You understand I have to be here, don't you? There are a lot of very important people here tonight."

I lay down, stretching, rolling my back against the floor so that he is faced with tits and baby belly. I bend my knees, letting them fall open so he can see just how good of a job the artist did painting me. My labia is four distinct colors—white, gold, orange, and brown.

When I meet his gaze again, the smile is gone. Anyone looking at him would believe he is very angry, but I know his face better than everybody. I know his expressions, his moods. He lusts me. I smile and roll back up to sit, then reposition onto all fours, waiting for the elevator to open, hoping he's still interested in a few hours when it's finally time to leave.

The elevator doors don't open. Behind me, I hear Master making a call on his cell. "I need you to cover for me."

I decide he is talking to George Kirkpatrick, his Number One.

"I'm taking Kitten home, it has been a long night for her."

I glance over my shoulder, see his lust and am immediately okay with the fact he is using me as an excuse to ditch out early. Turning my head back around to face the elevator doors, I try to not look smug as he makes two more calls, one to his security team leader and one to our chauffer. By the time he finally opens the doors, everything is in readiness for us to leave. He leads me through The Oasis to the back service corridor. He keeps walking, I keep crawling...down the long corridor all the way to the service elevator. We take it down to the ground level alley where the car is waiting.

Master helps me into the back seat and slides in next to me. The car isn't prewarmed, there wasn't time. I shiver and Master pulls me close, into the V of his thighs. I relax against his chest, and his arms close around me.

"Mmmm, purrrrrrr."

"Yes, this is very nice," he murmurs against my hair. "Do you know how badly I've wanted you all night?"

I shake my head.

"Maybe it's the auction. It always brings that night back to me, the night I bought you."

I smile, because I've been remembering it too.

His hands slide over my belly. "That night, I never dreamed we'd be here, *like this.*"

I roll my head so that I can look at his face.

"I'm happy, Kitten. Really happy. I know I don't tell you that often enough or how important you are to me. I should tell you every day."

I lift my face, pushing my mouth nearer, and he lowers his lips but the kiss doesn't quite work. We have to shift and resettle to make it work, but then we are kissing and all the questions and worries and thoughts I've had just disappear. That's what Master does to me. *Nothing else matters.*

His fingers are warm and silky smooth as they glide over my skin. He tweaks a nipple before sliding lower. He dips his fingers between my thighs and teases lightly over my labia. "I like the paint tonight."

I smile.

"You are so very sexy."

I press my lips to his neck, directly over his pulse.

"We should take pictures and send them to Thomas's email."

I go still against him. I don't want to think about Thomas, my Lord

Fyre and other Master. Not *now*. I only want to think about Master. I roll in his embrace, going onto my knees to face him. With practiced fingers I undo his bow tie, leaving the ends hanging on either side of his neck. I unbutton his shirt and kiss my way down his chest and belly as his skin is revealed. Reaching the waistband of his slacks, I unbelt, unsnap, unzip him…push down the elastic edge of his black briefs…his erection springs free, obviously very hard. I smile, meeting his gaze, and lower my mouth to tease him with kisses before actually licking his length. I swirl my tongue in circles around the head before taking any length into my mouth. I allow my saliva to collect so that when I do slide him in and out there is a slickness for him to glide against.

"Kitten." He sighs and when I look I see his eyes have closed.

He's told me often enough that I do this well, so I don't doubt my ability as I knead his thighs with my fingers, a little pain, a little distraction from the pleasure I'm giving him. His eyelids slit barely open, but enough for me to know he's watching me.

I bite, making him moan. If I didn't have his undivided attention before, I most certainly do now. The thought makes me smile. Withdrawing his length, I graze him slowly between my teeth, then lick him like a lollipop, up, down, side, side, swirl around.

The sweetness of a little escaped pre-cum coats my tongue. I whisper, "You taste good."

I bite again, this time a little harder.

"God, Kitten."

I lap and suck, take in his length and swallow, gagging, knowing he likes the sound when I gag. I make that sound again and again. He's close, very close when he pushes me back. Pouting, I don't understand until he says, "We're here."

With a heavy sigh, I join him on the seat, watching as he zips, snaps, and refastens his belt. He doesn't tuck or button, leaving his shirt open. As soon as the limo pulls up beside the curb, he opens the door, not waiting for the chauffer.

He helps me climb out but prevents me from dropping to my knees to crawl. "I want you. Now."

I imagine having sex with him in the luxurious lobby, the receptionist and doorman looking on, but that isn't what happens. We hurry to the elevator and as soon as the doors close, giving us privacy, we are kissing like sex-starved teenagers. His fingers lace into my hair and controls the kiss, letting it spiral out of control but then reining it back in with a tug, only to let it spiral again.

"I need you, Master," I whisper against his mouth, the kiss not stopping even for the words to fully form.

His hands slide down my back to cup my bare ass. "You do?"

"Yes."

His fingers move lower, prodding as his hands pull apart my ass cheeks to give him access. He finds my slit. "You're very wet, Kitten."

As much as I want him to, he doesn't stop the elevator. We ride all the way up to the penthouse level. Picking me up, he carries me down the short hall to our door and once inside we don't make it to the bedroom. He lays me gently on the sofa, commanding, "Roll onto all fours."

I roll over and position myself on knees and elbows. I automatically drop my head, pressing my cheek to the cushion. I arch my back and lift my ass. Behind me, I can hear him unbuckling and unzipping. I wonder if he will come to me still wearing his clothes or whether he will take the time to undress. The question is answered by the sound of his dropping pants, the belt still in the loops. His jacket falls beside the sofa, and I see he slid out of his shirt and jacket at the same time because the sleeves of both are tangled together.

He slides his fingers down my spine, making me shiver.

"Cold?"

"No, Master."

He slips his fingers along my crack, and the sensation makes me sigh. He finds the slippery slide of my arousal, pushing one finger into me easily.

"Wet?"

"For your pleasure, Master."

He withdraws his finger only to push in again, this time using two fingers. He teases, pumping his fingers in and out of me. I press back, wanting more. *Harder, faster.*

He lightly swats my behind. "Hold your position."

God, oh God. His voice is like warm, smooth bourbon, holding me in place when I would have rather moved. The command pushes through me, making my body react to him in ways it only reacts when he uses his Master-voice. I close my eyes, wanting desperately to move my hips back and forth, but for him I hold still and it is pure, torturous agony as I wait…he pumping me slow and rhythmically…me wanting him to force his fingers deep.

He slides his fingers all the way out, and when he pushes them back in I know he has added a third. He keeps the push and pull aggravatingly slow. I growl with frustration and squeeze my pussy tight, trying to hold his fingers in, trying to force them out, trying, trying, to get what *I* want.

He smacks my hip again, lightly, but there is a slight sting. "That is still considered moving. Relax for me completely. Submit to my will, Kitten."

I force myself to focus on my breath, trying to relax every muscle, but as my focus shifts from what he is doing to my twat, every muscle is tightened. He keeps pushing his fingers into and out of me, slow, slow, slow. I want to scream with frustration, but he's given me a job:

relax. I start with my shoulders, commanding them to relax, following the line of tension down my bicep, relaxing, relaxing. I allow the tension in my upper body to ease out completely, sagging with the relief it gives me, and then I turn my attention to my ass and thighs, allowing them to stop clenching.

"Very good, Kitten, but don't lose the arch." The hand he isn't pumping me with taps my spine where he wants it to drop.

I lift my hips and pull the arch tight, every muscle in my lower back straining to hold the position. Need shoots through my womb white hot. I feel like my spine orgasms the sensation is so great. "God."

"That's good, Kitten. Very good. Hold that for me."

I cry out, the need too great, the pleasure too great. I. Need. To. Move.

I feel the cushions shift as his knees press into them, he is straddling my legs, one knee on the sofa, the other foot still on the ground. I think he will finally give me what I need, I think he will finally thrust into me. I am left disappointed. He slides the fingers out and on the next press in, pushes in all four fingers.

I lose my battle of self-control, pushing back against him. I want more, I need more. I am sharply reprimanded, "Kitten! Do not move."

Oh God, oh God, oh God. I still, it's hard to do, but I do it.

"Do you want me to bind you? Force you to my will?"

We both know it is an empty threat. Until I have the babies, there will be no bondage. No real floggings or canings, or even good old-fashioned spanking.

I relax, letting him pump me with four fingers. I float on the sensation, knowing I will rise no higher, knowing I will not climax. I savor this simple pleasure, because it is what my Master wants me to enjoy.

I drift so well, I do not even realize when he eases the four fingers out and slides his penis in—until he chooses to push deep—deeper than mere fingers can go. My eyes fly open and I gasp, the sensation lifting me up as high as I can go and crashing me back to the earth in one fell swoop.

Grabbing my hips, he thrusts deep again, as deeply as he can thrust. It is still slow and easy, not forceful, just deep. My body responds with the same life-altering climb and plummet.

"God!" I shriek, growl. Primal emotion wraps my chest and squeezes.

He withdraws as my orgasm eases, and with slow methodical pressure fills me again, pushing deeper and deeper. He hits the wall of my insides and something breaks within me, not physically, but emotionally, spiritually. It is like the first night we were together. Exactly like the first night he owned me.

"God! God! God!"

Am I praying for grace?

Am I praying for release?

There is no release. There is only my orgasm, wrapping me, lifting me, dropping me, again and again, at my Master's whim.

"...there are quiet victories and struggles, great sacrifices of self, and noble acts of heroism in it—even in many of its apparent lightnesses and contradictions."

Charles Dickens, *The Battle of Life*

CHAPTER 2

THOMAS

Washington, DC

A wintery mix of rain, sleet, and snow falls simultaneously, my welcome to the capital city. I'm not sure how I managed to land in the taxi with a driver who is capable of cursing in three languages simultaneously, but it's actually comforting he does. Of course traffic is a nightmare, adding further to my tardiness, and if not for the weather I would walk and get to my destination quicker.

Washington DC is a far cry from San Francisco, or more specifically Lewd Larry's, the BDSM fetish fantasy nightclub that has been my home away from home for more than a decade as I've stayed hidden from those who wanted me dead. I'm still hiding, though now I hide in plain sight. Spy. Secret agent. Black ops soldier. Assassin. That's who I am, not what I do, and yesterday that truth dawned very clear in my mind as I left Garrett and Celia, the two I love more than life itself, behind for the call of duty. I cut off my shoulder-length hair and shaved my goatee, put on the black suit, tie, and bright white shirt that will be my uniform for the next—God only knows how many—months, years.

I don't recognize myself in my reflection. *Lex Karros.* My latest alias seems ridiculously contrived, like a Hollywood actor, but is actually more agreeable to my ear than Thomas Stephanopoulos, the name I used in San Francisco. The name my wife knew me by, my children, my lovers...

All except Celia...

Her eyes were closed, her head sagged so that her face rested heavily in my palms, and her tears dripped into my hands. I kissed the top of her head, trying to console her. "I'm sorry I've caused you difficulty with Garrett" but she didn't respond. "I don't know how to fix this. I need your loyalty, I need to know that I can count on you and trust you, but I don't want to ruin things between the two of you." Still, no reaction and I was feeling so frustrated. I was failing her. "No one ever promised you it would be easy serving two Masters."

Finally, she opened her eyes and met my gaze. She said, "Tell me what to do."

"Be good to Garrett. Love him while you're waiting for me." I kissed her, filling her mouth with my tongue, claiming her. Her tears left both our faces drenched. "I. Love. You. With. All. My. Heart. And. All. My. Soul."

"I love you, Lord Fyre. Thomas."

I cringed inwardly. I didn't want the woman I loved so deeply to call me a name I detested so much. I wiped her tears away with my thumbs, as I still cradled her face in my hands, and I told her a truth few knew. "Ari. My real name is Demetres Aristotle Velouchiotis. In private I'd like you to call me Ari."

She repeated my name, "Ari," and made my heart soar.

I don't regret trusting her. Even if someday that trust could get me killed. Hearing her say, "I love you, Ari," was worth everything to me. Taking a deep breath, I linger in the back of the taxi a moment longer and watch ice chips clink against the window.

"Sir?" the driver asks.

"Drive around the block a time or two."

She'd sobbed against my mouth as I caught her lips. She'd begged, "Please don't say goodbye."

I couldn't believe she was still professing doubt after I'd revealed my soul to her. "You carry my child and I have just professed the depth of my love to you, I will never ever tell you goodbye. You are my heart. I could not live if I didn't have your strength to hold me together."

It was the night I'd learned she carries my twins, and now I've left her.

As the taxi pulls back into traffic, I allow myself the luxury of a daydream. I imagine Garrett and Celia still sleeping and wrapped in each other's arms. I doubt that is the truth of it. More likely, Celia was so distraught over my leaving, Garrett had to restrain her. Under normal circumstances, I would think she might be locked in a body conforming cage she finds most comforting but since her pregnancy there is not enough room to contain her belly.

I expect Garrett to hold together the pieces until I return, knowing it may be years before I am able to. The question worrying me is whether I will be welcomed back into their arms when I do come home to them.

I know they can't understand. They couldn't possibly. I think only another soldier could understand the things that make me tick: danger, duty, honor, loyalty. And though the duty I rushed across the country to fulfill has little challenge and only a miniscule amount of danger, it does have everything to do with loyalty and honor.

I trust Garrett to honor our ménage. To keep both his and her love for me alive while I am away and to raise my sons to know me even though they may have to wait years to meet me.

I called them from the airport to let them know I arrived safely, and Garrett assured me they would be fine. I reassured him I would keep in touch and didn't ask to talk to Celia. I know my strengths. I know my weaknesses and for Celia I would turn my back on everything else. My sense of duty is strong but my loyalty to family is stronger, and so I dare not tempt myself with the possibility that there could be any escape from this assignment. There is too much at stake.

A glance through the window proves snow is now falling in earnest, large flakes that are quickly covering the pavement and sidewalks. It is easy to understand my driver's irritation with my refusal to exit.

The storm which is blanketing most of the nation east of the Rockies delayed my arrival by several hours. So much for being in the office by seven, seeing that local time is nine a.m. Lucky for me it won't be my new boss's first impression of me.

No, I am very well acquainted with the woman to whom I am very shortly to be in complete servitude. *Glorianna.* Not her real name of course, rather her agency name as director of The Guardians, a US supported covert organization. A decade ago she found me when I was a burned agent on the run. With over a dozen countries preferring me dead rather than alive, I'd faked my death and left my then agency support, the WODC based in Paris, to hide. She found me and offered me a fresh start. By becoming a *guardian* of US interests, a safe-keeper of *her* interests, I would have her protection.

I glance down at the damp newspaper gripped tightly in my hand. The headlines make the nightmare real.

SAN FRANCISCO, Senator Abigail Wainwright-Fuller of California announced her bid for president Saturday, a single woman hoping to unite the nation and a Republican portraying herself as being singularly dedicated to the task. A widow for over twenty years, she has chosen to dedicate her life to public service and if elected would be the fourth president to enter the White House single, following James Buchanan, Grover Cleveland, and Chester Arthur.

The Republican party may be embracing her, but there are many who do not want to see her elected based solely on the fact that she is female. That she is also a single woman is salt in the wound. I am here to be Glorianna's...*Abigail's*...personal aide, protector, and secret lover since she dare take no other, the reality of the situation being that she will be under intense scrutiny. A woman with many secrets, safeguarding the fact that we will be having kinky sex will be the easiest of my tasks.

In exchange for my service, she has promised me retirement from the profession that rarely offers an escape other than death. She has offered the same to my twin brother, Nikos, who for the last decade was deep undercover, fulfilling *my* obligations. If for no other reason than to see him free, to give him his life back, I would have taken this assignment.

My driver pulls up to the curb and glances over his shoulder. Reluctantly, I pay him and climb out. Lifting my face, I welcome the sting of ice.

As I approach the mountain of concrete steps that lead to her building, I know the only way I am going to get through this assignment is to trust Garrett and leave the worries I left in San Francisco behind me because there is no room for error in this town or with the woman I serve.

I run the steps, making quick work of them, and am not even breathless when I reach the heavy doors marking the entrance to her building. Inside the large foyer, I take off my trench coat and straighten my suit and tie before daring report to her office. She doesn't like excuses, and she doesn't accept tardiness. A metal detector and first line security officers pose further delay and the minutes tick by before I am allowed to even enter the elevators leading to her office.

Exiting onto her floor, I note two bodyguards, a man and a woman, guarding one of many doors. I assume their presence marks her office, since in all the time I have known her; I have never known her to be without an entourage of protection.

I should report to the reception desk and allow a secretary to announce my arrival, but I go in without waiting for confirmation. Neither agent confronts me when I pass them and pull open the door. I'm disappointed that I am allowed to stride into her office without challenge.

Glorianna is sitting behind her desk, as regally as a queen. With her blond hair tucked neatly into a French twist, she looks the image of Grace Kelly as I once saw her portrayed in a framed portrait hung in a retro shop. Her eyebrows are perfectly arched, her eyelashes incredibly long, and her cupid lips perfectly lined. I don't tell her how beautiful she looks.

I can imagine the world embracing her as England once welcomed Princess Diana but am not so certain the US is ready for a female president.

"You could be dead right now," I scold, closing the door behind me. I approach her desk. "I could be anyone, an assassin."

She stands, scowling at my tone and keeping the desk between us. "Except it is you. The agents wouldn't have let anyone else come in."

I shrug. "You're the one who believes someone wants to kill you."

Her eyes widen and her mouth opens to say something but she doesn't speak, seeming to change her mind. She walks around the desk, leaving a small distance between us. "I have you here to protect me now...even though you are late."

"Not even I can control the weather."

"You could have planned for it. Left earlier."

I close the distance between us, but make no move to touch her. Her breath hitches, and she licks her lips. How does she ever think we are going to work together? Our relationship has always revolved around pure, unbridled passion.

Looming over her, I can feel the fear she has of me radiating off her. Still. After so many years. "I'm here now."

"Yes. You are." She turns away, but I grab her elbow and swing her back around to face me, making her gasp.

"Perhaps we should discuss exactly what my obligations and duties are to be in my role as your *personal assistant*."

She tries to keep her tone light as she says, "Manage my schedule. Keep me alive. Make certain absolutely no scandals make the nightly news," but her voice cracks, shattering the illusion that she is as relaxed and confident as she pretends to be.

I lean closer. "By any method necessary?"

She nods curtly.

"Let's talk about your schedule, because I won't brook complaint when it comes to meeting *your needs*."

She swallows, sexual tension swelling the room. It is less my nearness than the chemistry we share. I doubt she understands the need that makes her want me so, nor do I profess to have any mystical insight on why I desire her.

She looks away. "What do you see as my needs?"

"Eight hours of sleep, three regular meals, two hours for sex."

"You just wiped out half a day." She chuckles nervously and shuffles through some papers on her desk. "That isn't feasible on the campaign trail, and you know it. I'll be happy with meals on the run and six hours sleep."

Noting she had no argument to two hours of sex, I shake my head and lean even closer. She takes a step backward, bumping the desk.

"We do things my way," I tell her, my tone warning against further argument. Leaning close enough to catch the scent of the perfume she'd dabbed behind her ear, I whisper, "Admittedly, it may be hard to focus two consecutive hours for sexual release. We might have to content ourselves with *quickies*."

She gasps as I rub my hands up her hosiery covered legs, sliding under her skirt to find she is wearing pantyhose, even though she knows how much I detest the things. "I think one of my first duties will be to shop for more appropriate undergarments for you, a garter belt and stockings for starters."

"Impractical. Floozies wear stockings."

She fidgets as my fingers hook into the top of her pantyhose and pull them down.

"The door!" she says panicky.

"Locked when I closed it." Chuckling, I kneel in front of her and rub my hands over the bare skin of her thighs. Leaving her pantyhose and panties at her knees, I push up her dark brown pencil skirt to reveal a golden triangle of pubic hair covering her privates. If there was any doubt as to whether she was born a blond, one only need look here. I push my thumbs through the soft down, exposing her clit. My breath fans over her bared sex when I dispute her. "Beautiful, intelligent women who want to be ready for sex on a moment's notice wear stockings."

I lick her sensitive flesh softly, noting her sigh. Of relief? Of pleasure? I suck and lick and tease the pink nub of her sex, making her knees shake.

"I can't do this, not standing," she says.

I pull my mouth away. "This?"

"*This*," she implores. "I won't orgasm."

I smile, pushing a finger inside her. "Sure you will. Pretend you're a man. Pretend I'm giving you the best head you've ever had. Shoot your load for me."

"I'm not a man."

"You're going to be President of the United States. I suggest you grow a pair between now and then."

She laughs though I've obviously shocked her with my crudity. I go back to teasing her clit, pulling the nub in and out of between my lips. She drops her head back and meets my rhythm with her hips. I slide two more fingers into her moistness, pushing deep to stroke her g-spot. Her moans tell me I'm on the right path.

I stroke harder, deeper. Her wetness makes a slushing sound as I pump her, and I can feel her need build as a thick tension envelopes us. Her clit grows thicker, harder. Her hips meet the rhythm of my fingers, pushing against me as her vagina clinches tight. Her fingers wrap into my hair, making fists as her back arches, and although I feel she is straining to not scream as her orgasm washes over her, I show her no mercy and continue licking, sucking, and tugging at her flesh until she folds over me, gasping my name and begging me to stop.

I release her clit and meet her gaze. "As long as we've reached an agreement about your schedule and my duties."

"I postpone death by living, by suffering, by error, by risking, by giving, by losing."

Anais Nin

CHAPTER 3

NIKOS

San Francisco

I'm a sex addict, among my many other addictions. I drink too much, smoke too much, chase adrenaline too much, and in Shanghai, enjoyed opium entirely too much...but in the absence of mind altering drugs, I am more than content with sex.

At Lewd Larry's I have landed in a sexual playground.

I can hardly believe my brother left me stranded here, but then again this is exactly where I should be. Work. Sleep. Stay out of trouble. That seems to be the order of the day and an impossible one to obey because I am surrounded by hundreds of beautiful women. Trouble seems inevitable. Especially when my gaze returns again and again to the one I've been told is off limits and she won't give me the time of day. *Morgana.* I've been trying to get her attention for two months now.

Seeing her duck out a back door, I toss my bar towel on the counter and tell the other bartender, "I'm taking five."

He doesn't argue. I've intimidated him from the moment we were first introduced. Our dress code is shirtless and my tattoos take center stage, tattoos now riddled with scars. He has a hard time meeting my eyes, and I don't mind that so much. No one knows my story here, and it isn't because they don't wonder, I can tell by their glances everyone wants to ask. They don't because there is a code of privacy here that I don't completely understand but am grateful for.

I find Morgana standing behind the building, huddled against the chill, smoking a cigarette. She spares me only a quick glance before turning her back to me. I light up, an excuse for being outside I suppose, but thankful for the kick of nicotine just the same.

We're standing under a canopy, but it is drizzling and the wind carries an icy dampness. It's too damn cold. I back closer toward the brick wall and notice she does the same. Her voice is soft and it is only belatedly I realize she is talking on the phone. "I'm bored out of my fucking mind. Please tell me there is something happening somewhere tonight!"

It seems absurd anyone could be bored at Lewd Larry's, but then I just as quickly remember from what I have been told that she has been here much longer than I. After a few more months I'll probably be just as blasé.

Today she is wearing black boots that cover her knee and a crème-colored latex corset dress that barely covers the curve of her ass.

She clicks her cell closed and takes a long drag off her cigarette. I start a conversation with the second topic opener that comes to mind, falling right after, *let me fuck you senseless* and before *I could give your evening a few exciting possibilities.* "You have no pet."

She pivots and I see that the front of her dress is split to allow her strapped on dildo to protrude through the flaps. It is the same color as the dress. Meeting my gaze, she tosses her cigarette to the ground and grinds it under the toe of her boot. I can see the thought drift through her eyes that she should ignore my comment altogether, but then I bend to pick up the discarded butt and put it in the proper receptacle. My action may or may not have been responsible when she answers, "I prefer to not be burdened."

I pass her my half-spent cigarette and she takes it, wrinkling her nose. "I favor menthol." She takes a long drag. "But I'll smoke clove if that's all that's available."

She starts to hand it back but I gesture for her to keep it and pull out another for myself. Lighting it, I inhale. My words are smoky as I request, "Make me your puppy."

She looks me up and down before snarling, "You are not suitable."

I snicker, seeing her gaze lingers just below the waistband of my black slacks. Hey, I can't help that I'm hard as a rock *and* well-hung.

"I would be, if you trained me."

Gaze still focused in the general vicinity of my obvious erection, she catches herself licking her lips and bites down, trapping her lower lip between her teeth.

Holding my cigarette between my lips, I drop to my hands and knees, batting my lashes and wagging an imaginary tail. I'm surprised when she laughs. It strikes me suddenly how young she is. It isn't noticeable at first glance. Her fabulous body, the protruding dildo, the four-inch heels that leave her barely five feet tall, all noticed, her confidence, definitely. But as she steps back laughing, stumbling into the brick at her back, I notice her face, the heaviness of her makeup and the youth she tries to hide.

"You don't want owned."

I assure her I do, my aching dick attesting to the fact even though it's not visible.

"I do, Mistress. I really do." My cigarette bobs between my lips.

"You really don't want me for a Master." She bends at the waist, giving me a glorious view of breasts trapped behind her latex corset. How had I not noticed before that the material isn't completely opaque? Her nipples are both larger and darker than I would have imagined.

"Please," I beg, not understanding myself why this woman captivates me so or why I am so willing to sell my soul into servitude to her for a single night wrapped in her nakedness.

She slaps me. Hard. Making my cigarette go flying. It lands in a puddle. The flame of her handprint flares across my cheek, waking up a violent desire to grab her…pin her…fuck her until she screams…but I don't do any of those things.

"You don't deserve to be my puppy. You're rude and insolent. And—"

My gaze collides with hers and I immediately recognize the signs of lust. Her eyes are dilated, her chest flushed. She licks her lips *again*.

Watching her breasts heave behind all that stiff, unyielding latex, I'd bet my sizable bank account that her pussy is dripping wet.

Seeing the direction of my gaze, she slaps me again before pivoting on her heel, prepared to go back inside. I stand quickly, pressing my length along her back as she tries to open the door. She's so fucking tiny, I have to bend to whisper into her ear. "Just admit you want me to fuck you already."

She gasps. It is obvious she isn't used to disrespect.

"If nothing else, training me would give you a way to alleviate your boredom tonight." I rub my rough chin against her smooth cheek and then I back away, giving her space. I'm not surprised when she pulls open the door and storms inside. I am left assuming it will only be a matter of minutes before I'm reported to security.

I am surprised when the door opens a bare crack and she demands,

"When your shift is over, report to the Puppy Pound."

* * * *

Puppy Pound? What did I expect? It's on the public level, a way for the vanilla folk to pretend to be kinky and perhaps get a small dose of what humiliation feels like. Vanilla, but definitely not PG. As soon as I check myself in I am told to strip down to my underwear. A wide leather collar and heavy chain are secured around my neck, and then I am locked inside a kennel cage barely big enough to fold my arms and legs into. For about a minute I am amused, but then two large dog bowls are put in the cage with me, one filled with foul smelling tuna salad and the other water. I gag.

Then I realize I am on display, mundanes walk by the cages, pointing and laughing, discussing which puppy they should adopt for the night. What was I thinking?

Two hours later Lewd Larry's closes and I am faced with the reality of Morgana's game. Humiliate me by making me believe I had a chance.

The pound guard hoses out all of the kennels but mine.

"You can let me out now."

He ignores me, continuing to go about his business like I'm not even there, and then turns out the lights. He's leaving me here. Brilliant. No doubt Morgana's plan from the start. Or Garrett's if she reported my behavior. Now, I get a night of cramped quarters to teach me a lesson, is that it?

Another hour. Two? The building is fairly quiet. An occasional security guard walks by, pretending to not see me.

With my face pressed against the wire of my cage, I doze, startling when I hear the main Puppy Pound door open. The sound of footsteps approach and I smile stupidly, recognizing the sound of Morgana's boots. Feeling sleep drool on my chin, I wipe hastily.

"Looks like all the good puppies are already taken." She walks by my cage without even glancing in. "Too bad for me."

She turns around and starts to leave. *Oh no you don't.* "Woof."

"What? Did I hear a puppy?"

"Woof. Woof."

She walks back toward my cage and bends over to peek in. "Oh," she says distastefully. "You are much too big. A stray. I was looking for a pedigree, something small." She indicates just how small with her hands and finally meets my gaze. Hers appear hungry and I take that for a good sign. I crawl around in a semi-circle, trying to show doggie-enthusiasm, wagging my ass and feeling ridiculous doing so but thankful I at least wore my black briefs and not the tidy-whities. I bark again with lots of gusto.

"I guess you might be a good watchdog."

I bark, and pant, and wag. *Let me out of this God damn cage and I'll show you what I'm good for.*

She squats in front of my cage, the strapped on dildo bobs at her waist. It glows in the dark.

"God."

"Puppy?"

"Woof-woof."

"I guess I could take you home for a trial run."

"Woof-woof."

"But if you don't work out, it's right back to the Puppy Pound for you."

"Grrrr, woof." I shake my head, putting my whole body into it.

She unlocks the cage and I decide quite suddenly to play a little, backing into a corner and pretending to shake.

Surprised, she asks, "What's this?" She claps her hands. "Here, puppy."

I don't go out. She scowls but doesn't close the gate. She walks away, calling, "Here, puppy-puppy."

I'm not stupid. I follow her, crawling, my ass wagging and the chain hanging from my collar dragging on the ground between my arms and legs. "Woof-woof."

She leads me to the elevators and we ascend to the fourth floor. The Attic. I've heard whispers all night from the vanilla customers intrigued by the infamous play area. Reservations only. The world's most skilled Dominants. I look at the petite girl next to me who hides behind a layer of thick makeup and a prosthetic penis. She is considered one of the world's *best*.

She doesn't look at me.

Exiting the elevator, she leads me down a dark hallway where the mood music is laughable, overlaid with canned screams and the sound of flaying whips striking skin. She opens the door to Room Two. It is a small room, made to look like a Victorian-age bedroom, except the room is dreary. Gray wallpaper with an intricate design of faded white roses, black velvet everywhere else, curtains, chair upholstery, bedspread. She leads me by the chain to look in an oval gilded mirror. Strangely, in her ghostly-colored dress and thigh high boots she looks perfectly at home in this room.

Her lipstick is black. I hadn't noticed in the dark Puppy Pound.

Meeting my gaze in the mirror's reflection, her eyes widen, and I think she might just be seeing what I'm seeing…two people perfect for each other. I look away quickly, not knowing where that thought came from. *I'm just here for the fuck.*

"Strip for me," she demands, but her voice is like thick honey, sensual, engaging, no threat behind the command at all.

I comply, shedding my briefs and trying to not smile. I've played these games before, mostly with European women, a little slap and tickle before getting down to the business of sex. Granted, I'm usually the one in control of such games, but I've been known to give over control to a woman wielding a riding crop.

She drops my chain and walks to an antique bureau that is stained dark, almost black. On closer look, it is intricately carved. A quick scan of the room reveals several similar pieces, none completely alike, a macabre collection. The tallest chest features twisted faces caught mid-scream. A low cabinet is adorned with cherubs. Another with skulls. The towering headboard of the bedstead is carved in a way that it appears a flock of ravens are preparing to take flight from the wood. I can't explain why the furniture makes my heart quicken.

Focusing my attention back on the woman, she seems to be searching for something. After a bit of rummaging she pulls on a pair of elbow-length black latex gloves. She walks toward me with a tube of lube in one hand and a butt plug shaped like a dog's tail in the other. Okay, this game has gone far enough. I crawl in a circle, facing her, my ass not.

"Remember, you asked for this." She smiles, lifting her brow in challenge.

I did, I'm man enough to admit that I did, and I'm not certain why I'm suddenly having second thoughts except for the morbid mood of the room and the juxtapose of the woman, so small, so doll-like, but so fucking sexual. She brims over with sensuality, bleeding it from her pores. As long as fucking ends up in the picture before our time together ends.

She pats the bare skin of her thighs. "Here, puppy."

I crawl to her.

"Lift your ass, puppy."

I lower my head and lift my ass. I'm immediately rewarded with a squirt of cold gel on my ass, but she doesn't slide the butt plug in immediately. I feel her fingers glide over my hip. The gloves are a highly erotic sensation on my skin.

She smacks my ass. "Higher."

I lift. Her fingers slide through the lube. A single finger penetrates me, making me moan.

"Is this what you signed on for, puppy? You willing to be my bitch?"

I close my eyes, reminding myself it is okay to play the game as long as I get what I want in the end. A second finger slides in. *Oh God.* She fucks me with her fingers.

I want to touch my aching cock so badly. It's been weeks since I've fucked, masturbation does not count.

"Don't you even think about coming, you naughty little puppy." She smacks my ass again, then slides in the butt plug. "Wag your new tail, puppy."

I wag, desperate to get off.

"Bark, puppy."

"Woof."

"That's a horrible bark. You aren't going to scare away anyone with that bark. You're supposed to be a guard dog. I think I'll take you back to the Puppy Pound."

I growl and bark and snarl.

"That's better." She smiles at me, and I am not certain if she reminds me of an angel or a demon, maybe both, or maybe angels and demons are really one and the same and only man has perverted the truth, wanting to believe there is more. She starts laughing which throws me a curve. Then she squats, pinching my cheeks between her fingers. "What is it about you?"

I wag my rubber tail, letting it smack ass cheek to ass cheek.

"You come in here, looking so dark and dangerous, mysterious. You have every sub within sight drooling over you, dying to be topped by you. And yet you are here, begging me to master you. Don't think you are going to top me from below, mutt. If that is your game, it isn't going to happen."

She kisses me, filling my mouth with her tongue. I kiss back, I can't help kissing her back, mouth and teeth and tongues in a desperate battle of wills. Sitting back on her heels, she looks at me hard before unhooking my collar and dropping the heavy leather to the carpeted floor. "You don't kiss like a puppy."

Standing, she walks behind me and jerks the butt plug out none too gently.

I stay on my hands and knees, knowing I fucked up. I was supposed to be submissive. How hard can *that* be? I whine, lay down, and roll over. I try my best to look needy and pathetic. *Submissive.* Keeping my eyes lowered, I don't even meet her gaze when she asks, "Why?"

I stare at the intricate design of the oriental rug until it blurs, trying so hard to think of something to say, knowing it wouldn't go over very well if I admitted that I've wanted to fuck her since the first moment I saw her. Finally, I whisper, "Punish me. Please." *God. Why did I say that?* There are hundreds who would willingly beat me to death if I turned myself in to my enemies and yet I kneel here, naked, before this slip of a woman.

I hear her footsteps, walking away from me.

No, no, no. Daring to look up, I watch her cross the room, expecting her to open the door and demand I leave, but she doesn't. She opens a large cabinet which displays floggers, paddles, canes, and crops. "Training a new puppy is hard work, time consuming. I'm not convinced I want to make that investment in you."

Lying on my back, hands and feet in the air, I nod and whine. She wiggles a finger, gesturing me to come to her. It is the most entrancing vision of a woman I have ever faced. *God. What is it about her?* I roll back onto hands and knees, and hurriedly crawl forward. I pant, hoping she can see how happy I will be to please her. *Hurt me. Hurt me. Hurt me.* She squats beside me, stroking my scalp. The sensation is delicious. I only notice too late she is also going to add small clamps to my scrotum. The bite of pain is quick and not so delicious. Normally, I like pain. Like it a lot, but it seems every healed bullet wound flairs anew with pain. Four. Five. Six clamps.

I drop to my elbows, moaning. She comments, "Low pain threshold. This should be interesting," and then she chuckles.

Low Pain threshold? You're joking, right? I flew halfway around the world with almost a dozen bullets in me, and didn't pass out. That's a pretty high tolerance if you ask me. But she doesn't know that, does she?

She stands, then retrieves a birch cane from the cabinet. When she walks back to my side, I drop my eyes, refusing to look at her until her boots enter my field of vision.

Without warning, she strikes my ass and though I absolutely refuse to cry out my knees buckle under me. She waits, impatiently tapping her foot, as I force myself back into position and try to remember how to breathe.

The wind whistles just before the birch makes contact with my skin, and I brace for impact. *Holy mother of God.*

I scoot away, not enjoying being on the receiving end *of this.*

She steps in my way and I collide with her boots. I look up guiltily. "You don't really believe you deserve to be punished, do you? All of this is merely a bitter pill to swallow, a means to an end. You're only here because you want to stick your nasty thing inside of me. You want to get off and go, maybe brag a bit about what it was like to hear Mistress Morgana cry out your name in ecstasy?"

I don't agree or deny. I do flush, sweating pouring from me, and hope she doesn't see it as an admission.

"I'm today's conquest. Tomorrow there will be someone new."

"No, Mistress."

"You and dozens of others in this place with the same fucking fantasy."

Her rage rolls off of her, and I realize this is going terribly wrong.

She knees me in the ribs hard enough to make me grunt. "Is that it?"

"No, Mistress." Unexpected emotion floods my chest, making it heavy, making it hard to breathe. I can't remember the last time I felt *anything*. I lean down to lick her boots. *I need to stay. Here. With her.*

She jerks her foot away from my reach. "I'll tell you when I want you to do that. Licking my boots is a privilege you must earn, and you certainly haven't gained any favors from me yet."

I swallow hard, not understanding the need making my body throb.

"Tell me what you need, mutt."

"Forgiveness." I whisper so softly, I doubt she heard me.

She taps my flaming ass with the cane, making me jerk. "You can't take it, but I'd bet my last pair of shiny, patent leather platform boots you love dishing it out though." Her voice is venomous as she asks, "Do you know how many cocky assholes I see every damn day?"

I shake my head, trying to not look at her guiltily.

"Too many," she says softly, and it seems her indignation has waved a white flag. "So, you're here seeking redemption for some crime?"

There's no forgiveness for the things I'm guilty of.

She grills me, "Did you cheat on a partner? Lose a bet? Trying to win a bet?"

I am ashamed of the evil I've done, remembering so many screams of agony. I'm a bad man. I've committed atrocities far beyond the imaginations of this woman. I give her no answers to her questions.

"Can you serve me loyally, mutt?"

"Yes, Mistress."

"Are you willing to wade the fires of hell to earn the privilege of serving me?"

"Yes, Mistress."

She jerks the chain attached to my collar, lifting my head, stretching out my throat. Seeing her smile wickedly, I know she is going to hurt me and enjoy doing so, because I recognize the look in her eyes as pure pleasure.

Minutes later, I am stretched out and tied, standing spread eagle. She seems exceptionally fascinated by my genital piercings and before I know it, I am wired, electricity coursing through my dick and balls. I think she enjoys my grunts of pain, my screams, because she claps and laughs when I curse her. Morgana raises and lowers the voltage on her whim, making me go up on tiptoe even though my ankles are bound.

Lowering the voltage to a hum, she lubes me and fucks my ass with her fingers. I don't expect the mind blowing jolt of pleasure. "Tell me you like it when I finger fuck you."

"I like it, Mistress." I growl, near orgasm.

The voltage goes up and I scream, any pleasure I'd felt prior gets ripped away by the agony inflicted on my dick. She is a fast little minion, untying me, changing my position.

I don't try to escape. I asked for this.

She chains me in an impossible position, my collar anchored at four corners of a small cage. My arms are stretched wide and manacled. My ankles are lifted into the air and attached likewise. I am balanced in a sitting position on my ass, my tailbone the fulcrum. Am I comfortable? Not a chance. Is she enjoying my discomfort? I would have to guess yes, she is enjoying my discomfort very, very much.

The front of the cage is opened…at least for now. I am insanely uncomfortable. Spread. Stretched. She attaches wires to my nipple piercings, the ring at the base of my cock, and my tongue piercing. I momentarily wonder about how safe this can possibly be. I struggle, but the effort is wasted. She has me bound more securely than I've ever been bound by my enemies.

She switches on the power, and I am lit up like a Christmas tree. Voltage alternates between tongue and tit and cock, without pattern. Each shock is a distinct painful jolt.

"Do you like that, mutt? I'll just turn the voltage up a little bit higher."

The pain makes me grunt involuntarily. She asks me questions that I try to answer even though the clip on my tongue makes it almost impossible.

"Do you have a girlfriend?"

"Nom."

"A boyfriend?"

"Nom."

"Are you in any type of relationship?"

I shake my head frantically as the voltage goes up and the pain becomes a relentless rhythm of agony. Time loses all meaning. I cannot relax and even though I know we are in a safe, sane, consensual environment, I begin to feel tortured.

And then it stops and through a haze of white hot need I watch her stride away.

She folds open the doors to a wall-mounted cabinet that at first glance is a dreary black and gray mixed-media, which depicts a cemetery scene. I'd thought it only gothic art and didn't see past the tombstones jutting through swirling fog. Inside there is a wide screen monitor. She turns it on and a scene from inside the club rolls, obviously footage from a security camera. She aims a remote at the wall, adjusting the frame until I realize I am watching myself. Flirting.

"You wish to top her?"

"Nom."

The electricity on my tongue, which has been a low annoying buzz suddenly stings.

"Fuck," I say.

"Funny. She's a very active submissive in the club. Why else would you be flirting with her if not to get in on some of her action?"

"My job." I slobber, forcing myself to enunciate. "Make customers feel good."

She alters the voltage's pattern, and I jerk as my chest and belly spasms.

My muscles are fatigued from being stretched in the position they are in. At least that is what I tell myself when I start shaking.

She walks to me and pinches my cheeks between her fingers. "So, if I make you my puppy you'll be able to give up all other women? All other men?"

Is she being serious? Or is this only part of today's game? Is this what I want? "Yes, Mistress."

I meet her gaze and any doubt I'm feeling vanishes. I've never felt the way I feel now looking at anyone. I think I lost my mind at some point but in her eyes I feel I can find the keys to my salvation.

She leaves me chained, saying as she leaves the room, "Sleep while you can."

Is she insane? My tailbone has gone numb, my body is held at an awkward, if not painful angle, and my neck is immobilized by the wide collar.

She won't leave me here. Like this.

Time ceases to have any meaning. My mind has split in two. Laughing maniacally seems to be my only recourse, and I decide I really have lost my mind.

I wake up to find her holding my bound body and kissing my face. I realize tears are streaming over my cheeks. Some part of my mind believes I am being held in the arms of an angel.

Have I been forgiven for my sins? Not a chance, but for a minute, just one, I feel relief from the weight I hold on my shoulders. Quick release snaps see me free. She removes the manacles from my wrists and ankles, removes my collar, and tosses me a hand towel. "Clean yourself up, mutt."

I collapse back, my shoulders on the platform, my legs dangling over the side. My entire body is shaking as I take the cloth in hand. I'm not sure where to begin but manage to wipe my face, then my body, removing as much saliva, sweat, and tears as I can without showering. I'm not certain how I find the energy to sit up, but I do. I even manage to meet her gaze.

"Think you still want to be my puppy?"

Hell no! This woman is more on edge than I am—dangerous—and I need to get out of this room while I have the chance. If this was a preview of her power, whatever comes next can't be good. I'd be a lunatic to stay, wouldn't I?

"Yes, Mistress." She pets the top of my head and I apologize. "I don't know why I'm shaking."

She bends at the waist to meet my gaze, lifting my chin with two fingers to keep me from looking away. "Sure you do. You've had people in just this place, ridden by adrenaline."

I lick my lips, the truth of her words making my mouth go dry. She can't know the truth, not possibly. If she was an agent, my brother would have told me.

"Are you a sadist, mutt?" She lifts my chin a notch higher. "Do you think this is the way to gain my trust so that you can play a power-switch on me?" Her voice seems verged on hysteria. "I. Don't. Switch. Understood?"

I don't blink. "Understood, Mistress. All I desire is to be your puppy."

She laughs in my face before spinning away from me. I sit still, quiet, watching her pace the room like a caged cat. She clicks her incisors together, and I know that she is thinking too hard. Almost to herself she says, "There's no fraternizing between employees. It isn't allowed. Period. I could lose my job, and I can't lose my job here."

Still pacing, she hugs herself in her arms, and it is as if she has forgotten I am in the room.

"Garrett wouldn't fire me." She stops suddenly and looks down at me. "Can you keep this relationship a secret?"

"Yes, Mistress."

She sighs, seeming to relax with my assurance. Her entire posture changes. She drops the strap-on harness to her ankles and steps out of it. She peels herself out of the latex panties she wears beneath the dress and drops them to the floor as well. In a slow, sensual tease, she peels down one long glove at a time, rolling them off and discarding them.

My heart speeds up as she walks away, turning her back on me. Her scent is thick in the room as she sits in front of her vanity and removes her makeup. I don't move, I can barely breathe as her true beauty is revealed. Pale skin, freckles, and a soft fringe of auburn lashes. She pivots on the cushioned seat, her knees wide enough to give me a full pussy view. She is shaved bare, her labia pink. "Help me with the boots."

Exhausted, I lumber off the platform and crawl to her. I take her ankle in my hand, lifting her foot to slide down the zipper. I tug off each boot one at a time, revealing bare skin, bare feet, toenails painted bright red. Without asking permission, I lift her foot and suck her big toe into my mouth.

She doesn't reprimand me, her eye lashes flutter closed and she sighs softly.

Encouraged, I worship each toe with my mouth, sucking, licking. I draw my tongue down the arch of her foot.

"Enough! Back off, mutt."

I sit back on my heels and note that her expression reflects the confusion I feel.

"I don't want to own anything until I know I've found the place where me and things belong together. I'm not quite sure where that is just yet."

Truman Capote, *Breakfast at Tiffany's*

CHAPTER 4

KITTEN

San Francisco

Pregnancy has given me new insight about myself. I'm a perfectionist. And a workaholic. Who knew? I would have never believed the truth of it but how else can I explain how hard I drive myself, pushing the limits of mental and physical exhaustion to new heights? At twenty-seven weeks, my back aches constantly and I feel grotesque, I'm constipated…and today all I can think about is strawberries. Strawberries! I sent Holly, my secretary, to the market to fetch them and immediately felt guilty for having her go. *But I needed strawberries!* And I ate the entire quart without sharing. I should feel guilty, and not solely for the sake of the strawberries. Today she has done her job and most of my work too.

I just can't concentrate. I keep wondering how long I should wait to ask her to run to the market and get me more strawberries. I'm a horrible, selfish person.

Awakening from falling asleep at my desk is the last straw and a sure sign I need to be home...in bed...sleeping, not having sex. Because despite what I consider my enormous, very pregnant with twins, not very sexy shape, my Master can't seem to get enough of my body. Especially now that my other Master, Thomas Stephanopoulos, has been called away on an assignment. A very *long* assignment. On the other side of the nation.

Garrett has taken advantage of the situation and feels that sex twice a day every day is not too often. Normally, I'd agree. Two times, three times, a dozen times. Let's go! I love sex. But not this week. Emotions, deadlines, and pregnancy on top of a full night crawling around in feline persona as Garrett's sex pet has taken a toll on my body. I know I can't keep up the pace I've maintained for the last year...and the truth is, no one except myself expects me to.

It's just—I *need* to work. I miss Lord Fyre so much. The pain is so raw in my chest. It seems like he only left this morning, it seems he's been away forever. I was twenty-three weeks pregnant then, and now I am into my third trimester. I am absolutely miserable. I'm *done* with the whole thing and have considered begging for a Caesarian section now just to put me out of my misery.

Staring into space, a field of turquoise is all that I see, my office wall at *The Darkness*, though I could as easily be at Lord Fyre's beach house, the place he took me to when I was solely his for three months. I close my eyes, breathing deeply, my hands held over my baby bump. I feel one of the babies stretch inside me, and I fight back tears. I miss their father so badly.

With my eyes closed, I still see the blue. Blocking out the ringing telephones, copying machines, and people chatter on the other side of my closed door, I can even see the shadows cast by the flickering flames of candles spent long ago.

There was a time when I was solely his, Garrett and I had separated so that I could spend three months finding *my darkness* with Lord Fyre. Our time was cut short. *God, our time is always being cut short.* But that particular time was because his estranged wife was having a baby. He rushed to her side and she wasn't even carrying his child. I wonder if he will be so noble when my time to deliver comes.

Fighting tears is useless. I want to cry. I want to sob and rant and rave and scream, and although it might be all right for Kitten to do any one of those things at Lewd Larry's, Celia Brentwood, CEO of *The Darkness* has to represent at least a modicum of respectability.

Silent tears slide down my cheeks as I embrace the memory of Lord Fyre paying tribute to my body a final time before leaving me for his wife. I laid across his bed face down, my body exhausted from a night well-spent and warmed from the attention he paid it with paddle, flogger, and his bare hand. I was surprised when he asked, "Are you ready for the birch cane, sweetheart?"

He'd never used a cane on me before. No one had. And I was so afraid. I almost safe-worded, but I didn't. I couldn't. I loved Lord Fyre so in that moment that I would have allowed him to do anything he wanted to my body.

Surrendering to the fear was the hardest part but once I did, once I said, "I am ready, Lord Fyre," I knew utter and complete peace.

He helped me to roll over, because my body was already settling into the pain of our previous encounter, and then there was no delay, no time to regret or renege.

The birch landed across the tops of my thighs. Once, twice…four times. Agonizing pain split me in two, making my body spasm in reflex. I screamed and covered my thighs with my hands, not because I wanted him to stop. Because I didn't. Primal instinct made me try to protect myself from more injury.

I was trying to force myself to relax, embarrassed I couldn't, when he flicked the birch against my stomach. My hands flew to the new source of pain. I wasn't consciously in control any more, my body reacted on instinct. He would have had to restrained me at that point to keep me from trying to block the blows, but I didn't know where or when the birch was going to bite next. I'd stopped screaming, I was resolved to more pain.

More pain.

Anything for Lord Fyre.

Anything to please him.

Because he was saying goodbye and as far as either of us knew, he was saying goodbye forever. He would never own me again. Never master me again.

He slashed the cane against the inside of my thigh and the pain tore through me, such ridiculous pain, I sat up. That was the reflexive move. That was the only way left to protect myself. I sat up and threw my arms around his neck, not begging him to stop, not begging him to stay, but begging him to remember me…without words…just with the language of my body, then he left me.

And now he's gone *again*.

At least this time I have his promise to return.

My secretary, Holly, buzzes my intercom. "Celia? Line three."

I sit up, wiping my face and grabbing a tissue before pushing the intercom button. "No calls, Holly. Remember?"

She answers, "I know, I'm sorry, but he said it was urgent and I thought… Celia, it's Thomas."

"Fuck, Holly, why didn't you say *that*."

I pick up line three. "Thomas?"

"Why aren't you answering your cell?"

He sounds frantic, and I wonder what is wrong but then I realize he is worried *about me*. I rummage in my purse and find my cell, my *Thomas only* cell, registered to an alias he created for me, Blair Harrington, which makes me feel so much closer to him, being part of his cloak-and-dagger world, even though I'm not, not really. I check the settings. "I'm sorry, I had it set on vibrate and I didn't hear it."

Seeing ten missed calls, I feel horrible for making him worry.

"As long as you're all right."

"I'm fine," I lie, because what would be the point of telling him that I'm mourning the lack of him in my day? "I miss you terribly."

"I miss you, *Sophia*. I love you. Do not scare me like that again. What in the hell are you doing at work?"

He calls me my birth name, and it makes me feel cherished. He is the only one who has ever called me Sophia except my mother. I shake my head although he can't see it or the smirk on my face. Neither he nor Garrett understand that whether I am miserable at home or at work—I am *still* miserable. "Stop worrying. Please. I saw Dr. Wang yesterday. Everything is fine."

"Just be careful. Twins almost always come early and often unexpectedly. I just want you to be prepared." He sounds wistful when he adds, "God, I wish I was there with you."

"*I* wish you were *here*. You sound so close over the damn phone. It's hard to believe you are two thousand miles away."

"Almost twenty-seven hundred," he corrects. "Closer to three thousand."

I growl. "You aren't helping."

He chuckles and I know he is teasing me. Still, it is very far and I am very sad.

"I don't have long, sweetheart, so tell me *everything* as fast as you can."

"Everything?" I can't think of a single thing to say beyond how much I miss him. "The babies miss you. They're kicking and rolling around all of the time now. I feel like my stomach is going to split open any moment and an alien with lash out and this will have all been a dream."

"It isn't a dream," he assures me. His voice sounds wistful. "I'll bet you are sexy as hell."

I chuckle, shaking my head. "What is it with men and pregnant women? Trust me, I am not sexy."

"*So-o*, Garrett thinks you're sexy too, huh?"

I bite my lip, feeling like I've said too much, but I'm also smiling, because I can hear the smile in his voice. I answer, "Maybe," before admitting, "It's weird. I just don't get it."

"Do you *feel* more sensual?"

"I feel fat."

"And?" he encourages.

"I feel…raw…you know? It's different now, when I'm at Lewd Larry's, when I'm crawling around. It seems like I can connect with my animal more now. So, yes, when I am in character, I feel sexy, primitive, feral."

"Then *that* is what he's responding to."

I sigh, holding onto the sound of his voice. It's so comforting—hearing him.

"He wants to move us out of the penthouse," I blurt out.

"I know," he admits. "We've discussed it."

They talked? Well of course they did, but knowing they did hurts a little. Not jealousy, never that, just a little left-out-ed-ness. "You think it's a good idea to sell the penthouse?"

"I didn't say that. I'm the guy that owns more properties than I can keep track of. And if it was me, I'd hold onto it. But I also understand Garrett's perspective. You have to remember he shared the penthouse with Tony. They lived there. They loved there. After Tony was killed, Garrett couldn't let go of their home, he couldn't move on. He's ready now. He wants a new place to start over in. A place to create fresh memories in."

Duh. I feel like a nimrod. "I didn't even think about that."

"So you will stop fighting him now?"

Garrett told him we're having a major war over this issue if he's mentioning it now. "Is that why you called me? *Master* asked you to?"

Thomas sighs heavily. I don't want to fight with him. I don't want to fight with Garrett. I just don't know that I'm ready to move back to suburbia and nosey neighbors.

"What are you afraid of, Sophia?"

"People talking. People saying that I don't deserve my babies because I'm a sexual deviant. I don't ever want Children's Services to show up on my doorstep to take my babies away. It's crazy, but I feel safer in the city than I would in suburbia."

I can imagine him nodding, understanding. We get each other. Why can't it be this easy with Garrett?

"First, you would have to invite them in. They can't just enter your residence. They won't be able to just take our babies without some provocation and then they would come with a court order."

"What if a neighbor complained?"

"Why would a neighbor complain? In suburbia, you will be Celia Brentwood not Kitten."

"Exactly," I agree. Can't he see that *that* in itself is a problem?

Thomas laughs. "I wish I was there to see your face, to hold you and tell you that reintegrating into *Vanillaville* won't be as horrible as you think it's going to be. To show you how much fun it is to go in and out from under the veil of darkness, sneaking around, being more than one person, being a different person to everyone you meet."

"That's you. I like being Kitten."

"You also like being Celia Brentwood, CEO of *The Darkness*. You like dressing for work in your stockings and garter belt, your high heels, and then hiding all that incredible naughtiness under a skirt, a button-up-the-front blouse and a jacket."

I don't deny the truth because he knows me better than I know myself, but that doesn't mean I'm going to admit it either.

"Do me a favor," he says.

"Anything," I answer.

"I'm sending you information for a house that I want you to go look at. Look at the photos and tell me what you think."

I sigh, resigned. If both of my Masters want this, I don't have much to say. I wait for the download on my PDA, frowning. It sits on the corner of a busy street in Russian Hill. This isn't suburbia. This is minutes away from *everything*. Garrett will never agree. He wants away from the city. The description reads seven bedrooms—which seems like overkill, even adding a full-time housekeeper and a nanny, but as I do the math in my head, I realize it is about right—and seven baths.

As I start clicking on photos of rooms, I do not want to know how much this house costs. It has wood floors throughout, like Garrett's condo, walls of windows, like Garrett's condo, and a gourmet kitchen, no, not even close to Garrett's standards. "The kitchen would have to be redone."

"Obviously," he agrees. "But there is room enough for him to make the kitchen of his dreams."

"Yeah." My heart drops. It seems Thomas has found the perfect place for us. I have no arguments. It is Garrett's penthouse only on a grander scale...a house...with an insane view of the bay and the Golden Gate Bridge. "Tell me what you know about it."

"I'm in Washington DC. I can tell you what the realtor told me over the phone."

"Peachy."

"Don't sound so glum. It's a modernistic Neo-Classical residence that boasts soaring double height ceilings in the living areas with grand-scale Palladian-style windows."

"I see that," I agree, looking through the photos, not admitting how really beautiful the windows or their view beyond is.

"Sleekly designed staircases and an elevator to service the four levels."

Four levels? Holy crap. That isn't obvious from what he sent me.

"Do you see the patio photo?"

I scroll. "Found it."

"It's directly off the kitchen, and those raised beds are filled with herbs and it's surrounded by citrus trees."

God, Garrett is going to die over this place.

"There are actually two patios, there's no photo for the second but I am assured by the realtor that it is a flower lover's paradise with mature trees and ample room for children to run and play. There isn't one now, but when the babies are old enough for it, we could add a play set."

I snort, imagining what my Thomas would consider a play set. Probably one of those extravagant wooden monstrosities with swings and slides, a fort on stilts, and a climbing wall. It would be perfect.

"There's a *very private* terrace off the master bedroom." His voice alludes to our shared memory of me tied over the railing at his beach house. My lower belly tightens in memory. I want him so badly, I ache.

Sighing heavily because wishing him home won't make it true, I tell him, "I'd like to see it."

"Really?" He sounds like a kid promised a pony.

"Really. I'm sorry I've been so difficult. It's perfect, but I don't think Garrett will agree to it. He wants *acreage* away from the city."

Thomas chuckles. "Unless he has changed, he's still allergic to grass and fresh air. He doesn't have to make the kinds of sacrifices he believes he does just because babies are entering our lives. I'll make arrangements for you and Garrett to have a private showing and text you the details."

I feel the wave of his happiness through the phone, and it makes me glad that I've made him so jubilant. "I love you, Lord Fyre. I miss you."

"Me too, sweetheart. More than you can know."

He hangs up, no final *goodbye*, no additional *I love you*, just the silence of the disconnect. I smile, strangely cheerful. *I made him happy.* I *pleased* him. Even from almost three thousand miles away.

"If ever there is tomorrow when we're not together...there is something you must always remember. You are braver than you believe, stronger than you seem, and smarter than you think. But the most important thing is, even if we're apart...I'll always be with you."

A.A. Milne, *Winnie-the-Pooh*

CHAPTER 5

THOMAS

Office of Senator Abigail Wainwright-Fuller, Washington, DC

Sitting behind a desk isn't my style, I have too much energy and end up feeling chained and caged, especially this morning. I woke up from a dream of Garrett and Celia and it has ruined my day. Last night I was able to view some photos of her Garrett sent to my email, and I fell asleep missing her terribly. I want to be there with her, experiencing her pregnancy with her, and instead I must trust that Garrett is taking good care of her, meeting all of her needs. I've never been a jealous man, but *in this* I envy him.

I called her. I shouldn't have, my mind has been distracted ever since.

Around me there is a bustle of activity as interns and aides all prepare for *Glorianna's* first big speech. They don't call her Glorianna of course. Nor do I to her face, but it is important for me to remember at all times just exactly who this woman is that I work for, how dangerous she is, and so in my mind she is always *Glorianna*.

Her entourage calls her Ms. Fuller; I call her Abbie, and it pleases me she blushes when I do so. It also pleases me that there isn't another person on the planet who would dare be so familiar with her. She is a fearsome woman with many enemies. It is with that truth in mind I do my job, the full-time safe-keeping of her person, in the guise of executive personal assistant, though I have three people who report directly to me. One maintains her schedule, one screens her calls and fields her emails, the third takes care of all the tedious details from dropping off and picking up dry cleaning to walking her little dog, a Bolognese named Zita. The mutt is her Achilles heel, making the animal a liability in my mind. She's too easily distracted by it and worries about it incessantly. Until I came to work for her in this capacity I had no idea she could be emotionally manipulated, but seeing her with Zita, I know she can be.

The hairs at the back of my neck prickle and my gaze goes immediately from Abigail, who is sitting behind her desk and staring at her monitor with furrowed brow, still working furiously on her speech, to Zita, who is curled asleep in a desktop doggie bed. From my seat, I concentrate, trying to pick up on any subtle nuance, any shift in pattern or deviance of sound. There are littered conversations, soft and monotone, some one-sided spoken into phones. Two televisions play almost silently, one tuned to CNN, the other BBC. From the other side of the door comes the normal sounds of a large corporate office building, ringing phones and chatter. Everything seems boringly in order, but I don't discount the premonition of danger. Trusting my gut has saved my ass more times than I care to remember.

Late morning sunlight streams through the windows, casting a sheen of gold across surfaces. *Everything is perfectly normal.*

I am just about to credit my paranoia to the guilt I've been feeling over the Celia distraction when through the open office door I notice a flower delivery guy in the outer office. One of the agents is giving him the third degree, messing with him.

The young man is sweating bullets.

Abigail stands, smiling, seeing the flowers.

My gaze travels from woman to agent to courier and the prickling sensation intensifies. Standing, I command, "Close the door!" and immediately race to Abigail's side.

I have no reason to believe the flowers are a threat. I know they have been scanned, checked and double checked. All I have is my gut.

Thankfully, Abigail had instructed every person present, including the agents, to follow my every command, and as the door latches closed an explosion blows it off its hinges. I cover Abigail with my body, pressing her to the floor. In a split second, splinters and debris are showering over us.

"Oh God! Oh God," Abigail swears beneath me.

Standing, I scan the room to make sure everyone is all right.

"Zita!" she calls out, and the yapping Bolognese jumps into her master's arms. "Oh, sweetheart, are you okay? Mommy's here, mommy's here. God, you're shaking like a leaf."

Grabbing Abigail's hand and helping her to her feet, I'd say she is quite shaken if her trembling hand is any indication. Three secret service agents shield her as we hurry from the office building and to a waiting car in case that was only a first wave attack.

Clutching Zita to her chest with one arm and holding my elbow with the other, she demands, "How did you know?"

"I didn't know, not for certain, and in times like this I really wish I'd been wrong and left standing there looking idiotic for my paranoia."

"Well, thank God for your suspicions or we might all be dead. Is there a body count from the outer rooms?"

Timothy Watters, one of the agents, answers, "Two confirmed dead, including the courier, and seven injured. It could have been much worse if not for *Mr. Karros.*"

Our gazes collide and not for the first time. Tim doesn't trust me, or so it seems, and I don't think he believes for a second I'm *only* a personal assistant as evidenced an hour later when he asks, "What's your story, Mr. Karros?"

"Excuse me?"

"You're obviously ex-military."

"I have some training," I admit, knowing my vague answers will send him digging through the paper trail of Lex Karros's invented life. He will find that I served the United States with loyalty, valor, and was a decorated Marine. That should soothe his curiosity.

We are driven to a hotel and locked into a suite for safe-keeping until a thorough search of Abigail's office and home reveals if it is safe for her to return to either. She asks, "How long are we going to be stuck here?"

"A few hours at least."

She paces in front of a large bank of windows. "I need to work on my speech."

I stride past her, pulling closed the curtains before stepping in front of her and stopping her mid-stride with a hard hold on her shoulders. "Talk to me. You shouldn't be this shaken over a little bomb. What's going on?"

"I don't know." She glances way.

I tip her chin back to me gently. "Tell me what you're thinking."

She pulls away and wraps herself in her arms, admitting, "Self-doubt, okay? Why am I doing this? Why isn't The Guardians enough for me?"

I watch her with interest because this is a new side to Glorianna, one I've never seen before. "Who's behind your run for office?"

She jerks her chin, looking at me.

I prod her harder. "Who's holding your strings?"

Affronted she retorts, "I am no one's puppet."

I laugh at her, and when she moves to slap me I grab her hand. "A strong reaction. An emotional reaction. You don't want to be controlled but you are, and now you're worried that this assignment might actually get you killed."

She glares at me, and I pull her against me.

"You're worried that has been the plan all along, a way to get you out of the way. That's why I'm here, isn't it?"

She lets out a short sob when my mouth crushes against hers. I might not be able to identify the who but I understand how it feels when you know someone else decides if you are useful or a burden. I know how it feels to be burned. I kiss her soundly but don't let the kiss's passion extend beyond a kiss.

"They want you to cancel your speech."

"I won't."

"Good. I'd be disappointed if you quit now." I kiss her nose, vowing, "I'll keep you alive," and knowing exactly what that means for me: over a year of campaigning, four more years if she's elected, and if she's re-elected…

I'm putting the cart before the horse, but I have to be honest with myself and the truth is the ménage won't survive if I am away for an entire decade. My sons will be strangers to me. I only have to remind myself of the years my brother already gave up for me to remember just exactly how bad my life could have gone. This is a small sacrifice by comparison.

I close my eyes and push my face against Abigail's neck, not wanting her to see my pain. She takes it as an overture and rubs against me, whispering. "Thank you. Thank you. Thank you."

She kisses my closed eyes, my forehead, my cheeks.

She unties my tie and unbuttons my shirt.

I will my body to respond as she lowers her mouth to one of my nipples and bites.

"Lex?"

I open my eyes in time to see her walking away from me…toward the bed. Christ. This could be my life for the next decade. I try to not feel sorry for myself as I watch her disrobing. I see that she took my advice and bought a garter belt and stockings.

I put on my company-issued smile and join her by the extra high bed, seeing a little two step riser beside her for assisting with the climbing into and out of the bed. She reaches behind herself to unhook her bra, but I stop her hands. Catching her gaze, I force myself to smile wider, leering a little. "Uh-uh, leave it on."

She frowns but relaxes when I lower my mouth to kiss the rounded and pushed up top of her breasts.

I whisper against the swell, "Do you know how beautiful you are?"

I rub my hands down her body to cup her ass then lower to feel where the garter's snaps attach to the stockings.

"These are very nice. I think you need a different color for every day of the week."

She relaxes in my arms. "Well, I'd have felt ridiculous if I'd have ended up at the emergency room today and had to been cut out of my clothes."

I don't tell her that if the flower delivery had made it inside the doors there would have been little left of her to take anywhere except a morgue. I push her body down onto the mattress and kiss my way down her spine. I palm her ass, then smack it lightly.

"This is how I like to see you." I step back from her, looking at her bent over the mattress. "Arch your back, lift your ass for me."

She complies and I smack her ass again and again. Through the sheer crème colored panty, I see her butt cheeks taking on a faint pink glow. Her bottom grows warm to my touch.

I smack her again, a little harder, increasing the intensity. She fidgets in her high heels, and I know that the last smack stung. I smack her again, and she moans.

I smooth my hand over her spanking-warmed bottom. "You like that, don't you?"

She shakes her head and I chuckle as I push my fingers between her thighs, feeling her heat, knowing before I even push the flimsy film of panty covering her twat out of the way that I am going to find her pussy slick with her wetness.

"Tell me that you like it when I spank you." I push my finger inside, finding her very wet. She pushes back with her body, not admitting anything.

I withdraw my fingers and holding her down, give her a spanking she will remember the rest of the night.

* * * *

I am amused watching Abigail square off against the homeland security field director who is trying to convince her to postpone her speech. Her voice rises, "I will not go into hiding! Now, will you be transporting me to the coliseum personally, Bruce, or should I hail a taxi and notify your superior of your lacking performance in light of today's events?"

She didn't sit, she didn't ask him to sit and so they stand nose to nose. I imagine her ass is on fire beneath her skirt, her pussy still dripping wet.

Going to her side, I know that *Bruce* doesn't have a chance in hell of winning this argument, as much because she is irritated by his insistence that she cancel the speech as by the fact that he arrived before I could bring her *to completion*.

Pulling my PDA out of my pants pocket, I scroll through emails animating the role of very prepared personal assistant. "The concierge has arranged a car, and it is waiting downstairs."

She meets my gaze and nods. "Thank you, Lex."

I am as much Lex as I ever was Thomas or any of my other aliases. Putting on a name is like putting on a suit. I am who I need to be in any given moment.

Bruce gives me a loathing look before directing his attention back to Abigail. "If you insist on this insanity at least make use of one of the unit's armored vehicles."

"It is your prerogative to make the offer of availability, sir."

The muscle in his jaw twitches. "Consider the offer made."

"I accept. Thank you," she says graciously, though her eyes still hold scathing challenge as she leaves the room in a hurry, her security detail struggling to keep up.

I chuckle, following close, selecting elevator buttons and opening doors as we reach them.

"Enjoying yourself?" she asks dryly.

"Actually, I am. Life behind a desk was getting a little boring." As we step outside into the cool evening air, I stay close and help her into the back seat of a black SUV that screams *government vehicle*. "I think I would have preferred the taxi."

"Too late now, I suppose."

Our gazes meet as the SUV makes its way slowly through the hotel's parking lot. She's scared. I don't know when I've ever seen her afraid. "I'm here, and I'm not going to let anyone assassinate you today, Abbie."

She smiles weakly. "Thank you, Lex."

Traffic is heavy as we make our way toward the coliseum, and it turns out that Abigail is the reason for most of it. Record numbers have shown up to see hear her first speech, and standing room only tents outfitted with large screen televisions have been set up in the parking lot to accommodate the overflow crowd. The entrance road is lined by people holding signs, *Fuller for President* on the left and anti-Fuller for President protestors on the right.

"Wow," she says, and I squeeze her hand for support.

"Are you ready for this?" I ask in a whisper, leaning near.

"I thought I was."

"You are going to be brilliant," I say as the SUV comes to a stop and her door is opened. A wall of suits create a barricade between *us* and *them* as we are escorted into and through the building.

I watch from the sidelines as she is hurried through the process, wardrobe, makeup, and meeting with a line of 'very importants' and then she is taking the stage, standing behind the podium to give her speech. She doesn't look back. Now she is in her element. She raises both hands, waving a greeting to the standing ovation crowd. She waits for the commotion to die down before saying jokingly, "And to think, for a moment I was afraid no one would show up."

The standing ovation begins anew.

"Be with me always—take any form—drive me mad! only do not leave me in this abyss, where I cannot find you! Oh, God! it is unutterable! I cannot live without my life! I cannot live without my soul!"

Emily Bronte, *Wuthering Heights*

CHAPTER 6

KITTEN

Buoyed by Thomas's call, I left the office early. I'm hoping to get at least a two hour nap before I have to leave for the club and come home expecting to find the penthouse empty. To my surprise I hear voices coming from the bedroom. I'm immediately on alert, ready to flee, but listening closely I recognize Garrett's and relax. After the month I've had, expecting danger first and normal second is becoming a habit I'm fairly unhappy about.

I guess no nap if Master is home...

I step out of my shoes, lay my jacket over the back of the couch, and stash my purse and briefcase. Unbuttoning my blouse, I start to disrobe but, hearing a second voice traveling through the walls—a woman's voice—stops me cold. I can't ever remember a woman being here. Except for his best friend Jackie, who doesn't count because she used to be a man and as far as I know still has a dick and balls in addition to breasts. No, a woman in the house seems like not a good thing.

I finish unbuttoning my blouse and shrug out of it, letting the material fall to the floor. Similarly, I keep undressing, peeling off skirt, hosiery and garter belt.

Master and the woman-who-shouldn't-be-in-our-house come into the living room just as I'm taking off my bra. The woman gasps. "Oh! Oh my."

She seems a little frumpy for Master's taste.

Master barely gives me a glance as he leads her past the wall of windows overlooking the city and the bay beyond. I realize he is pointing out features. "You are going to adore the kitchen, Italian marble, Sub-Zero and Wolf Appliances."

The woman's gaze stays on me as she walks past. Curious as to what is going on, I drop to my knees and crawl after them. Her eyes widen, and she bumps into Master not realizing he has stopped just inside the doorway.

"Oh! Sorry."

Seeing me, Master shakes his head and I sit although I am still some distance away. I can be a good little kitten. *When I want to be.*

I watch them through the wide threshold between rooms, Master opening and closing doors, displaying virtues. "Side by side refrigerator, a full freezer, wine cooler, two built-in ovens, gas cooktops, warming drawers."

The woman can't take her eyes off me, and I like it that she can't. To reward her undivided attention, I sit in a sunbeam and proceed to give myself a tongue bath. Her eyes go wide. "Oh my!"

"Yes, it's a wonderful kitchen. I'll miss it." Master doesn't have a clue that she hasn't heard a word he's said or even seen a single feature.

I think he must be interviewing her to be the new maid, and I chuckle at the fun I could have at her expense. He turns around and sees she is gaping at me. Over her head he glares at me as he clears his throat to get her attention.

She jerks and turns to face him. "You have a lovely home, Mr. Lawrence. We should have little trouble getting top dollar even in this tough economy."

What? Top dollar?

I hear a soft vibration from the general vicinity of Master's crotch and watch as he retrieves his cellphone, excusing himself from the woman I now realize is a real estate agent.

A real estate agent?

He wouldn't sell the penthouse! He can't!

Heart pounding, palms sweating, on the verge of a full-scale panic attack, I do the only thing I can think of. I create a scene. Lifting my head regally, I crawl past the agent, swinging my hips and making certain I rub against her leg as I pass. "Meow-meow"

I circle her ankles, rubbing my naked body against her. Glancing up, I see she has gone from drop-jawed to pale. In my mind, I translate *vanilla*. Even though I'd bet hard, cold cash that she advertises being *scene* friendly. *First the obstetrician and now her.* It angers me that everyone is so willing to use the alternative lifestyle angle to gain new clients without any understanding what it really means to be kink-friendly.

Reaching my kitten bowl, I eat the chocolate puff cereal that is kept waiting for me. I am careful to keep my eyelids lowered, but that doesn't mean I can't watch her reaction. I'm thrilled when I see her look of panic. She wants to run, but that wouldn't be professional.

Sitting back on my haunches, I spread my knees wide. The view of my pussy gets her out the door fast enough. I smile, pleased with my success, but the repercussion is Master's quick return to the room when he hears the door slam. Looking unhappy, he announces into his phone, "Let me give you a call back in five."

I look at him innocently, thinking *better make it ten.*

"Kitten?"

I look at him blankly.

"What did you do?"

"Meow-meow?" I cock my head to the side and bat my eyelashes. He growls. "Speak. Why did Ms. Kruegger leave?"

"She didn't say."

He shakes his head. "I can only imagine."

"Please don't sell the condo."

"Kitten," he says patiently, explaining again, "We need more space, we're having twins."

"You promised to wait until I'm comfortable with the idea, and babies are tiny. They take up almost no space. We won't need more space for years."

He sits on the sofa and pats his knee. Despite my irritation, I crawl to him and rest my chin on his knee, meeting his gaze.

"I know you don't think you are ready for suburbia, but it is going to be fine."

I sit back with a loud pout. "You move to suburbia, I'll stay here with my babies."

"Kitten, that's unacceptable and you know it."

Standing, with extreme confidence and determination, I tower over him, hands on my hips. "I'm not having this argument, I'm not moving."

He growls and jerks my hands, forcing me to my knees so fast I don't realize what's happening until I'm down. "Lower your head. Eyes on the ground. Hands behind your back."

I obey, too surprised by his show of dominance to do less.

Still sitting on the sofa, he fingers my collars, the one he gave me and the one Thomas gave me. I let out a breath I wasn't even aware I was holding. Very softly he speaks and I have to strain to hear.

"Twins, a full-time housekeeper and two live-in nannies will not fit in this penthouse."

Two nannies? I start to argue that I can take care of my own children and that we won't require nannies, but I stop myself because he's right—even if I give up a large portion of my hours at *The Darkness* and work from a home office in order to be home with my babies that still leaves the eight to ten hours we are at Lewd Larry's each night—we'll need help.

He strokes my head. "You have a very unfair advantage, Kitten."

I roll my gaze up to look at him as his hands descend to my shoulders, kneading them. His fingers slide down my chest to cup my much fuller breasts. God. Breasts! I have breasts for the very first time, and it seems strange. When I look in a mirror, I don't recognize my body but I think Master likes the changes.

He squeezes my breasts, testing the fullness of them. He rolls my nipples then pulls them, stretching them out and making me gasp. They're so sensitive. I don't like having my breasts touched, let alone played with, but the look he gives me keeps me from asking him to stop.

"I would do anything to make you happy. You're servitude pleases me. This pregnancy pleases me."

Emotion wells in my throat, and I drop my gaze to the floor as my vision suddenly blurs. I've had so many doubts since learning that Master is not the father of my babies and Lord Fyre is. Doubts Master might not love me as much…might not want me any more at all, my religious taboo-laden upbringing warping who I know Garrett Lawrence to be. He—the same man he was when he purchased me to be a sex slave, the professional Dominant who is so utterly mesmerizing that I've seen both men and women swoon in his presence, hell, the first time he touched me, I almost fainted, the man who gives lectures across the country on power exchange and polyamory—is not the man who would run away from a relationship just because it got a little hard, a little complicated.

Bending forward, he lifts my breast and takes my nipple into his mouth. Sensation slashes through me, pain verging on need, need verging on me begging him to stop. I imagine my babies, needing to nurse, and me turning my back on them. None of the books Jackie gave me said anything about breastfeeding being painful.

He nips, biting lightly.

"Oh God!"

He sucks harder, thinking I am enjoying the sensation.

Pregnancy is ruining everything. I don't want to have sex, I don't want to have my nipples sucked.

Finally, he stops and I suck in a deep breath of relief…but then he pulls my other nipple into his mouth.

"Oh God. Stop, stop, stop."

The thought rolls through my brain that 'stop' is not a safe word…is this really worth safe-wording over?

He leaves the couch, squatting beside me, still sucking. My breast has started to pulse and ache, but strangely my pussy is equally pulsing and aching. *I need filled.*

Master seems to know what I need because I feel his hand push between my thighs, his fingers teasing past my clit to find my dampness. He lifts my bottom, making room for his hand, and his fingers slide deep.

Yes, yes, yes.

I lift higher, repositioning without permission. *Bad, Kitten, bad.*

Obeying, disobeying, waiting for permission to do anything, all of our Master-slave protocols always weigh so heavily on my mind. How are we going to do this with babies in the house?

"Lean over the couch cushion."

I obey, laying my upper body on the sofa, lifting my ass to him.

Behind me, Master pushes his face against me, licking the length of my slit, his tongue probing my clit but not sucking, just licking. He teases lips and tongue over my labia, licking, licking, finding my anus to rim me gently.

"Oh God. Yes, Master." I should be silent. We're not in the bedroom. I can only speak so freely in the bedroom. How many infractions am I up to now?

I hear the door and jump, startled, but am trained too well to overreact. I stay in position. It doesn't matter who sees. Hearing the shuffle of paper bags and the toss of keys, which clink loudly into a ceramic bowl stationed on top of a small table near the door, I assume it is Enrique, the houseboy. But what if it was a nanny returning from the park with our babies?

I am acutely aware of the erotic tableau, Master pressing into my most sensitive places, making me gasp and moan. He stops licking, sliding over me to press kisses to my shoulder. His fingers slide over my saliva slicked ass. I arch, pushing against his hand, wanting him to fill me, anus, vagina, it doesn't matter. *I want this.* I suddenly feel like a cat in heat, so different than a moment ago when I didn't want sex at all. Every bit of me is still too sensitive—my nipples, my pussy, my ass—painfully so, but the *ouch* has turned into an *ohmyfuckinggod.*

"You make me so fucking hot, Kitten. I walk around with a

perpetual hard-on, thinking about you naked and when I see you, I just have to have you." He rims my asshole with his finger, and I push against the weight of his hand, wanting him to push that finger inside of me, needing it. I close my eyes tightly. I don't want to see if Enrique stops on his way into the kitchen with the groceries to watch. I don't want to imagine a similar scene with a nanny hastily covering our children's eyes with her hand. *We have to talk about this! Soon. How is this ever going to work with babies in the house?*

"I'm fat," I argue. "Not attractive."

"Not fat." He grabs my chin and forces my face around. He kisses me, then meets my gaze. "As far as I know, I've never had a pregnant belly fetish. To be honest, I've never really thought about it, but seeing your baby bump something snapped in my brain. At first I was afraid to have sex with you, afraid you might lose the babies...but as time has passed, I've realized those are foundless fears...and as your waistline has expanded, I've had to face this need inside of me."

What am I supposed to say to that?

"You are so sexy." He pushes his finger into me, stretching my anus, demanding I allow the intrusion, but my mind is still trying to wrap around his admission. "I'm not the only one. I see how some of our clients watch you as you crawl around The Oasis, your swollen belly so obvious, your hips fuller, your tits swaying."

He pushes his finger inside and I moan, trying to not think of the lingering glances I receive when I'm at the club and failing because I have noticed. I moan as he pumps his finger in and out of me. I'm so very tight, but it feels so good.

Master whispers against my ear. "They want you. They want to fuck you."

Yes, yes they do. I should feel ashamed, affronted, but as his finger slides in and out of me it is obvious my body finds it pleasing to think about.

"Oh God."

He slides in a second finger, stretching me more and I push against his hand, opening for him.

"Does it make you feel sexy? Desirable? Knowing those men would fuck you in a heartbeat if I would allow it?"

"No," I lie and he chuckles, making me feel like he doesn't believe me.

His free hand wraps around my middle, rubbing my belly, and one of the babies kicks against the weight of his hand. It feels so strange, knowing there are little babies rolling around inside of me, reacting to the attention Master is paying my body. *I shouldn't be enjoying this.* I should be cloistered in a nunnery for the duration of my pregnancy. Untouched. A silly thought I suppose since I've never been Catholic.

I push it away…all of it…all the random thoughts, and concentrate solely on Master's touch. Or lack thereof. He pulled his hands away, and I understand why when I hear the slide of his zipper. He doesn't make me wait long. I feel the head of his cock pressing against my ass.

This position, doggy style, is easier now that I'm pregnant and my belly is in the way, but usually he pushes into my vagina. It's been months since he's fucked me in the ass.

I like it when he does, but I feel so tight *today.*

Too much thinking, my head just can't drop into the blissful headspace I need to be in for everything to be perfect. I'm too worried about babies and nannies, or if Enrique is in the kitchen putting away groceries, or if he pulled up a chair and is watching from behind. *He wouldn't do that!*

Still, I'm thinking too much and am not surprised when Master commands, "Relax."

Hearing the command, need tightens low in my belly. His voice always does that to me, and I focus on the command, wanting to be mastered, wanting to feel owned.

He pushes in, just the tip of his cock, waits for me to relax, and pushes deeper. It still feels like only an inch. He's reached the tight internal muscle band that doesn't want to let him penetrate me.

He smacks my ass, and the sting takes me by surprise. Heat flairs over my hip and in that instant, while my mind is still focused on the smack, he pushes deep, filling me.

It's been so long since I've been spanked, smacked, flogged.

"Master! Please!"

I don't have to tell him what I want. He knows me. He smacks my ass again, pushing his cock even deeper, and this time I cry out. The sting. Oh God, yes, the sting flaring through my hip, but also the stretching and filling of my ass.

He pushes in, pulls out a little, to push deeper on his next thrust. I feel every inch of the glide as he goes deep. His hands close around my abdomen, holding me tight, controlling the rhythm with his hold on me.

I fight to not even register the flip-flops and bounces happening inside of me.

Stop touching my stomach.

Touch my clit.

Oh God, I want to come.

Impaled completely, I push back against him, feeling the soft hair that covers his thighs on the back of my legs. He sets a rhythm and his balls swing, a caress on my labia.

My ass contracts around his cock, and I reach to touch my own clit. He doesn't slap my hand out of the way and I wonder for a moment if he even noticed the infraction, but then my pleasure is rising, a blissful vortex lifting me.

I know the moment he starts to come because I'm right there with him, encouraging him to fuck me harder with the rhythm of my hips, pushing him, pulling him. "Oh God, oh God, oh God!"

"Love never dies a natural death. It dies because we don't know how to replenish its source. It dies of blindness and errors and betrayals. It dies of illness and wounds; it dies of weariness, of witherings, of tarnishings."

Anias Nin

CHAPTER 7

NIKOS

I am like a bitch in heat, waiting for her stud. Any glimpse of Mistress Morgana would do it for me, but as I wipe counters, take orders, and fill drinks, I am disappointed again and again each time I scan the room, seeking the bright flash of her hair.

"You okay tonight, man?"

My co-bartender has noticed my distraction, the sloshed drinks, and lack of conversation with our customers. "I'm fine. Just a lot on my mind."

Morgan and I have kept our meetings secret, waiting until after work to *play*, even going so far as to spend our days off at various hotels far away from town. It has to be that way, I know it does. I understand the rules in place here. I also know I *need* to see her.

She put me in a chastity cage our first night together. Now she holds the key to the plastic cage around my cock. I never realized before how many erections I have in the course of a day. Especially here. I could keep a permanent hard-on...if not for the cage...and now, I am forced to divert my eyes, divert my thoughts, or else there are painful consequences as the plastic denies my body's attempt at a full erection.

If she wanted my thoughts to be on her every moment of every day, she wouldn't have had to gone to such lengths. I would have thought about her anyway. Three weeks later and I still haven't fucked her. Even masturbation is out. I feel like I am losing my mind.

She tortures me, she allows me to serve her. She doesn't allow me to pleasure her, which makes me wonder who she is having sex with. She doesn't own a pet...and I doubt she's owned. What if she has a partner completely away from Lewd's? That thought makes me more insane than all the others.

I sleep at the foot of her bed, a good dog, and the entire time I want nothing more than to hold her, but she doesn't let me.

She's a nightmare of pain, but when I'm with her I feel some salvation is imminent.

Dozens of beautiful bodies flirt with me every night—men and women—I could have my pick of partners, so why am I so obsessed with this one?

I close my eyes, remembering our last scene. She'd put me in the damn box, my wrists and ankles secured in the corners, my throat caught in a center collar. I was spread, balanced precariously and completely at her mercy.

She unlocked and removed the cage from my cock but there was to be no pleasure in the moment. She immediately attached clamps to my scrotum. Stroking my face, she'd said, "Enjoy the pain I cause you."

She stroked my cock and I rose to the challenge, even when she added the low vibrating hum of electricity through my cock and balls her threat had seemed inconsequential. She worked me up, making my cock so hard it felt as if it might break off. Then she added more electricity and any pleasure I was feeling plummeted, my erection fell.

She slapped my sagging flesh. "You're such a huge disappointment."

She turned the electricity completely off and disconnected all the wires. My guts clenched, fearing the worse. I'd failed any chance of being *hers*. But she wasn't playing fair. I had no idea how to please her.

"Please, Mistress. I want to please you."

She collapsed the box's walls, leaving me still anchored at corner posts. Another snap and the half of the cage bottom folds down. "You want to please me?"

"Yes, Mistress."

"I'm going to fuck you senseless, mutt. If you want to please me, you won't come. You'll deny yourself all pleasure."

"Yes, Mistress." I was bound and helpless, my cock deflated. It didn't seem like such a hard request.

She zapped me with a long handled animal prod, again and again, on the inside of my thighs, the backs of my arms and legs. Each jolt is a painful surprise.

"Fuck," I cursed. "God damn."

She laughed at any attempt I made to pull my wrists or ankles free of the cuffs, and after a while all I wanted was free of her torture. She must have sensed the moment *I quit* because she backed off, walked away. She returned with lube. Standing in front of me, she spread a liberal amount over the prosthetic cock she had strapped to her hips. "Do you like it up the ass, mutt?"

"Yes, Mistress."

Leaning over me, her face close as she met and held my gaze, she spread lube on my anus. She rimmed my hole with her slick fingertips. "I don't believe you."

Slowly, she slid a finger deep inside of me and wiggled it. My muscles clenched against the intrusion.

"Say you love my finger in your ass."

"I love your finger in my ass, Mistress." I hated it that my voice cracked. Strangely, my chest felt heavy with emotion I didn't understand. I'd been fucked up the ass before. It wasn't that I was an ass-fuck virgin, but my body was responding with nervousness, fear. Vulnerability. I didn't understand why I was feeling the way I was or why it was so important for me to experience it with her, but it had seemed since the first moment I'd seen her that she had to be the one. I'd just seen myself controlling her.

Was it really that simple? The power exchange happening between us was mind-fucking me?

She pushed the head of her rubber cock against my anus, just pressure, not entering me. She sighed against my face. "Do you want this, mutt? Do you want me to fuck you?"

"Yes, Mistress."

She pushed harder, still not entering, and my cock sprang to life. Need harsher than I've ever felt welled in my middle. I pulled on my wrist restraints, wanting freedom and knowing if I was free that this game would end now. I would fuck her senseless, and she would beg for mercy.

Holding my gaze, she smiled and it was a wicked smile because it seemed she could read my mind. "You want to fuck me so bad, don't you, mutt?"

I ground my teeth together to keep from saying a word.

She slid the tip of her cock inside of me, opening me slowly. *Too slowly. God, just do it. Get it over with.*

She pulled back out, then pressed in, just the head, not even pushing past the band of muscles that would fight against the intrusion.

"Say you love my cock in your ass."

"I love your cock in my ass, Mistress."

She thrust hard. Stretching me. Opening me. She thrust faster, accusing, "You like being the Dom too much. You like controlling people. You like hurting others."

"I don't," I lied, forgetting to use the word *Mistress* as the faces of those I'd harmed flashed through my brain, one after another.

I didn't enjoy it. It sickened me. But I'd done the things I'd done despite how horrendous the tasks were. I'd stomached it. I'd done my job, but I couldn't tell her that, I couldn't admit anything of my past to her.

"You caused pain, and you laughed about it."

"No," I refuted, suddenly remembering where I was and who I was with. "Mistress!"

She thrust harder and harder, ripping moans from my throat as the pain I'd caused others and their screams welled up from a place in my memory I thought I'd locked down tightly.

"Don't lie to me."

I started shaking then screaming, matching the sound in my head, not because she was hurting me fucking me, but because I'd hurt myself so badly, doing the things I'd done. Irreparable damage. I am damaged. "I'm sorry. I'm sorry. Oh. God."

She kept fucking me, even after I started sobbing.

She kept fucking me, even after I'd recovered from whatever breakdown had wrapped me in its grasp for those moments when I'd wailed like an infant. I wanted free, but I couldn't escape her. I couldn't escape myself, my memories. I was held down, fucked hard, emotion riding me mercilessly as I was forced to feel all the pain I'd hidden from for so long. "Mistress. Please release me."

She grabbed my face, pinching my cheeks hard between her fingers before she kissed me cruelly. "You're the one who came to me, mutt. You said you wanted to be owned, wanted to be controlled. You want to be punished for all your past sins, don't you?"

God, yes. "Please let me go."

"I can't do that. I won't fail you, mutt."

She thrust hard and deep, seeming to rip me in half. I screamed and kept screaming but she didn't release me, not until I became calm. Resigned. Exhausted.

I lay there knowing that even if she flayed me, it would not cause me enough suffering to make up for all that I'd done. She came. The sound of her pleasure seeming like the sounds of agony etched into my brain, and I knew then what drew me to her.

We're the two most injured people in this place. Broken. Soulless. Do we hope to save each other?

"A rum and Coke." My thoughts are interrupted by a customer's order. I go through the motions, serving them, a moment's distraction from *her* but then I'm scanning the room, seeking her out and being disappointed again.

My shift is unbearably long and when it is finally over, I want nothing more than my bed. Reaching the upper corridor, I dread walking its length. I have to pass Mistress Morgana's room to get to my own.

I'm surprised when her door opens just as I pass by and she orders me inside.

I can't breathe I'm so overwhelmed by her beauty and my need. I watch her close and lock the door, feeling like I am trapped in a dream. Turning to face me, she looks me up and down.

Her eyes are rimmed red and puffy. I think she has been crying, but I don't ask. I don't say anything. She unlocks the cage holding my cock in check. "Go shower."

Dumbfounded, it takes her turning me toward the adjoining bathroom and giving me a shove to get my feet moving. I know I'm going to wake up inside some new nightmare, but for a second I enjoy this dream. I wash my hair and lather my body. I allow myself to enjoy running my hands over my bare cock. It seems like forever since I've touched the smooth flesh of it. My length grows firm, and I am sorely tempted to masturbate, but I don't. A quick inspection tells me I'll soon be due a full body wax, and I decide to make an appointment to have it done as soon as I awaken. I like being hairless.

I step out of the shower and dry off. I leave the towel behind, and rejoin Mistress Morgana in her room. It is obvious from her posture she is waiting.

I don't know what to do so choose to kneel at her feet.

Looking up at her, she is even more beautiful than the first time I saw her. She isn't strapped on and the lack thereof makes me feel that she has been *out* tonight. Perhaps, clubbing. She's heavily made up and wearing a black tea-length velvet dress topped with a leather bustier heavily decorated with metal and buckles. Even her clunky platform combat boots are held closed with dozens of shiny silver buckles. She confirms my suspicions when she sits down on the padded stool in front of her makeup vanity and commands, "Take off my boots and rub my feet. I've been dancing for hours, and my feet are killing me."

I crawl nearer and struggle with the many buckles before finally pulling off the boots that extend well above her knees. I am surprised by the stockings she wears beneath. Thigh highs, but far from silk. They are a heavy cotton or a cotton-wool blend, striped gray and black.

I take my time rolling them down her smooth, pale legs, enjoying the reveal of skin littered with light freckles. When I have both feet bare and pulled onto my thighs, I start massaging.

Her head drops back and she moans, but she doesn't pull away, she doesn't ask me to stop, even when I think that perhaps the sounds she is making is from pain rather than enjoyment.

I guess, "Your boots are a size too small, Mistress."

"Two," she whispers, not looking at me. "They didn't have the right size, and I had to have them."

I chuckle. "Vanity?"

She lifts her head enough to look at me. "Vanity is my favorite sin."

I wiggle my eyebrows. "I have lots of favorite sins."

She pulls her feet from my lap and sits up. I regret my honesty when she turns away from me and faces the mirror. I don't move for fear of being sent away and am surprised as I watch her. She begins removing her makeup. Using makeup remover and cotton swabs she starts with her eyes, carefully removing her fake eyelashes before erasing the wide dark oval of shadow. She switches to a towelette for the rest of her face. The transformation is amazing.

She's young. *Very young* I decide when our gazes clash in the mirror.

Without speaking, she stands and faces me. She unfastens the buckles holding the bustier closed and drops the heavy material to the ground. At her sides, she unzips the zippers hidden into seams and pulls the dress over her head.

I'm still on my knees when she walks naked and barefoot to the bed. She pulls a small set of steps out from under the bed to climb onto the high mattress. Once she is centered on the big bed, looking small and fragile, more bared than I think few have ever seen her, she asks, "So, are you going to fuck me or is this an unremarkable waste of the rest of my day off?"

I start to stand, think better of it and crawl.

"You are no longer a puppy. I command you to be the man I know you to be."

I stand and climb into her bed. I don't know when I've ever felt so awkward climbing into bed with a nude woman. Should I kiss her first? Should I take her into my arms?

I decide to take her into my arms but stall when she seethes, "You better fuck me like you know what you're doing."

"Oh, I know what I'm doing." I grab her ankles and pull her down off the mountain of pillows propping her up to flatten her out. She squeals, surprised, and I decide to not kiss her. If fucking is what she wants, fucking is what she's going to get.

I push her knees open and take a long look at clit and labia. I separate her lips to expose the hidden passage and find her moist. The lure of her pink, damp flesh is great. I want to taste her.

"I don't want foreplay," she says and tosses a condom at me. It lands beside us and I look at it dumbly. It's been awhile since I've used one. My piercings tend to get in the way. I move between her legs, kneeling. I open her a bit more, pulling her labia lips apart, and I can feel her muscles tighten. She's used to being obeyed immediately.

I may only have this one chance.

I dip my head and lick her, long and deep, liking it when her hips buck in surprise. I grab her hips and hold her tight so that I can go down on her properly.

A few nips and licks later, she begs, "Please. Just fuck me."

Her urgency speeds my pulse, heightens my need, but also makes me wonder what her motivation is. Maybe she doesn't ever like foreplay, but it feels like something *more* is going on. I sit back up and pick up the condom. She watches as I open it and slide it over my erection, taking care when smoothing it past my piercings.

Angling above her, I take my cock in hand and guide it in. She lifts her hips, taking more of my length faster than I intended, and the sensation of her tight twat sliding over my pierced flesh is mind-blowing but I don't want to slow this down. I thrust deeper, making her cry out, then pump her hard and fast.

She wraps her legs around me, but that's too restraining for the rough fuck I want to give her. Grabbing her ankles, I put them on my shoulders. By the sounds coming from her throat I know she doesn't mind.

I thrust forcefully.

"Harder!" she begs. "Faster."

I won't last long but I do as she asks, I also slide my hand between us to tweak her clit in a matched rhythm.

She cries out, "Fuck! Yes! Oh! Fuck! Yes, yes, yes!" and it pushes me to the edge. I keep tweaking and thrusting, pushing back the wave of need riding me hard. I want her to orgasm first. I want—

"God." I lose the battle and push hard into her, my jism filling the condom. I keep moving over her, but it isn't with the same force as before and Morgana grabs my hips, pushing herself harder into me, grinding, bucking, and then screaming with frustration and unquenched need.

"From childhood's hour I have not been, as other's were—I have not seen as other's saw—I could not bring my passion's from a common spring."

Edgar Allen Poe, *Alone*

CHAPTER 8

KITTEN

At Lewd Larry's, I am surrounded by luxury, especially when we are on The Oasis level. Master designed the member's only dining room with an air of mystery. Plush red carpet in a Turkish pattern covers the floor, and soft pink tube lighting creates a warm glow around the room. Classical background music offers a thankful reprieve from the frenzied dance music on the lower level. It is a place for pet owners and their canine or feline slaves to relax and play.

I recline on a floor pillow at Mater's feet, while he sips brandy with one of his top Dominants, George Kirkpatrick, known as Doctor Psycho. I'm not sure how he came to be known by that name, because he seems to be the calmest, most rational handler Master has on his staff, although tonight he looks fatigued. Dark circles rim his eyes.

I pretend to sleep, listening hard, waiting for him to tell George about the house. I know Thomas must have sent him the information by now and am slightly surprised we are here instead of there to have a look.

"I'm hiring two more Dominants," Master announces.

"So soon? We barely have the last batch adequately trained." George's voice seems concerned.

"I think it's prudent. With Thomas not here, me looking at an extended paternity leave…"

What? He hasn't said anything to me about taking time away from the business.

"…and you obviously exhausted."

George sighs. "I'm fine."

"When's the last time you had a day off?"

"If you remember, I had almost *a full month off*."

Technically, it wasn't exactly time off. I think it, Master doesn't say it. He doesn't have to. They both know that his extended vacation was anything but restful. He'd spent the time saving Thomas's brother's life.

I sigh, audibly irritated, and am surprised when Master nudges me with his foot, a gentle reminder that I'm not supposed to be eavesdropping.

I can't help my feelings. I don't like Thomas's brother. He's going by the name *Joshua* now, who knows what his real name is. I heard Thomas call him Nikos, but is that his true name? Or just another alias? Although it hasn't been said, I know he's a secret agent too, and no doubt dangerous.

I might have liked him had we met under different circumstances, but showing up on our doorstep in the middle of the night, riddled with bullet holes, and out of his mind on drugs, wasn't a good introduction. If not for Master's quick surgical skills and George's willingness to stay with him while he recovered and detoxed, the man might be dead. I know it's not a very Christian thought but if it had been his time to die, it might have been for the best. I feel like if he'd never arrived, Thomas wouldn't have had to take the job on the other side of the country.

As it stands, I hate *Joshua*.

I sigh heavily a second time and receive a verbal reprimand. "Kitten!"

I wasn't even listening that time. Really! I open one eye and meet Master's irritated gaze.

"Meow-meow?"

He leans down, whispering, "Maybe you should take a nap in the office if our conversation is so disturbing to you."

"Meow," I answer, remembering the day he first taught me to vocalize two meows for positive, one meow for negative. Then it was only a game between us, pretend, but since then my feline persona has become every bit as real to me as my real life. I smile at him before closing my eyes and pretending to sleep.

"You expect Thomas to be away a long time this time, then?" George asks.

There is a long silence but Garrett finally answers, "Yes, a long time. His position in The Attic will need to be filled with a permanent replacement."

Permanent. He makes it seem Thomas is never returning, but he is. I know he is.

Soft applause erupts around the room, making me realize something is happening, and I sit up on my cushion to see what. My attention is drawn to a small, intimate stage where it appears a couple is preparing to enact a scene. My mood immediately brightens.

Boredom has not been my friend of late. I like being center stage. I like being on the receiving end of flogger, cane, or candle wax, and being forbidden play since my almost-miscarriage scare, the most I can hope for is watching someone else have fun. I smile, envying the woman being bound.

I recognize the couple as regular players, Jacques and Panda, and although I've never met them I've heard Master call him Jako in passing. Onstage, he bends her over a padded wood sawhorse, stretching her up on tiptoe. He ties her wrists and ankles, then steps back and looks at her. He asks the crowd, "Isn't she lovely?"

With a press on the remote control he holds in his hand, the raised dais they stand on rotates. He stops it only when she is posed with her bare ass facing most of the crowd. He rubs her bottom, and I can see her tremble lightly. I can say from experience that being so exposed in front of an audience is a very emotional thing. Fear and shame are powerful aphrodisiacs.

Not finished with his ties, he attaches a section of rope to her ponytail and forces her head back, stretching her neck out and forcing her to look forward.

He separates a flogger from his belt and proceeds to warm her bared bottom with soft, thuddy strikes, which leaves her skin a beautiful shade of pink.

God, I can't wait to play again. With each landing of the leather thongs, my skin reacts with memory. I am left wanting. Needing. I rub against Master's pant leg and he tousles my hair. "I know, sweetness."

Our gazes meet and I know he does know, because lust is evident in his eyes. With a heavy sigh, I go back to watching.

Panda's Master starts teasing her clit with a vibrator, and she starts whimpering. I frown, understanding immediately that she isn't enjoying being aroused in front of an audience. I think for a moment that she doesn't want to come with spectators watching, but then Jako uses the remote to revolve them around so that she is facing us.

She looks miserable and terrified, her eyes rolling back and forth. I wish I could have talked to her before the performance so that I could have told her to shut her eyes and just enjoy the sensation, but then I think that maybe Jako might have forbidden her from closing her eyes.

He continues stimulating her clit with the vibrator while lightly flogging her ass.

Suddenly and unexpectedly, her nipples start leaking and a tear slides down her cheek. My reaction to her embarrassment is just as astonishing. Heart racing, I want to leave. I don't want to see this. I didn't even know Panda was lactating. Did she have a baby and I not realize?

Jako kneels in front of her and pinches her nipple. A drop of white liquid pearls onto his thumb and laughing, he lifts his wet thumb to her line of vision. "Look at that luscious milk coming out of you, Panda. See what your arousal does to you?"

She looks like she wants to die of shame.

"Are your breasts feeling tight as your milk drops for me?" He slaps her ass hard, expecting an answer.

"Yes, Master."

"Tell me you want me to milk you like a cow."

A sob catches in her throat, but she obeys. "Milk me like a cow, Master."

"Yes." He sighs, cupping her breasts, squeezing. "Show the audience what happens when you come for me, little cow."

He holds the vibrator back to her clit and lightly smacks her breasts with the thongs of the flogger. It doesn't take long before Panda's shouts fill the room. "Please let me come, Master."

"Not yet. Show them you're my dairy cow, Panda. Show them how much milk you can squirt for me."

He smacks her ass with his bare hand.

Her moan wavers.

"Please, Master," she begs to come, tears sliding down her cheeks to join the milk dripping on the floor.

"Are you my dairy cow, Panda?"

"Yes, Master. I'm your dairy cow."

I gasp as milk starts shooting from her breasts. Her scream tells me that she's coming, that her body is finding pleasure either because of or in spite of her humiliation. I shudder, not understanding how Jako could put her on display like that if she didn't want to lactate publically. I can't imagine my own Master doing that to me.

Daring to look up at Garrett, I see he is smiling, clapping, enjoying Panda's humiliation.

Flopping down, I curl into a ball and close my eyes tight. I don't want to see any more. I thought I'd grown immune to anything that could happen here that I might find unsettling. It doesn't matter if all of our kinks aren't the same, right? I wish I knew what Panda was really thinking, what she is really feeling. If this wasn't consensual, I've lost any respect I might have ever had for a Dominant I don't even know. *God, please don't let Master ever get the idea of doing anything like that to me.* I pout—disappointed in myself—for passing judgment so quickly.

The scene seemed to begin consensually, and she does have a safe word. Even if she had to resort to using the house safe word "alacadabra", she could have stopped the scene. Master and any number of security would have seen to that.

Hearing near footsteps, I open my eyes to see Matthew Farris approaching the table. He is Thomas's inside man, though Garrett isn't aware of that fact. I know he is Thomas's eyes and ears while he is away. I know he is also here to protect us. He ducks close to Master and whispers something in his ear. Whatever he said was lure enough to call Master away and *that* makes me slightly nervous. Reason assures me that if had anything to do with Thomas he would have drawn us both away, not just Master.

I dare another peek at the stage and see that Panda doesn't seem as humiliated as before. She is actually enjoying the attention Jako is paying her clit with a vibrator. It doesn't matter. I curl tighter in a ball, still seeing in my mind the milk seeping from her breasts and the look of horror on her face.

" . . . for not an orphan in the wide world can be so deserted as the child who is an outcast from a living parent's love."

Charles Dickens, *Dombey and Son*

CHAPTER 9

GARRETT

"Sorry to disturb, Sir."

In a private corridor I face Farris impatiently, wanting to get back to Kitten, and instead of him saying whatever he needs to say we are wrapped in this game of verbal protocol. "Is there a good reason for pulling me way from the night's entertainment?"

He looks at his shoes, but just for a second, then meets my gaze. It is that gesture that warns me I'm not going to be happy about whatever he has to tell me.

"I need to bring the actions of one of your Dominants to your attention, Sir."

Great. Already problems with the new hires? I can't seem to get a break here. I'm distracted when the door to The Oasis opens and I catch a glimpse of Kitten, curled on her pillow. It's obvious she's upset tonight, and the evening's entertainment seemed to only make matters worse for her. Distractedly I ask, "Which one?"

"Mistress Morgana."

My chin jerks and I meet Farris's gaze. "Excuse me? Did you say Mistress Morgana?"

The muscle in his jaw tightens. "Yes, Sir. I believe she is in a relationship with another employee."

"Who?"

"Joshua Lambert, one of the bartenders."

He knows only that she is one of my most trusted Dominants. Being new to Lewd Larry's, he doesn't know the history we share.

When I bought the warehouse that eventual became home to Lewd Larry's, I expected to have to gently evict a few homeless people and help them find somewhere else to live. After all, the place had been abandoned for years and it wasn't secure, broken windows and doors off their hinges. In a word, it was a mess.

I didn't expect to find a thirteen-year-old girl, curled up and asleep on the fourth floor. I really didn't expect to fall in love with her at first sight.

I woke her up as gently as I could, but she jerked away and held out a knife. Her bright red hair fell in tangles all the way to her waist, but it was her eyes, blazing a bright emerald green, that held my attention. She seemed fearless, and when she commanded me to "stay away" I believed she had every intention of using the knife if she had to.

She was so small.

In every way small. She stood barely four and a half feet and weighed less than eighty pounds. I know, because I took her to the emergency room…right after she ran and tumbled down an entire flight of stairs. She'd broken her arm in three places but didn't shed a tear.

What a surreal night.

She'd begged and pleaded all the way to the hospital for me to not take her. Of course, I guessed she was a runaway.

She'd offered me her body to keep me from taking her for treatment.

"I don't sleep with children."

"I'm not a child, *not anymore.*"

I knew by the tone of her voice she was trying to tell me she wasn't a virgin, and a rage went through me that anyone would take advantage of such an adorable child. I assumed it had been another vagrant since she was obviously alone on the streets, but as she revealed her story she explained it had been her step-father and she no longer lived at home because her mother hadn't believed her.

Her account felt truthful, but I made a few phone calls anyway and after two seconds on the phone with her mother discovered she not only wasn't welcomed back, but the woman didn't even want to hear whether she was dead or alive, sick or well. What kind of person throws away a child?

The night had turned into one of *let's make a deal.*

"I'll tell the hospital I'm your father *if* you let them treat you."

"I'll find you a safe place to live, someplace where you'll never have to worry about your safety or hunger ever again *if* you'll go to school and make good grades."

The first part was easy. The hospital didn't require anything in the form of identification once they found out I was paying cash. Getting her registered for school was slightly harder. Finding someone I trusted to give her someplace to live was next to impossible, and so a room was made on the fourth floor just for her. The Attic was just a dream then and room for one small girl was easy. Granted, a fetish fantasy nightclub wasn't the best atmosphere for a young girl, but it was better than the streets and I'd never planned on her staying forever.

I got her through adolescence, through high school *and* college.

I'll never forget the day she came back and demanded a job. She didn't ask, that wasn't her style.

I've spoiled her too much, I think. She's always gotten her way.

Fucking Thomas's brother is the final straw, a direct challenge to my authority. I assume she doesn't know the true identity of the bartender known as Joshua Lambert. She does know the house rules. Fraternizing between employees is strictly forbidden.

I can't overlook this.

I find her alone in her room.

"Is it true?" Our gazes collide. Her jaw muscle tightens, and I'm sure she is seeing the same sight on my face. "Do you have anything to say for yourself?"

She glances away, shaking her head, and stands. She doesn't think I see, but she half-smiles before turning back to face me, which only makes me wonder if he is out there waiting for her.

"You know you have to be punished."

She props her ass against the windowsill. "Are you going to fire me?"

"I should." *I can't fire him.* "You're demoted."

Her forehead tightens, making two deep lines between her brows. "You're demoting me?"

"You can't obey my rules—you're lucky you still have a job."

"Fine."

"I expect you to break off all relations with the bartender immediately."

She gives me a look, cold, calculating, if looks could kill...

"No."

"What did you just say to me?"

"I'm not going to stop seeing him. Fire me if you have to. Throw me out. I should have moved out years ago anyway. This was always supposed to be temporary."

I can tell by her face, she's bluffing. "Maybe you should *go*."

Her expression is a mixture of fear and disbelief that breaks my heart. She wants me to beg her to stay, I want to beg her to give up the damn bartender. Watching her, I suddenly remember so many standoffs as she was growing up…lines in the sand…she wanted a puppy, settled for a goldfish, she wanted to wear eyeliner, settled for lip gloss, she wanted—

"You're a hypocrite!"

"Excuse me?" I'm still trying to figure out what I can substitute for a man, another man would be fine, any other man besides Thomas's brother.

"You want to talk about the rules? All was fine and dandy when you wanted to start fucking Thomas but let any of your underlings get an itch and they get fired?"

"I didn't say you were fired! We were discussing you moving out of The Attic so that you aren't breaking the rules under my God damn nose!"

Morgana bats her eyes at me and smiles. Oh, fucking no. I did not just give her permission to keep seeing Joshua, but as her smile grows wider I know that's exactly what she thinks. She throws her arms around my neck and kisses my cheek. "Thank you for looking the other way."

I grab her and pull her into a hug she can't escape. "I don't want you seeing him."

"I love him."

Meeting her gaze, I know she believes she does.

I want to tell her he's dangerous. I want to ground her and lock her in her room, but I'm wise enough to know that it will take more than me standing between them to keep them apart. The most I can hope for is that Thomas's brother bores quickly. I kiss her forehead. "Be careful, sweetheart."

My heart is heavy as I return to The Oasis. Knowing he wants his brother to lay low, I'm going to have to call Thomas. He certainly doesn't want him to leave the premises. I'm going to have to allow Morgana to stay in The Attic with her lover. It's only a matter of time before anarchy reigns.

I go back to our table and find Kitten right where I left her. At least I can count on her to obey my will. Patting my knee for her to climb into my lap, I censor myself for being so imperialistic. *Am I being too hard on Morgana?*

I push my nose against the back of Kitten's neck, inhaling the scent that is distinctly her. With her pregnancy, holding her is made slightly awkward, but I pull her closer. She breaks house rules when she whispers against my face, "Is everything all right?"

I kiss her nape. "Nothing for you to worry about."

She angles her face so that she can gaze deeply into my eyes. She thinks I am lying.

I take a deep breath and force myself to relax even more, pushing away the emotion I am feeling. I assure her, "It had nothing to do with Thomas."

She nods and sighs, obviously relieved, and allows herself to relax against me.

I whisper against her neck, "I'm sorry I missed the rest of the performance. Was it enjoyable?"

I'm surprised when she tenses in my lap. I wrap my arms around her waist so she can't escape to the pillow at my feet. I squeeze her breasts. "They're getting bigger. They're going to fill with milk soon."

I know she was made uncomfortable by the scene between Jako and Panda, and I find it exciting that there is something new for me to trigger an emotional response to. I look forward to taking her home and discussing her discomfort at length, but then I see Joshua in the elevator with Morgana. He is on his knees, she holds his leash. I allow Kitten to move to her pillow, displeased Morgana has chosen to flaunt her behavior.

Later, at home, in bed, holding Kitten tightly, I try to think what recourse I have with Morgana. I'll just have to draw the line in the sand, forbid her from seeing him, but immediately remember the desperation Kitten responded with when I forbade her from seeing me—the kitten antics, the phone calls, the computer sabotage—and wonder if Morgana would go to such great lengths to try to keep seeing Joshua. I don't think she would, but then Morgana has never professed to loving anyone.

"Where are you tonight?"

"Morgana said that she's in love with Joshua."

Pulling away from me, Kitten sits up and turns on the bedside light. She is pale and worried. "That's not good. She has to stay away from him."

"He's been well behaved. There hasn't been a single complaint about him."

"He's dangerous!"

Her hands are fisted tightly into the sheets. I don't even think she likes Morgana, and yet she's obviously worried about her. Sitting up, I stroke her face. "Yes, he is."

"Forbid her from seeing him."

"I tried. If I force her, she'll leave."

Kitten shakes her head. "Morgana would never leave Lewd Larry's."

I blink at her, remembering when I let her go with Thomas, remembering allowing Thomas to take over ownership of her for three months and knowing he was a dangerous man. The only difference between Thomas and his brother is that I trust Thomas. I don't know what Joshua would have to do to gain my trust, but I don't trust him now. I can only pray he doesn't do anything to hurt Morgana.

Pulling Kitten into my arms, I kiss her forehead. "You asked what was on my mind, I told you, now I think you should help me forget my concerns."

She doesn't look happy that I've deemed the conversation over, but she complies with my request. Pushing on my shoulders, she presses me back against the pillows and licks a slow, sensual trail down my body.

As she circles my nipple with her tongue, I close my eyes and will myself to relax and forget the day. Joshua. Morgana. Thomas. Their faces flash through my mind unwanted. I crack my eyes open and focus on what Kitten is doing to me.

Soft licks over my ribcage.

Damn it, Morgana, what are you thinking?

"Bite me."

Our gazes meet. I've never asked Kitten to hurt me, or top me, though she's topped me often enough from below. She knows I'm not always dominant. With Thomas, I'm almost always submissive. I like the pain, the head games. As I watch her, she grazes her teeth over my ribs, not biting, not yet. I shudder, the sensation not soft enough to tickle or hard enough to hurt, but the look she has in her eyes definitely holds me still and ready.

When she sinks her teeth into me, I hold my breath not wanting the inhale or exhale to cause more damage than she has already caused. I think she doesn't have enough experience, probably no experience, inflicting pain, and I've made a mistake. She's obviously broken skin. It isn't so much the pain, but the warm slide of liquid over my flesh. Blood. My blood. There's something so special about knowing I am bleeding, about knowing I have allowed someone to draw my blood.

She watches my face intently, not pressing harder, or tearing free, or even releasing my flesh from her grip. I consider commanding her to release me, but don't. I want to see what she does.

When she does soften her bite, she licks the wound. She holds my gaze as she licks. There is something in the depths of her eyes, need, savage and unspent. I think she could tear me to shreds. Moving only inches away from my ribs into the soft part of my belly, she bites down again. I moan, the intensity of the pain greater at this spot.

She holds me in her mouth, not biting harder, nor relaxing her grip, and I wonder where she learned this from. I can feel her breath fanning across my skin, across the stinging field of pain she's created with her teeth, and I realize my body is tensed, ready for more pain, hungry for more pain.

Her hands slide over my skin, so softly it tickles, and I jerk against her mouth. Her fingers slide over my pelvis, over my thighs, lower to cup my scrotum. She squeezes, hard enough to make my breath catch and while she is squeezing, she bites deeper, harder, leaving me writhing and moaning against her.

"Enough?" she asks softly, and I look to see her licking my blood off her lips. "Do I have your attention now?"

I nod, unable to take my eyes off her as she moves to straddle me. She's completely and utterly mesmerizing as she pushes herself down onto my erection. She closes her eyes as I fill her. She commands, "Hold my shoulders."

I push against her shoulders, holding her up as she falls forward. I hold her steady as she starts to rides me. She kisses my forearm, licks, and then bites as she increases the pace of her hips.

I push more deeply into her as the pain holding my thoughts captive, scatter my pleasure. She rides me harder, faster. She bites deeper.

"Oh God, Kitten." I cry out as she pulls my orgasm out of my scrotum. "Holy fucking God."

"Man is only truly great when he acts from the passions; never irresistible but when he appeals to the imagination."

Benjamin Disraeli, *Coningsby*

CHAPTER 10

THOMAS

After two months in Washington DC I'm a different person, and the life I left behind in San Francisco seems like a dream. The world of politics is all-consuming, especially the one I've joined. There are agendas within agendas and every meeting is scheduled around a meal, breakfast meetings, luncheons, dinners, cocktails.

Abigail is in high demand and we go to wherever the interest is highest, decided by projected contributions.

Tonight finds us in New Hampshire, and she is expected to walk away with millions in donations for her campaign. I think we're all in for a long night as I estimate her half-hour speech taking more than two to deliver. After a while she launches into the speech, knowing the clapping isn't showing signs of dying down. As she talks the room grows completely silent, because everyone wants to hear what she's saying.

Trained in public speaking, she knows just when to project and when to speak softly for effect. She screams into the microphone, "It's time to bring our jobs back home."

Enthusiastic applause follows the statement and she speaks over it, knowing the clapping won't die down. She continues shouting into the microphone. "How can we support a global market when our local economy is failing?"

I realize I'm smiling. I'm proud of her. I'm even glad I'm here during what I believe will become a defining moment in history. I know that neither Garrett or Celia would want to hear such sentiment, but my bond with Abigail runs far longer and deeper than what I have with either of my lovers. That isn't to say I love Abigail, but I do respect her and I do believe she is the right person for the job. If my being here helps her to succeed in winning the election, my time and energy have been well spent.

Her speech ends and my clapping joins that of those standing on their feet. I'm still scanning for trouble, watching hands, facial expressions, but for now I feel like she is safe and when she finally comes off stage, I pat her back, professionally, and congratulate her.

Eyes wide, smile bright, she demands, "I want a clean getaway."

I hurry her away from the chaos, leaving her security detail trying to keep up.

It is a long drive back to the hotel. She is shaking with nervous energy and flushed with excitement. She is high on adrenaline and success. It is a dangerous mood, that could make her reckless, and I want to get her behind the safety of her hotel room door as quickly as possible.

"I want to celebrate," she says breathlessly. "Before the numbers come out, before I see any news report or any speculation, I want to enjoy how this feels."

The SUV hits a bump and our knees touch. It is like a lightning bolt shooting down my spine, and I know if I felt it, she felt it. There has always been an almost uncontrollable sexual tension between us, and it has only been the boring monotony of daily tasks that have helped us rein in our need in public spaces. I can feel her desire rolling off her in thick waves.

I shake my head in warning. Pouncing on the personal assistant in a jam packed security vehicle would not be a smart move. Thankfully, she glances out the window.

I look out the window on the other side of the vehicle, counting telephone poles, basically the equivalent of a cold shower but it does little good, and by the time I drop her off at her suite, I am ready to rip her clothes off, but that wouldn't do, not at all.

Two bodyguards are posted in the hallway and I go to my own suite, unescorted.

I take a deep breath, stepping inside. Waiting in the dark. *Hearing everything.* Soft voices in the hall, the two guards talking about today's big game, an interior door opening and closing on the other side of the wall I know is Abbie's room. A second later the sound of her turning the deadbolt to the door that connects our rooms seems as loud as a gunshot. Crossing the dark room to meet her there, I turn the deadbolt on my side and open the door. We collide, both of us needing to get to the other desperately. We are a tangle of limbs, mouths connected, kissing with intensity I have rarely experienced.

I had thought to go to her in her room, but as she pushes me back like a gale force storm, I am fine staying in my suite. Wrapping my arms around her, I slide the zipper to her dress down her back and start to pull the fabric off her shoulders but her hands are wrapped in my hair, holding me tight and preventing the move.

I pull my mouth away from hers. "We have all night. Let me help you out of your dress."

Bright light shines into my suite from hers and through the

doorway, I see her room is lit up, every light on, enough illumination for us to not break anything in the dark and for me to see the primal need reflected in her eyes. She whispers, "I need you *now*."

I pull back from her, grabbing her forearms and holding her tightly, but gently away from me though she tries to move forward, wanting back in my arms, wanting to *control*. I chuckle when she pouts. "Slow down, my love. That is all."

But it wasn't *all* I wanted.

I'm too long from Lewd Larry's and the way of life I have there—dominance and submission in all of its glorious perfection—at my will. I've never considered myself a sadist, dominant yes, curious about what makes humans so willing, so needy, to be controlled, but finding joy in causing another pain? No. Although sometimes, it is necessary.

God, I miss it. At first I thought I was only longing for my lovers, Garrett and Celia, but as the weeks have passed…I need more than just a lover's caress…I need to control. And although I have shared a few scenes with Abbie, those amount to nothing more than bedroom games and compare little to what I want to do to her tonight.

I'm not at all certain how she'll respond, and the mystery itself is alluring.

I gaze upon her face. Cast in shadows she appears much younger, more vulnerable. Perhaps it is her widened eyes, her parted lips, or the quickened pulse in her throat. I wonder if she can feel my need or my restraint.

Her eyes hold questions and though only seconds have passed, it feels much longer. I close my eyes, enjoying the pulsing throb of time. I feel caught in the moment, and it feels much the same as the heart-stopping second before I pull the trigger. My target is in sight and then…

And then…

I open my eyes and look again upon her face. I whisper, "Abigail."

She wets her lips with her tongue but doesn't speak.

Ducking my head down, I kiss her. But more than that I savor each nuance of the kiss, her taste, her scent, the crush of our lips against each other. I suck her bottom lip into my mouth, pulling on it gently. Need pulls between us like thick taffy, but I refuse to give into the moment. There has been too much quick pleasure between us, barely sated need. Tonight I want more, and I hope she is able to give me what I need.

"I want to see you."

I've requested the one thing she never allows. Of course I've seen almost all of her body naked, but only sections at a time. She hides her body from me, hiding it behind nightgowns, robes, or the veil of darkness. I suspect she is shamed, self-conscious, or embarrassed. And though it is true that she doesn't have a twenty-year-old's suppleness, I don't think she should feel anything less than beautiful.

She pulls away and turns her back to me. I take it as an invitation, though I'm certain she didn't mean it as one. I slide my arm around her middle, pulling her hips tight against my groin. With my other hand I unzip her dress the rest of the way and slide the fabric down her arms.

Dress trapped between us, I unhook her bra and pull it away, dropping it on the floor.

She tenses when I start to ease the dress over her hips. I kiss her neck and shoulders and keep lowering the fabric until it falls to pool at her ankles. I start unfastening the row of hooks holding her girdle closed.

"Lex?"

I whisper against her neck, "Relax," and with a hiss the body shaper slides free and I drop it.

I run my hands over her bared breasts and stomach, enjoying her curves.

"Can we please get into your bed?" she begs, trying to lead the way.

I hold her back, running my hands lower, feeling the silky weave of her pantyhose. I roll them down, squatting as I do so. I help her step free of each shoe and pull the stocking away from each foot, leaving her standing in her underwear.

She trembles slightly, and I like it that she does. I kiss the back of each of her thighs before tugging the waistband of her panties down and helping her out of them.

Standing, I take her hand and lead her to an armless desk chair. I tell her, "Sit," and my tone of voice brooks no refusal. Sure, she could disobey. There is the choice after all, but I think she's intrigued now that the fire of passion has cooled a bit.

She sits, her bare bottom sliding against the satin of the chair. It is a sensory jolt reflected in her facial expression. Her discomfort at being so exposed is evident in the challenge of her arched brow.

I turn on a desk lamp and angle the shade to cast its light on her stomach and juncture of her thighs. She starts to stand, saying, "That's enough. I don't know what game *this* is, but I don't—"

I push her back down, her bottom hitting the cushioned seat hard. Our gazes clash. "This isn't a game. I said that I want to see you, and I intend to see all of you. I want every inch of your flesh bared to me. I want your emotions raw. I want to see your soul."

Her gaping mouth slams closed.

"You are going to do everything I ask you to do, Abigail. Do you understand?"

Her lips part but she doesn't speak, she only nods.

I kneel in front of her. "Separate your knees."

She does but barely. None too gently I push her knees wide, making her gasp. I angle her legs to either side of the seat, looking closely at her. Her downy fine pubic hair curls over her clit. The pink nub barely peeks through. Her hair below is only slightly darker blond than the platinum blond on her head. Touching her lightly, I tease one of the curls away, considering asking her to shave it but as quickly decide against it.

I tease the nub of her clit with my thumb, drawing the moist evidence of her desire back with the hood of skin trying to hide the hidden bud.

"Lex, you're making me uncomfortable."

"No words, Abigail." I meet her gaze, saying, "Tonight is only about what I want. What I want to take from you and what I want to give you. This moment I want to look, and if that makes you uncomfortable, then I want that too."

I return my gaze to her clit. Looking, just looking, and knowing by her rising heat and scent that she is growing moist beneath the coils. That if I only reached out, I could dip my finger into her wetness. I don't. I flick her clit, making her jerk, making her cry out. I shake my head. "Sh-h."

I flick her clit again.

And again.

"Stop it, Lex! That hurts."

I caress her cheek, gazing deep into her eyes. "Accept that I want to hurt you tonight."

I notice she is panting, and I believe that she wants this as much as I. She has been playing with me for years, blindfolds, silk binds, a little slap and tickle, but never pain. We have danced around the potential of what could happen between us if only we allowed it, perhaps if only I forced it. Is that what I'm doing now?

Forcing this to happen?

Her arms are clamped tightly around her middle, hiding what she sees as imperfection. I continue holding her gaze as I pull her arms way, exposing her further. I rub my hand over her belly, rolling the flesh under my hands. She squints her eyes closed tightly. "Please. Don't. I'm self-conscious enough of my fat."

I don't stop touching her, kneading her. "I'm going to gag you if you don't shut up, Abigail."

Her eyes fly open and she shudders, but she doesn't say anything else. I keep massaging her belly, feeling her discomfort. I pinch a roll of flesh, letting her know with the action that I am taking a measure of her. What I don't see as an imperfection is utterly humiliating to her, or at least that is the way she is responding. A flush of red creeps between her breasts and up her throat.

She is too strong a woman to ever cry, to ever let such weakness show, and while I admire her strength, I also want her to let go of her emotion.

I cup her ample breasts, lifting them, weighing them in my palms. She has such heavy breasts. It's surprising really once they are free of their fabric cage just how large they really are. Crushed beneath foundation products meant to hide, not enhance, and her jacket, she lessens her femininity and grasps at a more male driven power. As if anyone could forget that she is a woman.

Standing, I look down on her and she sighs with relief, thinking we are done.

"Stay there. Don't move," I warn.

Crossing the room, I open the closet and pull out one of my bags. My toy bag.

Inside there are restraints, gags, nipple clamps of all sizes and designs, whips, floggers, riding crops, and paddles, lube, and a couple dozen dildos and vibrators also in various sizes and designs. Just unzipping the bag, my pulse speeds up a bit.

"I like a look of Agony, Because I know it's true— Men do not sham Convulsion, Nor simulate, a Throe—"

Emily Dickinson, *I Like A Look Of Agony*

CHAPTER 11

KITTEN

Thank God for work. Even though I'm exhausted and didn't sleep a wink. I left the house early, citing a mid-week employee meeting. Knowing Garrett, he's still asleep. Dawn to dusk, then rising for work. It's quite the nocturnal life we lead, except I'm trying to lead both a normal life and night-time life. I know it's something I'll have to find a better balance to once the babies arrive, but for now I need both the club and work, anything to keep my mind off the fact that Thomas is away.

Jackie finds me working late at *The Darkness* and although I'd usually be thrilled to see her, when she opens my door and pokes her head in, I wish I'd locked it. Then I could have stayed hidden. Except my car is in the parking lot and she would have guessed I was in here. *She* would kick the door down.

"How about some dinner?" she asks.

"Did Garrett call you?"

She comes into my office and poses with her hands on her hips, stretching out her full height—all six foot six inches of her—six ten, counting her stilettos. "What? A friend can't show up unexpectedly to take a friend out for some dinner?"

"He thinks I've lost my mind because I insist in coming here after a full night at the club."

She walks over and sits in one of the upholstered wing chairs on the other side of my desk. "He might have a point. How are you feeling?"

"Pregnant."

"I'm worried about you. Ever since Thomas left...you work too hard...I don't think that's good for you or the babies. Have you looked in the mirror lately? Those dark circles under your eyes mean you need sleep." She shakes her head. "I admit there's no love lost between me and Thomas, but I never believed in a million years he would abandon you."

Bristling, I demand, "Is that your way of asking *what the hell is going on*?"

"Whoa, sistah. It's me, Jackie, no ulterior motive for prying into something that isn't any of my damned business except for my love for you. I worry."

I snort.

"I would jump up and down and clap with joy—behind your back, of course—if you were to tell me that demon was gone from your and Garrett's life forever, but I do love you, and if you are hurting you should have someone to talk to about it."

My shoulders slump as I release a heavy sigh. "It isn't so much that I'm hurting. I'm resigned. I feel like I've been waiting for this to happen since I first met Lord Fyre. Being with him was so chaotic, so intense, it didn't seem like it could possibly last forever...and having both of them, Master and Lord Fyre, well, that was just too good to be true, wasn't it?"

Jackie takes my hand and pats it. "Nothing is too good for you, honey. You deserve the best of the best every minute of the day."

"That would be having both Master and Lord Fyre here."

I guess it is Jackie's turn to snort, because she does, loudly and derisively.

"He's coming back," I defend, not knowing how much Garrett has told her about the situation, and being sworn to secrecy about Thomas's work as a covert operative makes anything I say compromising. "He was just offered a job he couldn't refuse."

I meet Jackie's gaze, and the look she gives me is one of pity. She really doesn't believe he is coming back. Is that what Garrett told her? Panic fills my chest as doubt floods my mind. *No. No! Thomas is coming back. He would never lie to me.*

Standing, she comes around my desk and taking my hands, pulls me out of my chair. She wraps her arms around me. I will not cry. Jackie doesn't know anything about it. Garrett would have no more compromised Thomas than I would, not even to Jackie. With my mouth muffled against her ample breasts, I say, "Dinner would be good."

As it turns out, the sun hasn't set yet and it is a perfect spring day. The air smells sweet after the recent rains. Crossing the parking lot, I ask Jackie, "Do you think anyone would be at the Primal Birth Center? I know it's not one of our regularly scheduled days but—"

"Is something wrong?" she interrupts. "Tell me you aren't in labor!"

I laugh at her obvious distress. "Nothing quite so dramatic, I assure you. That's at least a month away. I just wanted to talk to someone."

"I thought that was why I'm here," she says cheekily. After we climb into her car and buckle up, she turns toward me, asking, "Is Garrett still being an ass about wanting you to have a Caesarian section?"

I smirk. "Well, of course. But that isn't what I want to talk to someone about."

"I'm all ears," she says brightly.

Starting the car, she drives through the parking lot and out onto the main road while I try to figure out how to even broach my concerns and what I'm feeling. "Did you see Panda and Jako's performance last night?"

She shakes her head. "I wasn't at the club last night."

It is only after she tells me that I realize I didn't see her last night. "Well, you missed a show."

Her eyes widen, and she smiles at me. Zig-zagging through traffic, she demands, "I need details!"

God, where do I start?

It isn't the onstage scene my mind drifts to. Last night Master wanted to talk about the scene, hours later, and I certainly didn't want to discuss it.

"It was fine," I'd said, leaving him in the bedroom to go to the bathroom.

He followed me, and I peed in front of him.

I don't know if it's a normal thing to have your partner not give you any privacy for bodily functions, or just a kink thing, but I'm used to it. I washed my hands and brushed my teeth, the whole time debating whether or not I wanted to shower.

I decided I did. I'd felt dirty ever since Jako and Panda's scene, but I hadn't wanted to invite intimacy so I'd climbed under the covers and soon we were talking about Morgana...I thought the Jako-Panda scene was forgotten.

"What bothered you most, Kitten?"

Was it that obvious that it bothered me so much Master had to keep needling me? To escape the question, I opened the shower door and turned on the water. "It didn't bother me. I don't know what you're talking about."

"Yes, you do." His hand on my elbow kept me from entering the shower. "Talk to me."

Holding my elbow tight, he used his free hand to stroke my breast. He drew teasing circles around my areoles with his fingertips, leaving my nipples tingling with a strange sensation. "Are you worried about how you are going to feel about your own milk coming in?"

I cringe just remembering. Jackie is waiting aptly. There isn't any way to tell Jackie what happened other than to just be blunt.

"Jako milked Panda onstage."

"Really?"

I can tell by her tone she isn't disgusted by the image.

"Yes! *Really.*" My heart starts racing and I begin talking fast, probably too fast for her to understand anything I'm trying to say. "And now Garrett wants me to nurse the babies, and I'm scared to death he's going to want to humiliate me onstage the way Jako humiliated Panda, and honestly, my mind just can't go there. I can't do that. I won't do that!"

"I don't think Jako and Garrett share a single aspect of dominating style. So, I don't believe that should even be a worry in your pretty little head."

I hate being patronized.

She wasn't in our bedroom last night. She didn't see the look on Master's face when he cupped my breasts, when he kissed them. When he licked them.

"I can't wait to watch you nurse our babies. There's nothing more natural in the world. You realize that, right?"

My mouth went dry and I felt like my tongue had swollen double. I couldn't answer. In my mind I was seeing him milk me like Jako had milked Panda.

As the water of the shower ran over my head and into my eyes I'd allowed myself to cry, even though I didn't know why I was crying. With the water still running over my face, I washed my hair, and realized only when I felt a cool draft that Master had stripped and joined me in the shower. I'd kept my eyes closed, saying nothing when he soaped my breasts and abdomen.

Cupping my breasts, he took first one and then the other into his mouth, sucking each nipple gently. "Are you going to share our babies' milk with me, Kitten?"

I didn't know what to think or say in response to that question. I know I thought I was going to have a heart attack, my heart was pounding so hard in my chest.

He'd sucked harder, drawing my flesh painfully into his mouth, and raw need pooled low in my belly.

"Does it make you as hot as it makes me, Kitten? When I think about pounding you with my dick as hard as I can and making you come while I suck the milk from your breasts..." He slid his fingers between my damp slit, finding me slick with arousal. I was disgusted by my body's reaction. So disgusted, I came almost immediately. I came against his fingers, while he was sucking my nipple, and I was imagining my milk flowing over his tongue.

"You can't understand!" I face Jackie, angry that she can't understand how I'm feeling. *My God, how can she? She's not a real woman.*

I can tell by her expression, she's hurt. She really does want to understand. But how can I explain it?

I was disgusted by my orgasm, I was disgusted by the fantasy Master had shared, but I couldn't deny the lust that wrapped me so tightly it hurt.

"We had a fight."

"About Jako and Panda's scene?"

"No, because he made me orgasm. I didn't want to think about it, not any of it. Not about Jako and Panda, or about Master sucking milk from my nipples, or even my babies sucking milk out of my nipples, but he did make me think about it—all of it—and I came thinking about it. I'm such a pervert."

Jackie pulls off onto the shoulder and puts the car in park. "You're just a little bit perverted, and that's okay. Tell me about the fight."

"I was screaming and crying—and coming—and Master was holding me tight against his chest while I came. He didn't let go of me when I finished. He just kept holding me, and I was fighting to get away from him. I started cussing him, calling him every vile thing I could think of, and when I collapsed against him, exhausted, all he had to say was, 'Feel better?' Well, of course I didn't want to talk about it."

Jackie pats my hand, trying to be a good listener I guess, because she doesn't say anything and the silence is only making matters worse.

"Please say something."

"You have no idea how lucky you are. How blessed."

I hmmph.

"You are a very sensual woman, pregnancy doesn't change *that*. I think he was just trying to help you understand your strong reaction to Jako and Panda in the only way he could."

"I don't want to understand that it upset me so much because I was turned on by it!"

She shrugs.

"We have sex all the time, and I think it's *because* I'm pregnant. Like he can't get enough *of me*. And it's only because of *this*." I point to my stomach. "What's he going to do when I'm not pregnant anymore? Not want me?"

She shakes her head. "I don't see that happening."

"And what about these?" Through the fabric of my shirt, I cup my breasts and bounce them in my hands. They are obviously larger than ever before, making Jackie laugh. "What if he becomes one of those fetishists who wants to share the supply? What if he's so turned on by that, he wants me to *keep* lactating?" As I ask the question, I realize just how uncomfortable I'm made by the thought. Actually, it disgusts me. "I can't do that."

She glances at me, and her face is a mixture of humor and concern.

I keep thinking about the scene with Jacko and Panda, about how upset and horrified she looked when everyone laughed at her public humiliation. I repeat, "I can't do that. I won't be a cow for him."

Jackie nods and when she says, "I understand," I bust out laughing. *How can she?*

I hoot hysterically.

"Maybe we should do a late dinner after we stop by the Primal Birth Center," she suggests. "Maybe you can find some answers there, talking to a *real* woman."

I know she's hurt, and I don't know how to make that part better. I don't argue. I just let her pull back into traffic and start driving. I'm still giggling when she pulls into the center's parking lot. And too soon I am in a small room with Sally Woodward, one of the birthing centers doulas, and Jackie is outside waiting in the relaxation garden. I'm not sure why it surprises me that Sally has a baby tucked into a cloth sling hung over her neck and shoulder, but it does. It also makes me uncomfortable. I can't remember the last time I was this close to a baby.

After inviting me to sit and both of us getting settled on low-to-the-ground padded benches, I have to ask, "Is that comfortable?"

She laughs. "For me and the baby. I can get my work done while he sleeps."

I nod, wishing there was an easy way to start the discussion I want to have, and decide I'm in the wrong place. I should be back at Lewd Larry's, trying to find a kinky woman who has had a baby, someone who is dealing with the lifestyle and motherhood. I don't know what possessed me to seek out a *vanilla* woman.

While I procrastinate the baby wakes up crying. Sally lifts her shirt, pops her breast out of her bra and tucks her nipple into the baby's mouth so quickly, I'm stunned. I gawk like I've never seen a woman's bare breast before.

"Does my nursing Liam bother you?"

I shake my head, but keep staring awkwardly.

"Does it bother you seeing my breast?"

Looking away, I blush and giggle. "No. I've just never seen…"

"Come closer."

She pats the extra-wide bench she's sitting on and I join her, looking down at Liam's mouth latched tight on her nipple. The baby's mouth is a deep shade of red, he's sucking so intently.

"God, that has to hurt."

"Some. At first," she admits. "But *that is* what nipples are designed for."

We both laugh, though admittedly mine still has a ring of nervous hysteria.

"So, what brings you to the birthing center today? You said you have a few questions?"

I look away, embarrassed. *God, why did I come here?*

Sally pats my thigh. "Don't worry. I've heard it all. You can't shock me."

I swallow hard, meeting her gaze. "I used to feel that way."

She tilts her head, obviously curious.

Taking a deep breath, I nervously admit, "My—" I stumble over the word *Master* and replace it with "boyfriend" but the word falls flat and sounds wrong as I struggle to form a coherent sentence "…owns Lewd Larry's nightclub." I leave out the *Fetish Fantasy* part of the club's name.

She blinks.

Does that mean she's heard of it? Hasn't heard of it? *Oh, hell.* I skip the part about Jacques and Panda, waving a dismissive hand, I say, "Not important. Anyway, my boyfriend is *really* into sex now that I'm pregnant."

She looks at me like she's waiting for the punch line of a joke.

"I mean, *he's really into it.*"

"Oh! *I see.*" She blushes, eyes widening. "First, don't worry about being the first woman to come to my office with this problem. Not that it's a problem, unless you are saying 'no' and he isn't listening?"

I shake my head. "No, no. Nothing like that."

"I've talked to enough women to know that there are two types of men, the ones who don't want anything to do with their wives until after the baby is born and men who just can't seem to get enough of their wives while they are pregnant. Not that there isn't a happy medium somewhere in between the two, it's just those women don't complain."

I frown. Is that what I'm doing, complaining? "I think I'm just confused."

She nods. "Okay, let's talk about that part."

"I feel like I'm *bad* because when he is so obviously excited, feeling the babies move inside of me, it's a turn-on for me too."

"Ah, like feeling sensual while you are nurturing a new life inside of you is taboo?"

"Exactly."

"I think that as a society we've desexualized pregnant women, but just because there is a baby inside of you doesn't make you any less sensual, and many women do find that they are a lot more horny once they are past that first trimester. I did. I wanted sex constantly while I was pregnant. I wore my poor husband out."

"Really?"

"Really."

I am mesmerized by Liam sucking his mother's nipple, but not in a sexual way, just because he is so intent. It looks like very hard work. His face turns bright red, he passes gas and then sighs, releasing her nipple. I gasp, realizing he did more than let out a belly full of air.

"Does that happen a lot?"

"Often enough." She de-slings him and lays him out between us, then grabs the near diaper bag. I get my first up-close-and-personal lesson on changing a baby boy's diaper. Sally keeps up with the conversation. "It's hard to not feel sexual when you are pregnant. A woman's nipples are more sensitive, and just the rub of her cloth bra can make her body react by becoming horny."

I nod. I hadn't thought about it because I'm so focused on Garrett's sudden new pregnancy fetish, but I'm not saying no, I want it as much as he does, and she's right, even when he isn't nearby I feel horny a lot of the time.

"Just be thankful your boyfriend is one of those men who gets turned on by pregnancy and not turned off."

I hadn't thought about that.

"So, I shouldn't be worried that his interest is going to become a crazed fetish and he's going to want to keep me pregnant *all* the time."

Sally laughs. "Well, let's hope that isn't the case! I think after you give birth you will find he's just as happy with you regaining your pre-pregnancy shape. Is this helping at all? I feel like you came in pretty desperate, that more was going on than just your boyfriend's increased libido."

I blush, admitting, "He freaked me out by saying he wanted me to share the babies' milk. I couldn't believe he was even thinking *that*."

She lifts the baby to her shoulder and pats its back. Smiling, she says, "Don't worry. That's also quite common. I don't think it necessarily means he really wants to, although it might, but it does seem to be a common theme for women who want to talk to me, so you can be assured he isn't being abnormal."

Vanilla women have these conversations with her? I'm not sure if that makes me feel better or worse. I suddenly don't feel nearly as kinky as I did when I first sat down with her. Sighing, I relax.

"Do you want to hold him?"

Terrified, I shake my head, standing and backing away. That I'm not ready for.

"Tell me you'll at least stay for a session? This afternoon our topic is Sensual Labor."

My eyebrows arch. I'm intrigued. Within minutes Jackie and I are directed to an outdoor "room" that is a paved circular space with a thatch roof. A step-down pit area is lined with pillows, and many of the couples are already seated. Most of the women are reclining against their partner's chests, making me wish Master was with me.

In *this* we're at an impasse. Still. He isn't open to considering Primal Birth as an option even though Dr. Wang is willing to be a supportive member of a birthing team. No, Master will be happy with no less than a hospital, sterile operating room, and if he has his way, a Caesarian section.

Descending the three steps down into the seating area, I take Jackie's hand and catch her reassuring smile, but I still feel defeated. Without Master's support I feel like I'm wasting my time being here. A group of four women are seated in the upper level, drumming. The rhythm is soothing and seems to float on the warm breeze.

It's nice here. Calm. Peaceful. So different from the constant supercharged sexual atmosphere of Lewd Larry's or the heavy mood at the penthouse, made even worse since I've refused to consider moving. I don't know if I would feel differently if Thomas hadn't left town. Maybe I would. If the three of us were able to go house hunting together, it might be easier to consider suburbia because I'd know that we were moving as a ménage.

But then, maybe it wouldn't be better at all. Who knows.

"Deep thoughts for a woman who's supposed to be meditating," Jackie whispers against my ear. I realize suddenly that she's rubbing my tension filled shoulders and guess she's probably been massaging me since we sat down and I just didn't notice.

"It's Master. He might not be here in person, but he sure is loitering in my brain."

She snorts. "You need to start charging that man rent. You're thinking so hard, you're wearing me out."

I smile, chuckling.

Anne, the workshop facilitator, moves to the center of the room and immediately starts swaying rhythmically and chanting. In our seated positions we follow her lead, bending and reaching our arms like branches caught in a gentle breeze as we imitate her basic intoned, "Ohhmm," repeating it after it fades to nothingness. I close my eyes, and the facilitator's voice becomes a measured comfort to my mind: "Chanting engages all the parts of yourself. As your mind memorizes words and melody, your heart applies a deep primal emotion born on the tide of beginnings. Tune out the chaos of your life and open your soul to the deeper wisdoms that our society stupidly left behind. Rise up and embrace your authenticity. Rise up and embrace the sacredness of the journey you have undertaken in the moment you created life."

As the other couples stand, Jackie helps me up and I lean back into her. We sway together, our chant changing, following the facilitator's lead. It swells and thickens. Likewise my heart expands and I feel a sweet lifting of spirit, a natural high.

Anne encourages, "I want you to let your mind go on an erotic fantasy, the goal is complete and utter surrender. Coaches, you can assist your partners by massaging their breasts, kissing their necks, even rubbing their genitals."

My eyes fly open. Jackie and I don't have that kind of relationship.

Jackie presses her cheek next to mine. "Relax. This isn't sex, this is massage."

As her hands run over my breasts, kneading, rolling their softness beneath her strong palms, it sure as hell feels sexual. I close my eyes tight, trying to forget that it's Jackie touching me.

I'm shocked when Anne tells us, "During your labor, I want you to orgasm often. Use the pleasure your partner can give you to help you ride through each contraction, not only pain free but joyfully."

Is it normal for the kinky one in the room to feel completely and utterly vanilla?

Jackie's hands slide down over my abdomen. Her touch does feel good, relaxing. I can imagine Thomas embracing the idea of me orgasming through the pain of labor and I allow my mind to drift, imaging his hands sliding under the curve of my belly, massaging, teasing.

Anne says, "An orgasm is twenty times more relaxing than a tranquilizer."

My pussy tightens with need as Jackie's fingers drift lower, teasing my mons through the stretchy yoga pants I'm wearing. My arousal makes me uncomfortable, but as I crack my eyelids open to see how the other couples are reacting to today's instructions, I see that they are all participating enthusiastically.

"Sexual arousal will expand your vagina as much as two inches, which is why it is so very important for both of you to be comfortable with clitoral and vulva massage during your labor. Some of you may have a doula or midwife present. Now is the time to have a frank discussion with them. Discover their comfort level and decide whether they wish to step from the room to give you privacy during your contractions or if they are willing to stay."

Jackie's hand slides between the juncture of my leg, pressing against my labia, and need shoots up my spine. I push back against the pressure, enjoying the pleasure of her touch.

Anne confides, "For several days prior to delivery, I felt like the time was near. Using olive oil, I massaged my perineum every few hours. My husband brought me to orgasm several times each day, and when my contractions started we concentrated on reaching orgasm as the contraction peaked. Yes, there was pain. I won't say my labor was completely pain free, but the pain and pleasure blended. It was so erotic. My heart and mind and soul connected with my husband's in a way that was so powerful. The energy of our sexuality cradled us. My husband admitted that to him the experience was like being high."

"God, I wish Garrett was here. If he could only hear what the birth could be like—"

"Take a few moments to reground, talk to your partner about how they're feeling, and in a few moments we'll start the next exercise."

I don't want this activity to end, but as the facilitator eases us back down we slowly retake our seats. I look shyly at Jackie and she laughs.

"Girl, I told you I could be a good coach."

"So, how do I convince the hospital staff that I need to orgasm through my contractions?" I smile, still slightly embarrassed, and we both laugh at the image, making jokes about their shocked principles, but it really isn't funny. "I wish Garrett would just open himself to the idea."

The facilitator asks suddenly, "Who has done their homework? Who can tell me what endorphins are?"

A dozen hands go up, and she takes two answers.

"Endorphins are hormones, the body's natural pain-killers."

"Endorphins transport you to an alpha-state."

She smiles. "Exactly. Endorphins are responsible when someone reports they had a painless childbirth."

Smiling faces radiate hope around the room. Of course we all want a pain-free labor and delivery. I feel my own face tightening as I imagine a sterile room, masked doctors, and a bloody scalpel. "Oh God."

Jackie pats my hand, looking concerned, and I force a smile.

The facilitator keeps speaking. "The more endorphins you produce, the better you will feel. You'll be able to surrender to the experience. Likewise, the baby will enter the world more relaxed, calm, and I know you all want that for your baby."

Oh, I do. I do. I rub my belly, feeling my babies move and roll inside of me. I have to figure this out, I have to find a way to get Garrett to understand how important this is to me.

"With memory set smarting like a reopened wound, a man's past is not simply a dead history, an outworn preparation of the present: it is not a repented error shaken loose from the life: it is a still quivering part of himself, bringing shudders and bitter flavors and the tinglings of a merited shame."

George Eliot, *Middlemarch*

CHAPTER 12

THOMAS

Standing in the shower, with hot water pounding my shoulders and steam rising around me, all I can think about is naked bodies, specifically the arch of Sophia's back, the curve of her hip; the flat plain of Garrett's stomach, the veins that stand out on his erect penis. It has been only minutes since I had sex with Abigail, but my body hardly registers the contact. I *need*—not sex—*loved* on. I close my eyes and feel the ripple of my abs under my soaped hands, imagining *Sophia's* touch. I turn my face into the spray, pretending the tears leaking from my eyes are just water runoff. I never imagined being away from her and Garrett would be *this hard*.

Sophia is thirty-four weeks. Unless I can wrangle it, I will miss the birth of my sons. I will potentially miss out on much of my children's lives…I feel doubly cursed. And there is even more guilt because in wishing I could walk away from this assignment, I feel I could walk away from my brother and my commitment to him.

"Lex!"

By the tone of Abigail's voice I can tell something is wrong. Throwing open the shower door, I rush out, grabbing my Glock, ignoring the towels hanging in reach.

Weapon leading, I visually sweep the room but see no threat, just Abigail's pale face trained on the television. Dripping, I go to her side. "What is it? What has happened?

She doesn't reply and so I turn my attention to the television screen for answers. A headline flashing *Breaking News* runs across the bottom of the screen, and as I watch the film footage playing behind the news anchor it takes a moment for my mind to register what I'm seeing. My wife, Lattie, is behind a podium giving a speech at a Sudan peace rally when the sound of gunfire fills the air. She drops down, ducking behind the podium. I hold my breath hoping she was not shot. As the camera's view zooms closer, I see that she is crawling to a row of seats staged behind her where moments before dignitaries were seated. They've all fled. All but one. As she reaches him I see the sniper's target was her father, but that makes no sense to me. Yes, he's powerful, he controls a significant part of the country, but he has no real enemies. I swallow hard and sit in a nearby chair. I didn't like the man and he definitely didn't like me—actually, he wanted me dead—but I certainly didn't want *him* dead. "What in the hell?"

"Wait. Watch," Abigail urges, as we continue watching events that have recently unfolded. Obviously, she has already seen the footage once and instead of telling me, she lets me see for myself as four masked men appear at the back of the stage. Heavily armed, they grab Lattie and drag her off the stage.

The news anchor's voice has been a monotone *blah, blah, blah,* not really registering as I try to understand what was happening. I force myself to listen. "It is not yet known why Lubna A'isha Charbonneau was taken following the assassination of her father, Charles François Charbonneau. There have been no claims by any group taking credit for the act of terrorism nor has there been any demand for ransom. Headlines across Europe are calling her a hero, and it is being speculated whether she will be one more martyr to fall in this region of turmoil."

Lubna A'isha. The last time I heard her birth names seems like a far off dream. As soon as we reached American soil she became Latisha. Balling my hands into fists and breathing hard, I turn to Abigail. "I have to go to Sudan."

"She could be anywhere. We don't even know who has her."

The full reality hits me like a blow to my head, and I drop to my knees realizing the entirety of the situation. With François dead and Lattie missing, I have no idea where my children are or who is caring for them. "My children."

"God, Thomas."

"I have to get them out."

"I'll send an extraction team. Do you know where they would be?"

I shake my head. My wife wasn't even supposed to be in Sudan. The last I'd heard she was in Ba'hai but she'd promised to enroll the children in school in France. "They could be anywhere."

My cellphone rings and I look at the caller ID with irritation, expecting it to be Abigail related, but then I see it the number for the SAT phone I left with my children. "Hello?"

"Papa!"

My son's frantic whisper rips through me. Every imaginable horror races through my brain, hearing my son's terror over the phone line. "Hektor? Are you someplace safe?"

"Men are here, searching the camp for something. They are screaming at everyone and hurting people! I'm scared."

I fear the *something* might be my children, but that is horribly paranoid. It is more likely that François was involved in something that has gotten him killed and put Lattie in grave danger.

"Are you with your brother and sisters?"

"I have Athena-Sophia with me, but Nikkos and Olympia were with Isaam and Badriya." His whispers alone tell me he is very afraid and believes he is in danger. I don't know if it is good or bad that he is separated from his brother and sister, but at least I know the quadrant of the world they are in by his telling me they are with my wife's sister and husband. I can also triangulate the SAT phone now that I know it is still in his possession. *Thank God.*

"How far are you from the well?"

"We are here. We arrived two days ago. We were packing to move out this morning, but the men came and started tearing everything up."

"Don't draw attention to yourself. Hide if you can. I'm coming for you."

I hear a shuffling, and then the phone goes silent.

I know it is too late but I shout, "Hektor!" anyway. My mind and body goes into work mode, I keep my cellphone in one hand in case Hektor is able to call back and use a second cellphone to make a call out to some very dangerous men on the other side of the globe, mercenaries willing to do whatever needs done for a price.

"*Pepé*, it's *Wiley*, I need a favor." *Pepé* is for *Le Pew*, not because he smells but because I've never known him to not be under the influence of obsessive love, and *Wiley* because I tend to survive even impossible circumstances as does the cartoon coyote.

"Name it, brother."

"My four children are stranded in the base camp of a man named Charles François Charbonneau. I want them out of harm's way immediately."

Pepé whistles.

"What have you heard?"

"The same as you, I'm certain. Charbonneau was killed last night. His daughter kidnapped."

"But *you* know what happened?"

"No. There wasn't even a rumor on the wind before it happened."

I growl. "Pepé!"

"Charbonneau was trafficking very rare finds from a recent dig and butted heads with some desert pirates. He had something. Something very valuable. Maybe he thought it was worth dying for to keep. I think someone is willing to do anything to get their hands on it."

"Shit!" The only thing keeping Lattie and our children safe in that corner of the world was her father's hired guns and with him no longer there to pay them, there is no protection for my children, and worse, they may turn on my family if there is money to be had from another source.

Pepé interrupts my thoughts. "You sure those kids are in that camp?"

"Yes. They'll be there. There is a well three hours north of Khartoum. Do you know it?"

"Sure, sure."

I use my phone to send a data file of their most recent photographs. "I need you to get them out of the country. Now."

His voice is gruff when he tells me, "I'll contact you when I have them in my custody." The line goes dead, and I listen to the silence. I called the right man. I called the only man for the job. I just hope I called him in time. Silently, I pray for my children.

I pray the feeling in my gut that my children are the target of the search to be used to put pressure on my wife is incorrect. Why Lattie continues to place my children in harm's way, I will never understand, but I know I am finished with whatever game she is playing.

I watch the television screen replaying the assassination footage. In the foreground Latisha is standing at a podium speaking. "Politicians want us to believe the war has ended, but I say to you, as long as women are being raped and murdered as they forage for firewood, as long as young men are being castrated and left to die in the desert for being born the wrong race, as long as violent raids terrorize those seeking sanctuary in refugee camps… The. War. Continues."

In the background, many of the diplomats come to their feet leading a standing ovation. The next moment her father is falling. The remaining dignitaries frantically run off the stage, taking cover.

Latisha looks over her shoulder, sees her father's slain body, and reacts by facing the camera. Anger and fear makes her eyes wild. Her nostrils flair as she cries out, "The. War. Continues."

A second later she drops to her knees and crawls to her father's fallen body. Film coverage breaks away after she is grabbed by the hooded men.

I feel Abigail's hand on my shoulder. Looking up, I see her holding out a towel. I'd completely forgotten that I am wet and naked.

"You spoke to one of your children?"

I nod and numbly take the towel. "My son, Hektor. He said that men were in the camp, searching it."

"Men? Insurgents or soldiers?"

"I'm not sure he'd know the difference. He knew enough to be afraid." My gaze collides with hers as I wrap the towel around my waist. "Did you know?"

"That Charles François Charbonneau was targeted for assassination? No."

She worded her answer too carefully, making me suspicious. "But my wife, you did know something?"

"There are threats against your wife every day. She is not a popular person in Sudan."

"The people love her. She is a hero to them."

"Yes, and by being so, she has alienated herself to others."

Abigail's cellphone rings and she supplies curt answers. Meeting my gaze she says to me, "I have a team in Djibouti."

My breath catches in my throat. Following the attack of nine-eleven, our bases in Europe and Asia were abandoned in favor of a military presence closer to the Middle East. Djibouti is one of several places the military could locate in Africa that could serve as a point of operations in the US's attempt to fight terrorism and secure US oil-interests.

"They have recovered four children, two boys, two girls, claiming to be American."

I don't ask what in the hell they were doing in the camp at exactly the right time. I don't even challenge the lies Glorianna told me moments ago. I just utter, "Thank God."

"They are sending photos for possible identification before taking them on to London."

I nod, understanding that London is a safe refuge while they wait for transport to the US. We stand stiff and anxious, hovered over her PDA, waiting for the photos and when the device vibrates in her hand, she jumps then laughs nervously.

The first photo loads and it is Olympia. I breathe a heavy sigh of relief. "My daughter."

She scrolls through three more photos, and I am uncertain only about the infant. The truth is I haven't seen Athena-Sophia since her birth and seeing proof of her growth...

I am overwhelmed with emotion. *God. Oh God.*

Through tear-blurred eyes I deduce it is the correct baby, dark wavy hair, slanted Asian eyes, a female of the correct age.

"Yes, they are all mine."

"Thank God." Abigail grants authorization to transport to London and from London to Washington, DC. When she is finished with the details she comes to me, pulling me near, consoling me. "By tomorrow you will be reunited with your children."

I look at her blankly, still numb and uncertain. The truth is I don't trust a single thing she says. Ever. I manage to whisper, "Thank you," against her neck.

With my children out of danger, I can focus on the next hurdle and immediately contact Pepé. "My children have been recovered. When you reach Khartoum, you will focus on intelligence recovery. I want to know who has Charbonneau's daughter and where they are keeping her."

* * * *

Secret CIA Airbase, undisclosed location

It is dark outside, thick fog, and pouring rain. Still hours before sunrise. Inside the hangar, the lights are bright and the air chilly. I'm comforted that Glorianna insisted on escorting me, but her presence isn't really necessary. Waiting is the hardest, but finally a military air transport lands. We wait for it to taxi into the hangar. We wait for the hangar doors to close. It is only minutes, but it seems like hours before the airplane's door opens. A Marine exits first. He takes the hand of a young boy, my son Hektor, and leads him down the steps.

I hurry to his side and kneel beside him. He strokes my cheek.

Using both of his small hands, he grabs at my shorter hair. "You are my father."

"Yes. My hair is cut, my beard shaved, but I am still the same man."

"I have missed you, Papa."

"I have missed you, my firstborn son." I hug him close. "I'm taking you home with me. It's time we are together again."

He nods against my shoulder, whispering, "I would like that. I have missed school, Papa. Do you think my friends will remember me?"

I kiss the top of his head. "I'm certain they will."

Seeing a second Marine approach, I stand. He holds both Olympia and Nikkos's hands, and as soon as they see me, the children pull free and run to me, Olympia almost bowling me over. "Papa! Papa!"

I pull my children to me, hugging them all at once. I blink rapidly, holding back tears I wouldn't be ashamed of if they fell, but thinking it better that I not let my children see them. They need to feel safe and protected. They don't need to know how bad everything really is.

A third Marine exits the plane, and I see she is carrying a toddler. With my children close, I stand, preparing to take my fourth child, but Athena-Sophia clings to the female Marine's neck, refusing to come to me.

Hektor holds out his arms, and the baby goes readily to him. He is just a child himself, but he carries her like he has taken care of her often. Sighing heavily, I shepherd my children to a waiting SUV. Abigail walks over as I get my children settled in the backseat. She smiles sadly. "It was fun while it lasted."

I look into her eyes, not understanding.

"You have four small children to raise. You don't think I'm going to force you to stay with me, do you?"

Actually, I hadn't thought about Abigail at all, my only plan being to get my children home and settled.

"When their mother is recovered..." I don't finish the sentence. The look in her eyes is a reflection of my own doubt. I think we both know that without a ransom, without even a hint of who is responsible, the likelihood of recovering her is slim.

"I expect you to go home and *stay* with your children. No heroics." She buries her face against my chest, hugging me tight before releasing me. "I may be searching for a new assistant but I do expect to see you again. Alive."

I look through the vehicle's window at my children. They don't know anything about what has happened to their grandfather or mother yet. To them, this has been a big adventure. What will I tell them if I don't do everything I can to rescue their mother?

I wink at Abigail. "I'll see you again."

"I will wear my heart upon my sleeve. For daws to peck at."
William Shakespeare, *Orthello*

CHAPTER 13

KITTEN

I wake up with Master spooned around me. I keep my eyes closed, feeling him against me, the long line of his chest, the solid press of a morning erection. I think he is still asleep but I'm unsure. I drift in and out of slumber, realizing he follows my movements as we sleep, staying curled against me, holding me, protecting me. Sometimes he wakes me, kissing away tears I shed while sleeping. I try so hard during the day, while I'm awake, to be strong and not show my emotions. I miss Thomas so much, but I try to not let those feelings show. I can't help what happens while I'm sleeping. Every morning he makes love to me, again at night before turning out the lights. I think he hopes he can erase the pain of missing him.

"I know you're awake." He presses his hard cock against the crack of my bare ass, as if I hadn't already noticed his hardness.

"I'm tired of being pregnant." It isn't actually a denial of entrance. He lifts my leg, thrusting into me shallowly from behind. Behind us, the alarm clock goes off, announcing it is five p.m. It is a soft harp sound meant to wake us up gently and will gradually grow louder if Master doesn't turn in off. He ignores it.

"I know, baby." He kisses the back of my neck. Short, gentle thrusts as his hand slides around me and between my legs to rub my clit. "It won't be long now."

"I'm scared," I admit, squeezing my eyes closed. I hold back tears. Stupid, irrational tears. I shouldn't miss Thomas as much as I do. Master is more than enough for me. He takes such good care of me. There isn't any proof that Thomas would be able to prevent a Caesarian birth, but I'd feel like I at least had an ally. In my darkest moments, I worry Master won't even be there to hold my hand during the birth, but Lord Fyre would. He would move heaven and earth to be with me. The question is will he be able to convince the senator?

He pushes harder against my clit, making circles against my flesh, and my thoughts flee

"There's nothing to be afraid of. Women give birth every day. It's a natural part of life."

My body responds to his touch, the simple pleasure lifting me higher...higher. I ride the wave of bliss, waiting for the crash but orgasm spirals on. I make sounds in the back of my throat, high pitched, seemingly agony filled, but so far from pain. Master increases the pace of his thrust and reaches his own climax as I cry out. "God, Master. Oh God."

Too soon he rolls away to start his day with a shower.

I sit up, disappointed. It seems more and more I just want to lie in bed. "You don't listen to me."

He turns slowly to face me. My tone might have been a little harsh. "Did you say something? I didn't hear you."

"Please come to the Birthing Center with me tonight. I really want you to know how to breathe with me, just in case I can have a natural birth."

Master returns to the bed and sits beside me and even though he strokes my face softly, I can tell by his expression I won't like what he's going to say. "Kitten. Love. I do not want you to get your hopes up about something that has very little chance of happening."

"I have to have hope, Master. If I don't have hope, what else is left?"

"Me. Us."

"Yes," I agree, because we are what matters and I can't bear another fight about this. I wait until he is behind the closed door of the bathroom and I hear the shower running to sigh heavily. The closer I get to my due date, the more I worry—as much about having to have a Cesarian section as about whether or not Thomas will be able to get here in time for the birth.

Opening the drawer in the bedside table, I withdraw the cellphone that is my main connection to Thomas. He hasn't text in two days. I text him: *Are you there?*

Moments later I receive: *I'm in London.*

"London?"

Master comes out of the bathroom, towel in hand still rubbing his hair, and I try to hide the cellphone in the sheets.

"I know you text Thomas, I know he texts you. What about London?"

"He's in London."

"Hmm."

"That's it? Hmm?" I'm irritated Master isn't as upset by this as I am. I want to know he's in one place, safe, and that no danger is involved. I keep thinking about Nikos lying on our dining room table, riddled with bullets, and Master operating on him. *It could have been*

Thomas. It could have—

"He's working—for a senator who is running for president—I assumed there would be travel involved."

As my ire rises my cell vibrates. I look at the screen. "He said, 'I wish your Master watched television. Tell him to google Charles François Charbonneau.'" I look at Master, shrugging. "Who is Charles François Charbonneau? And what does that have to do with London?"

Master frowns and leaves the room. I follow him to the kitchen, where he left his laptop set up last night. While he powers up, I pour him a cup of coffee and salivate. I would really love a cup of coffee.

I turn, hearing the sound of a news reporter and see Master watching a news feed. I sit the coffee on the table, catching a glimpse of what he's watching. I immediately recognize the woman standing behind a podium as Thomas's wife.

"That's Latish—oh my God!" On the video, a man has been shot and Lattie ducks behind the podium, but only for a second and then she is yelling at the cameras. It seems everything happens so fast. She drops to her knees, crawls to the man who was shot, and is then grabbed and dragged off the stage. The video clip ends. "What just happened?"

Master runs his hand through his hair, looking shocked. "I think that was Lattie being kidnapped."

"Kidnapped? Oh God." I sit down hard in the kitchen chair next to Master.

"The man was her father." Master replays the video. "You said Thomas is in London?"

"That's what his text said. Why?"

"This video was taped in Sudan."

What does that mean? Does he think Thomas lied to us? Or will he fly from London to Sudan? I don't want to know. I really don't. But I do. If he is flying into danger...

God, protect him.

Master takes my hand and squeezes it. "I'm sure he'll be fine."

I nod, hoping, praying. *Please, please let him be fine. Keep him safe.* I gesture at the monitor. "I don't think I want him involved in this."

Kissing my knuckles, Master pulls me out of my chair and to him. I sit on his lap, hugging him hard. He holds me as tightly as he can, and I realize he's scared too. I cringe at every thought going through my head, and I imagine his thoughts being just as dark.

I start crying. "Why can't he just be a normal guy? Why can't he just be safe with us every day?"

Kissing my temple, he asks, "Would we love him as much without the danger and intrigue?"

"I would. I would!" I cry harder against his shoulder, all of the pain I've been holding in leaking out in wracked sobs. "I want my Lord Fyre back. I want him back."

Master stands me up and leads me to the library. I'm still crying but my body responds to the walk down the long hallway, just knowing a scene is coming. Inside the room, Master holds out a box of tissues. "Blow."

I take a tissue and do as I'm told.

He points to a stool. "Sit."

I look around the room with interest. This impromptu scene has left no time for an elaborate setup, and Master is all about setting a specific mood. As it is, I am sitting on a low, wooden stool in his library.

Cuckoo-clang-cuckoo-clang-cuckoo-clang-cuckoo-clang-cuckoo-clang-cuckoo-clang. The on-the-hour announcement draws my attention to a new acquirement. A carved bird, which popped through a small door bobs with its "cuckoo". I used to have a collection of clocks—mantle clocks, pendulum clocks, grandfather clocks, cuckoo clocks—I realize quite suddenly I haven't missed them. God, the ruckus they used to make. How did I ever sleep? I appreciate the silence when we are here at the penthouse.

By the sixth *cuckoo*, I'm annoyed by the sound.

"Like it?"

Is this a trick question? We are in the library after all. It makes me wonder.

"It's beautifully carved."

He snickers and I think by my avoidance of the question I probably gave him more information than I intended. I don't know why I'm worried. It's only a cuckoo clock.

"Do you think if I bind your wrists lightly that you would be comfortable for a while?"

Bondage? Really? I hold out my arms and bounce with glee. I couldn't be more excited if I tried.

Smiling, Master comes forward, holding out a wide length of silk. He binds my wrists one to the other, leaving them resting in my lap. He is careful to not tie my wrists so tight that it would slow my circulation. To my collar he attaches a chain that is anchored to the base of the stool. "You can move from the stool to the floor and from the floor to the stool if you get uncomfortable."

I appreciate his concern about the babies and blood clots, but it only makes me more impatient to give birth. I want to be tied in uncomfortable positions and used roughly, but I'm not complaining. I am bound. For now, that is enough.

He leaves me sitting and walks over to his desk.

"I know you love clocks." He lifts the cuckoo clock, and I look at it with new interest. As he carries it toward me I realize this is no ordinary clock. It folds open like a book, and the interior is mostly hollow. "I'm going to box your head inside of the clock. Do you agree to this scene?"

Curious and excited, I nod. I've seen slaves being led around Lewd Larry's with their heads trapped inside wooden boxes, and I've never figured out the fascination. I've heard some skin-tingling stories about insects or small mice being put inside the box to torture the one caged though I've never seen it done.

He fits the clock around my head and closes me in. I hear a click as the sides lock together. I am trapped in the dark, although as my eyes adjust some light comes through the opening around my neck. Master doesn't say anything. I don't like not seeing him, I don't like blindfolds, and I'm finding I don't like being boxed in much better.

My heart starts racing. *I don't like this. I really don't like this.*

I feel his gentle touch on my shoulders. "Relax. I'm right here."

I try to relax, dropping my chin to seek the light coming through the opening. Feeling my panic rise, I can't help but think how ridiculous this is. I've been bound and caged in dark rooms plenty of times and never panicked. What's the difference? This box on my shoulders is like a little, dark room for my head.

He opens the face of the clock and looks at me. "Do you want me to leave this open?"

Yes, yes, yes. I squeeze my hands into tight fists. I can do this, damnit. "No, I'm fine."

He closes the face of the clock, pitching me back into darkness. "I will be here. I'm not going anywhere."

Heart racing, breathing hard, I war with myself in the dark, fighting panic. I don't know how long I sit there. I almost safeword a dozen times but finally, after what seems like hours, I win. I sigh with relief, realizing I'm fine. I'm going to stay fine. Master is right here, and he won't let anything happen to me.

Cuckoo-clang.

I jump, almost falling off the stool. Master steadies me with his hand on my elbow and I realize my hands flew up to grab the clock, but bound as I am I only end up hitting the box and jarring my head. *Cuckoo-clang-cuckoo-clang-cuckoo-clang-cuckoo-clang-cuckoo-clang-cuckoo, clang, cuckoo-clang* .

"Eight o'clock," I say, really, really hating cuckoo clocks.

Master opens the face of the clock and holds a bottle of water up to the opening. He helps me to take a drink. "I'm very proud of you, Kitten."

I know he is. I can hear it in his voice.

With a lot of assistance, he helps me to lay on the floor, adding cushions beneath my knees and lumbar. He attaches a spreader bar between my legs with loose cuffs. I'm curious why now, after so many months of almost no play, he has come up with these ingenious ideas of how we can play. Better late than not at all I suppose.

He props my shoulders up with another cushion, explaining, "I want you to be able to watch."

It is a strange sensation, watching him from the round hole of my head-clock. Kneeling beside me, he bends forward and licks my clit. I'm not sure what I'm supposed to be seeing, because my big belly is in the way, but I like his tongue on my clit so I don't say anything. My hips start to move with the rhythm of his tongue, but he pulls away.

Going to the other side of the room, he pushes toward us a large, oval antique mirror and angles it so that I can see everything. "Better?"

I nod.

"You should have told me you couldn't see."

"Sorry, Master."

He smiles but walks away. I look at my spread genitalia and the view he would have of my big, swollen belly. Not sexy. Not sexy at all.

It seems like he is forever returning, but that is part of this game, the isolation.

When he does return, he bears lube, a small clear cylinder, and a hand vacuum pump. I lick my lips, new anticipation making my need spike. After slathering a thick coat of lube over my clit and labia, he positions the clear cylinder over my clit. With the valve open, he starts pumping. From past experience, I know this is just the warm up. It feels like he is sucking my clit with his mouth, but the view in the mirror tells me it is all manual tool. With his fingertips he teases my labia, then slides a finger inside.

I close my eyes, his touch feels so sweet. My body hums with pleasure. He takes me so close to orgasm, so close…

He stops pumping and closes the valve. The next pump sucks my clit, leaving it clearly distended inside the tube. It stays that way. He pumps again, stretching it more.

"Oh!" My hips jerk, orgasm so close. *Please, please, please.*

Smiling, Master leans over me and closes the door to the cuckoo clock. "That's enough for now. Rest awhile, Kitten."

No, no, no. I want to come.

* * * *

I'm floating, flying…

Cuckoo-clang-cuckoo-clang-cuckoo-clang-cuckoo-clang-cuckoo-clang-cuckoo-clang-cuckoo-clang-cuckoo-clang, cuckoo-clang, cuckoo-clang.

I jerk back to the reality of the library at ten p.m. Damn, I despise that clock. Master rubs my shoulders. "Don't hate the clock. Feeling all right?"

"I *was* feeling wonderful."

He chuckles.

"Damn sadist," I murmur under my breath.

"What was that, sweetheart?"

"Nothing, Master," I answer, smiling sweetly.

Master removes the box from my head, and I am comforted that he has dimmed the lights and lit candles around the room. The mirror is still in position, giving me a view of my clit sucked inside the cylinder. It looks huge inside the glass tube. *Shit.* I worry it will be painful when he removes it, like when he removes the nipple clamps, and am surprised when it doesn't. However, when his lips close over the engorged flesh I buck away.

"Oh God!"

"A little sensitive?"

"Yeah."

He releases my ankles from the spreader bar so that he can position himself between my legs before moving back into position. "I'll be gentle."

The new angle is better, and he does lick with a softer stroke. Taking hold of my bound wrists, he pulls my hands down. "Use your fingers to hold yourself open for me."

I press against my flesh, pulling apart my labia, which makes my clit stick out even more. "God!"

He chuckles against my flesh, just his breath sensation enough. He licks my fingers and my labia, lapping my flesh. I like the way his tongue feels when it runs over my fingers and then my labia and back again. He laps closer and closer to my clit, almost touching but not. Oh

God. I want my clit in his mouth. I wanted sucked on. As if he's reading my mind he gives me what I want, but my clit is so super sensitive I squeal. He turns his attention back to my fingers and labia.

His tongue glides over the tops of my fingers, slips under them. I imagine him tasting my juices. I can feel my slickness beneath my fingers.

Unexpectedly, he reaches into his pants pocket and retrieves his cellphone. "Hello?"

When he switches the cell to speaker a jolt of adrenaline speeds through my veins knowing it is Lord Fyre.

"I'm leaving in a few minutes."

Leaving? London? Master and my gaze collide. We're both holding our breath. This seems like so much more than just a simple update phone call. *Where are you going? Sudan? Please don't let it be Sudan.*

"I need you to run to the grocery."

Run to the grocery? Is that code? Do he and Master have code words set up that I don't know about?

"Sure, no problem." Master shrugs. *Obviously not code.*

"Kiddie Kibble, diapers, formula, a few bottles, and juice."

The line goes dead, leaving Master saying, "Hello? Are you there?" until the phone in his hand starts beeping. Looking at me he says, "Did you understand that?"

I shake my head. "If it's code, I don't know it."

"Then I guess we take him at his word." Master releases my wrists.

"Maybe it's the store that's more important than the items," I suggest, standing up. I realize my legs are stiff and bounce a little.

"I shouldn't have had you on the floor so long."

"I'm fine. I lay on the cushion on the floor at the club hours longer every evening. Those are pretty specific items. Maybe Thomas is just worried we won't be prepared for the new babies. He's so convinced they're coming early."

"Kiddie Kibble?" Master asks.

"High sugar, over-processed cereal. You've seen the commercial with the talking elephant, right?" No, because he doesn't watch television. I shrug. "Can I come with you? I can probably help you find it."

"That probably isn't a good idea."

I give him the look that says *you have to be kidding*. "Thomas wouldn't send either of us into danger. It's a grocery list."

"You're right." He squeezes my arm. "Get dressed."

An hour later we are standing in a monolithic superstore, the only one in town open twenty-four hours. The store is deserted, not a big surprise since it is so late, but still I expected a few people to be here. When I had a more normal life, it wasn't odd for me to do my shopping at night. As we push our cart through the aisles, I think we both are expecting someone to jump out and deliver a secret message Thomas couldn't give us over the phone. By the third aisle we are wired tight and all it takes is an employee pushing a dust mop to make us both jump out of our skin.

"Oh, crap!" I start laughing, Master laughs too, and we hug each other tight, half-holding each other up, because we're laughing so hard. The employee doesn't even pause to look at us. I'm sure it's just a normal evening for him, and he probably thinks we're drunk.

"Okay." Master releases me. "Cereal aisle."

We stand looking at the towering shelves of boxes. There are hundreds of kinds of cereal. Hundreds. It takes a step back and a long scan to find Kiddie Kibble, only to discover there are six different flavors: chocolate, chocolate chip, strawberry-banana, razzle rainbow, peanut-butter, and the original.

"Which one?"

Master puts one of each flavor in the cart. That's one of the reasons I love him, he's very thorough and leaves nothing to chance. I guess that would be two reasons.

We smile at each other, both of us pushing the cart. This is new, a completely different experience for us. Enrique always does the grocery shopping. I wonder if this is what Lord Fyre planned all along, a normal task in our kinky life to ground us and prepare us for the babies. I sigh contentedly.

Then we reach the formula aisle. "Oh, crap."

We stare at the choices. How can anyone just pick one?

"This might take a while." Master picks up one of the pre-mixed cans and starts reading ingredients. I pick up a different can and start reading.

"What are we looking for?"

"The healthiest choice."

I nod. Sure. That makes sense. "Would they make unhealthy baby formula?"

We share a look. *This is ridiculous.* After an hour of reading, we've grouped the different brands into nine types: cow's milk based, soy based, rice based, amino acid based, lactose-free, gentle, elemental, and special formulas for premature babies and toddlers. We end up with one of each kind in the cart.

At the diaper aisle, I leave him reading labels while I go to the front of the store for a second cart. With bottles, diapers, and juice still on the list, we're going to need it.

Two hours later we are back at the condo, staring at the vast amount of product we bought piled everywhere. "Now what?"

Master looks at his watch. "It's after one, we really should be at the club."

I shake my head, silently begging him to not go.

"We don't have to go tonight. I can call George and ask him to cover if that would make you happy."

I nod, relieved and realize I'm exhausted. It seems like I've been awake days instead of hours. "Can we take a nap?"

He waggles his eyebrows. "I might let you sleep."

"In the depths of winter I finally learned there was in me an invincible summer."

Albert Camus

CHAPTER 14

KITTEN

I am shaken awake by Master. I blink blearily. "What time is it?"

"Ten."

Ten? In the morning? I sit up, rubbing my eyes. "My alarm didn't go off. They expected me at the office an hour ago."

"I turned off your alarm so you could sleep well for once, and I left a message at your office that you wouldn't be in today."

I distinctly remember it being close to five when Master gave me permission to fall asleep. I blink at him and scratch my head. Not understanding, I lay back down, mumbling, "I don't think you should have called my office."

I'm too tired to argue. All I want to do is to go back to sleep.

Master sits down on the mattress beside me and rubs my back. "Kitten, sweetheart. I need you to wake up and get dressed."

By his tone I feel like something is wrong, and a rush of adrenaline makes me immediately alert. "What is it? What's wrong?"

"Thomas is home."

My heart leaps into my throat. Happiness races through me. Throwing off the covers, I hurry out of bed and would rush from the room if Master didn't grab my elbow to hold me back, but he does. "Get dressed first. His children are with him."

"God. His kids?" *Kiddie Kibble. Diapers. Formula. Bottles. Juice.* It all makes sense now. My heart sinks, remembering the news footage of their mother being kidnapped. "My God, those poor kids."

Master leaves me alone in the bedroom and I dress as quickly as I can, black yoga pants and a lime green tank top that molds around my stomach. It's what I had laid out to wear to my Primal Birth class…when? Last night? Did Master call Jackie? God, I hope he called Jackie so she wasn't worried. "Shit."

I hurry out, slowing when I hear giggles coming from the kitchen. *Giggles?* Catching sight of Master pouring milk into a bowl sat in front of a beautiful little girl with waist-length curls and huge brown eyes, I stop stark still. "Uncle Gar? How do you always know our favorites? Strawberry-banana, yum-yum."

"Chocolate Chip!" shouts a small boy seated at her right.

Master ruffles his hair. "When did you grow so big, Nikkos?"

The boy smiles at him, and I clutch my chest. His hair is shoulder-length and very curly. He has the same wide eyes as Olympia. Their mother's eyes, but the boy's smile is pure Lord Fyre. "God."

The sons in my belly choose to start a kicking match in my stomach. I push against a spot that is growing increasingly sore. Darker hands slide around me from behind, rubbing over the wiggling mound that is our babies. I close my eyes and lean my head back against his chest. "Thomas."

Leaning around me, he kisses me and I kiss him back, but then I remember his children and I pull away, explaining, "They might see."

"My wife's people are Muslim, my children's uncles have many wives. They will think nothing of my marriage to you. They will honor you as their other mother."

My marriage to you. My heart skips a beat, and I am left speechless and blinking like an owl. I don't know what to think or say.

"I just feel *wrong*. God, Thomas, is there any news of Latisha?"

His eyes narrow slightly before he looks away from me.

"Thomas?"

He crosses the room to look through the wide windows at the skyline.

I follow him, not wanting him to think that I don't want him. Never that. I want him desperately. "I've missed you. I'm so glad you're home."

He meets my gaze and opens his arms to me. I hug him tightly, not ever wanting to let go. Now is not the time to argue or to even consider the questions swirling through my mind. Soon enough there will be time to worry about how Latisha and the children fit into our lives.

I hear Garrett's voice and a response of giggles coming from the kitchen as Thomas leads me out of the living room and back to the bedroom. I'm not prepared for this, not at all. My heart races, and I don't know how to tell Thomas that I just can't do this. Not here. Not now.

When he closes the door between us and them, I feel no better about the situation.

He hugs my face in his palms and looks at me. I have never been looked at so closely, and his scrutiny makes me blush.

"You are so beautiful. I just want to make sure the image I held in my mind these last months has been truth."

I smile, but the tightness in my shoulders doesn't lessen.

"Have I lost you completely then?"

I jerk. "What? No!"

"Good. I was worried." He kisses my eyelids, the tip of my nose, my lips. Against my mouth he whispers, "I have missed you."

He slides his hands down my throat, tightening around my neck gently. I hold his gaze, I don't flinch or move. I trust him, breathing in, out, waiting for him to cut off my air completely—because he can, because I'd let him—only he doesn't. He slides his hands over my shoulders, down my arms. Bending, he kisses my belly, dropping to his knees. Cupping my buttocks, he pulls me into him. He presses his face into me, holding me tight. I realize after only a moment that he is crying. I don't move. I just breathe, in, out, while he sobs into me, my stomach, our babies, muffling any sound. I imagine him screaming, even though I can't hear it. I've been here—this broken. *God, oh God, comfort him.*

I don't cry. I don't let myself. I wait for him to stand. I wait for him to hold me again. I wait for him to allow me to comfort him, and then decide to just comfort him. I run my hands through his hair, pulling him closer, hugging his face into my stomach tighter.

I kiss the top of his head, molding around him, falling to the ground with him. He rolls with me, dragging me on top of him. Straddling him, my heart breaks for him as I kiss away his tears. I kiss his mouth. I kiss my way down his t-shirt covered chest.

Holding his gaze, I kiss his belt buckle before I unlatch it. I pull loose his belt, unbutton and unzip his jeans. I keep looking into eyes as his erection springs free and fills my mouth. Sliding my mouth up and down his length, I don't think about anything but his pleasure. I know exactly what he likes, how much pressure to apply with my lips and teeth. I know when to lick, when to bite, when to circle, when to plunge his length as deep as I can take it into my throat.

He grabs my face and pulls me up until I am kissing his mouth. He holds my face while I shimmy my slacks down over my hips. As soon as I am bared enough I lower myself onto his hard shaft. I ride him, gritting my teeth because my clit is over sensitized from the earlier pumping. I close my eyes, embracing the pain, eating it up, and pushing down hard against Thomas, feeding it back to him.

"Oh God," I cry out as pleasure punches through my discomfort.

Thomas brushes away tears that have fallen onto my cheeks. Tears, which have nothing to do with my clit, and everything to do with the pain I see etched on Thomas's face. I slow my pace, riding him gently.

He says, "Talk to me."

"I love you."

"I love you. I need to know that I am coming home to you as your husband."

My heart skips a beat and then another before I press my lips to his, promising, "You are already my husband." Quoting the Book of Mark, I whisper, "And they twain shall be one flesh. So they are no more twain, but one flesh."

A look of sadness crosses his face that I don't understand, but then he says, "I have to leave for Sudan immediately," and I understand completely.

I gasp. "No! Please, no! Stay here. Let the Marines rescue your wife or the senator's people."

He holds my face. "You are my wife now. All that I own is yours."

I pant, verging on hysteria as his meaning dawns clearer and clearer. He doesn't know if he will be coming back alive. I try to pull away but he holds my hips tight, forcing me to keep riding him. I know my pleas are pointless. If it were he or Garrett, I would go. I would do everything I could to rescue them. Latisha is his wife and the mother of four of his children. He loves her. He has to go. Collapsing over him, sobbing, I hold him as tight as I can for as long as I can. *God! Oh God, bring him home safely.*

"I want *you* to raise my children. With love. With God. All of my children."

I sob harder against his chest, and he lets me cry until there are no more tears left. An hour passes, maybe two, I don't know what Garrett did to entertain the children so long, but I appreciate the fact he did, allowing me this time with Thomas.

We dress in silence. My heart is breaking, but there isn't anything I can say or do to keep him from leaving us again. This is our relationship and as much as I hate the fact of it, I want him to return to us, even if it is just to tell us goodbye, again and again and again.

* * * *

After dinner, I know that Thomas will be leaving soon. If he looked at his watch once, he looked at it a dozen times. I think Garrett knows what is coming. He spent most of the day reinforcing the bond he once shared with the children. When Thomas takes his children back to the guest room, we both tense, knowing the time is near. I'm worried about having the children left in our care and ask him, "Do the children know their grandfather is dead?"

"No."

"Do you think they wonder why their mother didn't come with them?"

Reentering the room, Thomas answers, "Their mother is still in Sudan. That is the truth, and that is what they believe."

"They're going to ask questions, Thomas."

"I know that."

"What are we supposed to tell them?"

"Nothing." He joins us, sitting on the edge of a sofa opposite us.

"Until there is something to tell them, I don't want them upset."

"Thomas. They are children not idiots. You need to tell them something before you go away."

"What would you have me say to them, Sophia? That their grandfather was shot between the eyes and half his skull blown off? That their mother was kidnapped and will likely be tortured and raped before she is killed?"

"God. No!"

Going to Thomas, Master presses his fingers to Thomas's mouth. "Sh-sh-shh. We'll take care of the children. Go find Lattie *and come home to us safely.*"

I wrap myself in my arms, hugging myself, trying to not scream. I can't believe any of this is happening. When is enough *enough*? You would think I'd be numb to it all by now, but I'm not…and I completely understand that he has to try to rescue his wife.

No! I don't.

"Don't go," I beg again, arguing. "This is why we have a military, right? Send in the fucking Marines."

I race to him, throwing my arms around him, begging, "Don't go."

He kisses the top of my head. "I have to. She's the mother of my children."

I want to remind him that this woman left him and took his children away from him. God! God damn! I know he has to save his fucking wife. I know. He wouldn't be the man I love if he wasn't *that guy*.

Master stands and my heart catches, knowing it is time to say goodbye.

"Papa?" We all look toward Hektor. He is pale and obviously shaken by what he has just heard. None of us realized he was sitting hidden behind the sofa until he stood.

God, oh God. I believe the child heard every word, and my heart breaks for him as tears well in his eyes but do not fall. He walks slowly to his father. Thomas hasn't moved. It is like he is frozen in place until his son reaches him. Only then does he squat so that he is eye level with his son.

Hektor puts his hands on his father's shoulders. "You are strong, Papa."

"Like Superman," Thomas assures him, the words catching in his throat, and it seems the assurance is one he has given the child many times before. Hektor smiles, but a tear slides down his cheek. Thomas catches the tear with his thumb.

"Have the men who have my mother sent proof-of-life?"

I gasp, wondering how a child so young can understand such things, but even as my brain questions it I realize he has had a life much different than the children I have ever known.

"Not yet," Thomas whispers.

I turn into Master's arms, and he pulls me against him. Forcing myself to not lose it, I tremble against him and am barely comforted when he kisses me on top of my head. I can't take my eyes off the boy. He looks crestfallen.

"Find the men who did these things. Kill them, Papa."

Thomas presses his forehead to his son's. "I will avenge your grandfather."

Hektor kisses him. "Thank you."

Thomas takes his hand and leads him back toward the bedroom. We can hear him speaking softly as they walk. "I need you to be strong for your brother and sisters. I need you to be a good boy for Uncle Gar and Aunt Celia while I'm away."

Aunt Celia. Oh, fuck. I've never been an aunt. I've never taken care of children.

Garrett joins me on the sofa, and I reach for his hand. I realize only when he stretches his fingers that I am squeezing his hand so hard that I'm hurting both of us. "Sorry."

"Sh-h. Are you okay?"

"I'm an aunt?"

He chuckles and I wonder how he can laugh. "Consider the next few days practice for being a mommy."

I bend over my knees, suddenly light-headed and nauseated. *Oh God.* "Can we do this?"

He pulls me back to a sitting position and wraps his arm around me. "Relax. I've had the kids for a long weekend before. I have a little experience with my nephews and niece."

"Nieces," I correct.

"What?"

"You have two nieces."

Beside me, he nods then kisses me. "You're right."

Thomas reenters the room, clearing his throat to let us know he has. We both look toward him and he looks down, sheepishly. I've never seen Thomas look so vulnerable. "Both Olympia and Nikkos are awake as well. I believe a story from Uncle Gar will go a long way toward helping them sleep."

Master stands and crosses the room, saying, "I can do that," but he stops in front of Thomas and pulls him into his arms. He says something to him, speaking so softly I can't hear what he's saying, but Thomas nods and then they embrace, kissing, a long kiss that has the feel of desperation, and I realize Master is saying goodbye.

This is really happening.

I grab my chest as pain shoots through my sternum.

I'm going to have a heart attack and die.

I watch Master leave the room, and it seems like it is in slow motion. Thomas starts to walk toward me, but then everything speeds up and he is rushing toward me. I collapse against him.

"Breathe, Sophia!"

I try, I really do, but it hurts too much.

"Don't die, Ari! Please don't die."

He pulls me into his arms and holds me tighter than he has ever held me. "I'm not going to die, Sophia. Have some faith in me."

"I do have faith in you." I hold onto him for dear life. *Please don't go. Please don't go!* "I've missed you so much."

"I've missed you unbearably, my love." He slides his hands around to cup my protruding stomach and his unborn sons kick against his palms. "I will come home to you. *To them.*"

Neither of us mentions Lattie, that he will be returning with a wife, or how that will affect the ménage, and as he bends to kiss my baby belly I pray none of that will matter—and none of it will—as long as he comes home.

After he leaves, I stand with my forehead pressed to the door, crying silently. I can't risk having his children hear me, I don't want to upset them, and so I scream silently. I feel Garrett's body heat without knowing he'd come back into the room. He molds behind me, shoulder to knee, wrapping his arms around me. He doesn't speak. He just holds me.

Later, in the bedroom he finds documents left by Thomas laying on the nightstand. He doesn't ask "What's this?" because it is very clear just what it is, a Certificate of Marriage, declaring Sophia Jane Marie Alexander and Demetres Aristotle Velouchiotis as wed. *He used his real name?* His birth name. It is dated for three days earlier and witnessed by Abigail Wainwright-Fuller. The official stamp declares it was filed as a part of public record yesterday.

Our gazes clash over the paper. He knows I attended no wedding; I certainly didn't get formally married. I sigh heavily as he looks over the other documents, bank account information, stocks, bonds, deeds, a Last Will and Testament.

I insist, "He's coming back."

He nods. "I don't doubt he's coming back. Was this a power play to make certain that I know you are more his than mine?"

"That's absolutely ridiculous!"

"Is it?"

"He's returning *with* Lattie," I insist, gesturing helplessly with my hands. "This is some damn formality in case the worst happens, but the worst isn't going to happen. *They* have a family together."

He lifts his eyebrow and I know what he's thinking, exactly what he's thinking. Thomas and I also have a family together. Will he try to fit two wives and six children in one home, allowing Garrett to visit as Uncle Gar? Will he set up two households, one for each wife? Will he, Lattie, and their children live separate from Garrett, I, and our children? I rub my forehead, realizing my head is pounding.

Folding the papers, he lays everything back on the nightstand. "I'm going to sleep in the guest room with the children. I don't want them to wake up alone and be frightened."

"Do you want me to come too?"

I'm both disappointed and relieved when he shakes his head.

"In victory one does not understand the horror of war. It is only in the cold chill of defeat that it is brought home to you."

Sir Arthur Conan Doyle, *The Adventures of Gerard*

CHAPTER 15

THOMAS

Three hours north of the capital city of Khartoum, Sudan

It was a last minute decision to bring Nikos with me, and having him at my side as we look out over the semi-arid land sprinkled lightly with scrub and few trees, I am glad. Pepé and his men have already been here for two days, claiming Charles Francois's abandoned base camp as their own. It is deserted except for a few nomadic families.

In the distance I recognize Lattie's sister and brother-in-law, Isaam and Badriya. After a long moment Isaam recognizes me and rushes to my side. His wife follows, but stays behind him. She is heavily veiled in the bright, colorful cloth that is typical of the Rashaida nomadic tribes of northeastern Sudan.

Isaam speaks in rapid Arabic, "Soldiers took the children."

"I know. I know," I assure him, patting him on the back. It is obvious he has been beside himself with grief. I imagine Lattie left the children in his charge for the day it would take for her to travel to the city and back again. "They are safe in the United States with friends of mine. Have you heard anything about Lubna?" I defer to Latisha's desert name, because although Isaam has heard me call my wife Lattie before, Badrida has not.

Badrida's eyes go wide and fill with tears as Isaam shakes his head. I suspect he expects the worst has already happened and if she is not already dead, she is praying for it to come swiftly. "We only heard the report that Charles is dead. His men left almost immediately."

"Hektor said that other men came, that they were looking for something."

Badrida averts her eyes and I know the next words out of Isaam's mouth are going to be a lie. "Only the soldiers who came for the children. You said they are safe now."

I leave the couple to walk with my brother. "Did he know what they were looking for?"

I realize dumbly that although all of my questions were asked in English, Isaam had responded in Arabic. "No. Whatever they want is still a mystery."

The sun is setting, a brilliant orange band cutting the violet sky in half and setting the normally dull gray landscape ablaze with color. For just a moment there are bits of green and yellow and purple, which seem to be nonexistent during the heat of the day.

Young boys lead the camels in closer to the camp for the night. The camels' dung hangs heavily in the air and brought closer, the animals' muskiness is overwhelming. I am glad the winds pick up as the sun sets, and I inhale a deep breath of fresh air carried from far away. After a few days time I would become accustomed to the smell, but I hope to not be here that long.

"How could you leave your children here?"

I turn to see what my brother is looking at. His gaze rests on a young mother, heavily draped, sitting near a small fire, cooking, two small daughters crowded against her. She rotates a large kettle with two smaller pots over the fire and stirs the smaller pot with a knife. In the background the sides of the tent flaps in the harsh wind. Both mother and children hold their scarves close to their faces, protection from the blowing sand, but also to prevent any accidental exposure of their features.

I don't like the judgment I hear in his voice. "How is this different than how we were raised? They raise camels and goats. We raised horses and sheep."

"We had a real roof over our heads."

"Yes, tile, to protect us from the elements. It almost never rains here. All they need is a tent to protect them from the sun and sand."

"And their education? The women are kept completely illiterate and the men fare only slightly better."

"Francois had a tutor brought here from France. Honestly, most of the time, they were in Dubai, they lived like princes and princesses. When they are here, with Lattie's relatives, it is so they can have the best of both cultures. And, we agreed that at age eight they would be sent to boarding school, either in England or in France."

He shakes his head. "I would have thought that our experience would have turned you off boarding schools. If I ever have a child I would shelter it from that world."

I used to think the same thing. When did my point of view change?

"Boarding school teaches structure, self-reliance."

He shrugs. "They're your children."

"What does *that* mean?"

"You deserted them to the Infidels. Tell me you haven't sold their souls to the agency yet."

"You're right. I deserve your judgment and someday I may face God's judgment, but if I deserted my children here it was because I have no intention of my children carrying on the family tradition." I don't mention that *Glorianna* has already campaigned for my unborn twins or how I plan to keep her plans from materializing.

"If we get your woman out of this mess alive, promise me you won't allow her to bring the children back here. Raise them in the US, or Europe, or even Greece, but please, safeguard them from this life."

"The people here have a different life, it is not a matter of being better or worse."

"Promise me, Ari, or I will leave now and never look back."

The vehemence in his voice makes me believe him. "I want my children to know and respect their mother's customs, but I will be raising them. I won't leave it up for debate. If Lattie wants to stay in this desert, pursuing her own agenda, she can, but she can't protect my children here, and although I don't see the horror you obviously see in my children having a simpler life, I do want them to have a modern life with all the conveniences and opportunities for education they would miss out on by being forced to return here."

In my mind, I can hear their squeals of delight over their breakfast cereal.

I have missed school, Papa.

I wonder now if I lied to my brother. Did Charles have a tutor brought over from France? Have they been living in Bahai? All I have is Lattie's assurances. God, I don't want to be angry with her, but I am. More, I'm angry at myself for trusting her. Again. I don't want to believe she was a woman who would lie to me at every chance to get her way.

Once…a long time ago…she seemed so sweet, so innocent.

When I brought her to the United States, I never considered keeping her for myself, I never dreamed she might fall in love with me, but faced with her jealousy, I reasoned she must. Obviously, we were both so much younger, her barely more than a child. Seventeen. She knew little English but she knew enough to demand, "Where you go?"

She asked every morning when I'd return to our home, our bed, and I was always too tired to make love to her. I was training Garrett then, teaching him everything I knew about being a Dominant. He was wearing me out physically, and emotionally. I'd never been in love with a man and didn't recognize what was happening between us as falling in love. I'd tell her, "Work."

It wasn't all truth, it wasn't all lie.

One morning she pointed at bruises around my neck. "Not working. You tell me truth now."

That night I took her with me to a BDSM club and she was left stunned. I worried about her silence during the drive home. I filled the void, talking non-stop, telling her about Garrett's plans to create Lewd Larry's. I explained, "It isn't real torture. It's fun, play."

She'd looked at me incredulously.

"Can I show you?"

I'd pulled her waist-length hair up, catching it in an elastic ponytail holder, shaping the frizzy mass into a loose bun. She was trembling, worried. I undressed her slowly, helping her step out of her shoes and then unzipping the back of the summer dress she was wearing. Naked, she stood proudly and magnificently before me. She lifted her chin and despite her youth I'd never seen such a strong woman.

I caressed her cheek, then kissed her gently.

"No!" She cried out. "I want you to do to me what the ones at that club did."

I'd slapped her, hard enough that my hand was left stinging. I pushed her against a wall, lifting her up by her throat, cutting off her air. Her legs wrapped around my waist, instinctively trying to fight and save herself. I kept the pressure tight but gave her enough air to keep her from passing out. I'd wanted her to remember. I'd wanted her to enjoy the game we were playing. Mostly I'd wanted her to understand the need, the addiction of rough play. Then, I didn't yet see it as a lifestyle.

I'd filled her, thrusting hard into her, with her trapped between me and the unyielding wall. I tightened my grip on her throat, not allowing her to breathe as I thrust hard into her and knew the moment her orgasm exploded through her.

I let her take in long gulps of air but held her still against the wall. I thrust into her at a slower pace, building my own pleasure, not knowing if she would hate me from that moment on, or if she could start to understand.

Catching my face between her palms, she'd admitted, "I thought I was going to die."

"I wouldn't let you die."

She'd kissed me, asking against my mouth, "Next time will you lash me?"

I'm still chuckling at the memory when Nikos finds me sitting under the stars, far from camp. Silently, he sits beside me and gazes up at the splendor that is the desert night sky. So many stars, seeming so close, almost touchable, make me wish for simpler days. It bothers me that he sees only Infidels and not the lovely, gentle people my wife's family represented. To the north, south, east, and west wars and skirmishes—either religion or power based—rage on and somehow the nomads avoid the worst of it.

"How did you meet her?"

"I was sent for her father, renowned anthropologist, philanthropist, and premier arms dealer. I was captured and awaiting execution when she released me with my promise to help her get to America. It wasn't supposed to be complicated."

"Meaning you weren't supposed to fall in love with her."

I nod in the dark.

"In the States, did you raise your children Orthodox or were they brought up Muslim?"

I don't want to fight with him. Not here, not now, not while I am already dragging myself through the coals, second guessing every decision I've made over the last decade. I wonder if he's even been inside a church since joining the agency. "When Lattie left this desert she turned her back on her heritage, on her faith. She embraced all the United States had to offer. And I raised my children in the church with her at my side."

I expect more questions, arguments. I don't expect him to admit, "I think I'm in love."

I glance over at his silhouette, realizing that although his head is tilted back, he isn't gazing at the stars at all. His eyes are closed. Since I found him in her quarters at Lewd Larry's, I jump to the conclusion he's speaking of Morgana. I rub the back of my neck, considering all the complications that could come from his admission. Garrett is going to kill me. I chuckle under my breath. "Lust."

He turns his gaze to me and although it is dark, I can see clean through to his soul when he says, "I've never dreamed of more, never even considered I might ever have the chance at a life other than what I've known. I know what I am, I know what I'm not, but when I'm in her arms I start to believe I might be more."

I know that feeling. The papers I left with Sophia were as legal as any piece of paper can be, but they were not truth. I want Sophia to be my wife. I want her to be my children's mother. That fact doesn't take away from my love for Lattie, I will find her, I will deliver her to safety, but I won't be living with her as my wife ever again.

We share a heavy sigh and go back to gazing at stars we don't see while we think of the women we'd rather be with.

We spend the night together on the sand and share a sunrise. With each passing second, we both become more focused. Intent. Nothing happens in this land without everyone knowing it, and my enemies could be massing just out of sight. We have to keep moving and agree to head into the large, modern city of Khartoum.

Once there, traffic is congested and the heat is unbearable. The entire team is on edge. We're being open, obvious, stirring the shit with a big stick, and generally painting a big target on ourselves in the hopes of flushing out Lattie's captors.

No one is talking about what happened. It's a sad day when bribes can't even buy information. One thing is obvious. Fear. It's permeated the very culture.

Of course there have been newspaper reports and some radio broadcasts, covering the assassination of a prominent archaeologist, but I could have stayed in the United States and known more about what is going on here than actually being here.

Meeting up with Pepé about midday, we catch a break. "The BBC reported Charbonneau sent a colleague photographs and documentation on his latest discovery the night before his assassination. They believe there may be a connection."

I'm skeptical. "What was it?"

"A scroll."

"A scroll?"

"It could prove to be the most important find since the Dead Sea scrolls. It might have actually been written—" He whispers the last part. "—by Christ."

Beside me, Nikos snorts and quickly covers his nose with a cloth handkerchief and pretends to sneeze.

Pepé excitedly tells us, "No one is talking because to do so would be blasphemy."

"Where is the scroll now?" I ask.

Pepé shrugs. "No one knows. Like your wife, it has vanished."

"Someone knows *where she is* and *who has her*," Nikos says gruffly. Sweat drips down his cheek, and he swipes it away with the handkerchief. He's not overly impressed that we didn't come in guns blazing, he is hot and uncomfortable in the white dashdashas and turban he wears to cover his tattoos. Dressed as a businessman in suit and tie, I am no more comfortable but am the less grumpy of the two of us.

If the scroll is what the kidnappers seek, they are correct in believing Lattie will know its whereabouts. *She won't tell them.*

Nikos stands and paces, while the rest of us sip tea. It seems to him we are doing a lot of sitting around, getting absolutely nowhere, and as I sip my fourth cup of tea I can see his point. I have to believe patience will pay off. My only comfort is that everything happens slowly and methodically here—even torture—and though it is a sickening thought, I don't believe I have to fear her imminent death. We still have time to find her alive.

That's still my plan a week later.

It isn't so unusual to awake to gunfire, but on our twelfth morning starting with zero leads a quick glance through the upper window of the hotel I'm staying in reveals an American security detail shooting rounds into the air to announce their arrival. "Great."

From behind me Nikos asks, "What is it?"

"The Calvary is here." I take the stairs two at a time, Nikos trailing close, and run through the lobby. The last thing I want is innocents injured because of some hero's idea of how to flush me out. Nikos and the rest of the team stay in the shadows, guns trained on the Humvee caravan, while I step into the brilliant sunlight with my hands on top of my head. "Looking for me?"

One of the soldiers steps from the Humvee, machine gun pointed up. We walk toward each other. "Are there others inside that are of Guardian interest?" His accent is thick Russian.

"Only one," I answer, jerking my chin. Only Nikos revels himself, hands already clasped behind his neck to show he is no threat. He walks slowly to my side.

"We don't have all day. Get in."

Nikos and I climb into a rear seat, the Russian gets into the front passenger seat, and the vehicle is moving before we're fully seated. Another agent already seated in the back runs a scanner over the back of my neck, easily locating the identification chip embedded just under my skin. He speaks into a collar mounted receiver, "Agent XKM-one-zero-one confirmed."

He scans the back of Nikos's neck and says into the receiver, "We have a problem."

Nikos and I lock gazes. He admits, "I have trust issues," but if he was implanted with a chip I was unaware of it.

"When?" I ask him in Greek.

"While you were making nice with the senator and I was asked to wait in the hall. It happened before I knew what was going on. It could have as easily been a bullet through my brain."

I doubt that.

"No one asked permission to track me like a hound. I took it out."

I shake my head, sighing heavily. *My brother.*

"I am the only child of parents who weighed, measured, and priced everything; for whom what could not be weighed, measured, and priced, had no existence."

Charles Dickens, *Little Dorrit*

CHAPTER 16

GARRETT

I awake to screams and realize immediately I'm alone in the bed. Heart racing, I hurry down the hall through the living room and into the kitchen where I find Olympia and Nikkos sitting at the bar happily eating cereal and Kitten and Athena-Sophia both sitting on the floor crying. Actually, Athena-Sophia is screaming bloody murder and Kitten is crying silently. Both have tears dripping down their cheeks.

It is obvious what has happened, a bowl of cereal and milk hurled across the room, Kitten on hands and knees, trying to wipe up the mess, and Hektor, squatted, trying to console his sister with a bottle. But as the chubby toddler bats the bottle away for the third time, it is obvious she isn't having anything to do with it…or anything else when her brother holds out his arms to her and she hits at him too.

"Hey, hey. None of that." I scoop up the baby.

"Ommy, Ommy, Ommy." She wails.

"She is crying for our mother," Hektor explains.

"Ommy means mother?" I ask.

"Yes, and *Abbi* is dad but we always call father Papa, all of us except Athena-Sophia, she does not know Papa."

Now that I have the screaming, combative baby in hand, Hektor climbs onto a stool and pours his own cereal. Standing, Kitten gives me a look and a heavy sigh before rinsing the cloth in her hand and returning to the mess in the floor. She looks exhausted, like she hasn't slept at all.

The baby bites my shoulder and I am certain draws blood.

"Hey!" I shout at her, startling her into silence. "No biting!"

Eyes wide, her bottom lip starts quivering but she is silent and not biting. So it's a start.

From the floor, Kitten asks, "How long do you think he will be gone?"

I hear the desperation in her voice. The children have only been awake minutes and already she is overwhelmed. What a mess this is. I shrug, not knowing. How long could it possibly take to storm the castle and rescue the girl…hours? Days? "I wouldn't think very long."

"Don't leave me alone with them."

I assure her I won't. How could I?

* * * *

After four days, mornings are slightly calmer. Athena-Sophia has accepted a sippy cup in lieu of a bottle. Although it has a soft nipple, it is shaped like her older brother's sports bottle. He convinced her she is a "big girl" or at least that is what he says he has taught her to say when she lifts her arms over her head and cries out, "*Kah-beer Sha-bah.*" I am trying to convince him to only speak to her in English so that she will understand Celia and I as well. For now, every time she throws her hands over her head and cries out, "*Kah-beer Sha-bah,*" one of the other children imitates her but says, "Big girl."

Nervously, I leave the children at home with Kitten and Enrique while I drive to the private Greek Orthodox school in the suburbs to enroll Hektor in second grade and Olympia in kindergarten. It doesn't go well. First, I am told Hektor will have to take a placement test, seeing that he's been away almost two years. I think he will be devastated to not be able to rejoin the friends he left behind.

"Fall is always a time of transition for students," I am assured by the principal.

Olympia will be welcome join the other kindergartners, even though I feel she should be entering as a first grader. I am assured many parents wait until their children are six to start their formal education.

"*Mr. Stephanopoulos* will be very disappointed if I report back to him that the children will not be able to start classes immediately. Seeing that they have been in Sudan for almost two years he wants to get them acclimated to all things American as quickly as possible and reintegrating them into school to reestablish friendships is his first priority," I bluff with Kitten's sanity in mind. I pray the school will allow them to get started immediately.

Watching the principal's face reveals nothing more than a man adept at hiding all thoughts and emotions. His eyes are a different story, and the gears are obviously turning in his mind. My relief is overwhelming when he finally says, "Perhaps Monday morning would be best for all concerned."

Having taken much longer than I ever anticipated, I drive like a bat out of hell back to the penthouse fearing the worst—tears, blood, destruction of property—and am pleasantly surprised when I find that Athena-Sophia and Nikkos are down for naps and Olympia and Hektor are sitting quietly with Celia drawing pictures at the kitchen table.

Seeing me, she smiles.

"Monday morning," I say.

Evidently she revealed my errand to the children because they both give loud whoops of delight and dance around the room, chanting, "School, school, school!"

"I think you made their day." Celia leaves her chair to hug me. "I think we seriously need to consider the bigger house Thomas asked us to look at. It's been awhile, but hopefully it's still on the market."

I shake my head, feeling things are too up in the air right now.

Later I revise my thinking as I spend another night tucked between children, thinking about Celia sleeping in the other room alone. It occurs to me that after the twins arrive, every night could be like this. How did Thomas ever do it?

We need more bedrooms now, space just can't wait…and a nanny…

Quietly, I creep out of my bed to find Celia isn't in bed. I find her in the dark living room. I turn on the small spotlights that are meant to highlight our artwork. It provides enough light without being jarring. Sitting on the couch, wearing a nightgown I didn't even know she owned, she stares into space.

I sit down beside her and coax her into my lap. "Are you all right?"

She shakes her head. "I never dreamed he'd be gone this long."

I don't admit I'm just as worried, even though I assumed it would take time to find Lattie and arrange her release from the kidnappers. Five days seems like forever because our world has been turned upside down. I worry that Kitten has gone back to not eating and not sleeping.

"Our bed is so lonely without you in it," she says.

"I know." I kiss her temple. I consider sharing two of the four children with her, but she'd probably kill me if I suggested any such thing.

"If we get the larger house, they could each have a bedroom," she implores and there is a desperation to her tone. "Or the boys could share a room and the girls could share a room and we'd have enough room for a nursery and a nanny's suite."

"I know." I take her hand and kiss her knuckles. "Let's look at the house Thomas emailed us about."

She shakes her head. "That house is too big."

I hold up fingers as I start counting off. "Our room, Enrique's room, a nanny's room, the boys' room, the girls' room, and the nursery. Seven bedrooms seems like a lot until we really consider what we're looking at."

"Enrique?" she asks skeptically.

"I will have to rein in Enrique's more risqué behavior, but I can't imagine moving without taking him with us."

"You're right. He's part of our family. He has to come." She wraps her arms around me and hugs me tighter than she ever has. She whispers, "I'm so scared. What if he doesn't come back?"

I kiss her, holding her face. There isn't anything I can say or do to reassure her. She rearranges to straddle me without breaking the kiss. Being of the same mind, I push down the front of my pajama bottoms only enough to free my erection. There is a honeyed sweetness to it when she lowers herself over me and takes my length inside her.

She rocks over me quietly, gently.

I can't remember the last time I was forced to be secretive or quiet. Our joining seems most naughty. She giggles, and I think she is thinking the same thoughts.

"Sh-h," I whisper against her face. I lift my hips to meet her soft motion.

"We can't get caught, I'll die of embarrassment," she admits softly.

"I just need you so badly."

"I know. Me too." As the pleasure builds between us, I finally have the strength to admit to her, "Everything is going to be okay, sweetheart. No matter what."

"Each player must accept the cards life deals him or her: but once they are in hand, he or she alone must decide how to play the cards in order to win the game."

Voltaire, 1694-1778

CHAPTER 17

CELIA

I try not to think about Thomas, or the preparations he made before leaving. I can't bear to think of him not coming back to us. I'm exhausted, mentally and physically. Thankfully, Hektor and Sophia will start school on Monday, even Nikkos is starting pre-school, leaving me only Athena-Sophia to care for during the daytime.

Garrett left me alone with them while he went to look at the house Thomas told us both about. I'm not sure who was happier, him or the real estate agent, when he called this morning to arrange a showing. They determined to meet an hour later and although Garrett wanted me to go too, I saw everything I needed to see online. There are enough bedrooms that however everyone gets arranged, I will get to sleep with Garrett.

When Olympia and the two little ones conk out on sofas for their mid-day naps, I find myself with a young shadow. Hektor has been bored a lot lately. Getting crayons and paper, I sit with him at the kitchen table.

"I heard you call Olympia *Amira* last night. Is that a middle name or a nickname?" I have a sneaking suspicion it is Arabic. The more I learn about the children's last two years it seems Latisha wanted to erase their identities.

"It is her desert name. I was called Halil, Olympia was called Amira, Nikkos was Naji, and Athena-Sophia was Ayah."

"That seems very confusing."

Hektor shrugs. "A name is a name, each place you dwell gives you the opportunity to be someone other than you were before, a better person."

"Who taught you that?"

"Papa," he answers, intent on his coloring.

"Your mother was half French, did she talk to you in French?" I ask hopefully. I really need a common language to try to get closer to Athena-Sophia. The constant wavering between smiles and wails of frustration is wearing on all of us. "Does Athena-Sophia speak French?"

"I think some, but Athena-Sophia rarely talks."

"Well, you are amazing," I assure him. "How many languages do you speak?"

"Five. I think. Not a lot in some of them. I am best at English and Greek, but after we left the United States our mother only spoke to us in French or Arabic. But there is a difference between the desert Arabic and the Arabic in Egypt. So that's five."

"Well, you have me beat. I speak English, French, and some Spanish but very little."

Hektor laughs. "*Hola! Yo hablo engles? Hablo poco español.*

Podemos ser amigos?"

"Yes, I think we will be very good friends." I tousle his hair. "Your Spanish is very good. Much better than mine. You could say that you are well on your way to knowing six languages. You are very smart."

Hektor beams, eyes sparkling. He draws swirls on a piece of paper that I think is Arabic script. "What does this mean?"

He blushes. "It is a house blessing. To keep you safe."

"Thank you." I ruffle his hair, overcome by his sweetness. He seems so much older than seven, but then he's been through so much. I can't imagine how difficult it is for him, sliding between cultures, torn between parents, and now both parents gone. I hide my emotion by starting lunch.

Garrett returns as we are finishing up, finding Enrique loading the dishwasher and me sweeping. He takes the broom and pulls me into a hug. "We have a new house." He hands Enrique the broom. "Watch the kids? Cartoons, popcorn, you can handle them for an hour, right?"

The kids love Enrique, he loves them, and as sure as I am of that leaving them alone makes me nervous. "Are you sure about this?"

"We'll hurry back."

It's hard to not get caught up in his excitement and enthusiasm as we race across town. "You aren't going to believe this place. It's the penthouse times ten, and my God the view of the bay and the bridge!"

Pulling into the driveway, he presses a garage opener and we pull inside. It's a three car garage, no more parking garage. The inside garage entrance leads directly into a walk-in pantry and then the kitchen. He waves a hand dismissively. "I'll redo it, it's fine."

As I take in acres of granite, I can't imagine what he needs to redo, but it's *his* kitchen and I know it isn't even close to his standards. It seems like we're running a marathon as he leads me through the dining room, living room, out onto a deck that overlooks the backyard and the bay and the bridge. "It's breathtaking."

"But not the best part."

We go upstairs and he pulls me down a long hallway, pointing through doors. "Bedroom, bedroom, bedroom, bedroom, bedroom, bedroom."

We're both out of breath as we take the elevator up. We exit into a smaller but still big room. He points as we walk. "Second living room, office."

Opening a double door he leads me into a palatial room. "Master bedroom."

Our gazes collide, and we both smile. Neither one of us has to suggest it, we start tearing off our clothes. There isn't a bed or single piece of furniture. The carpet is a luxuriously, sinful shag. As I drop to my knees, I ask, "Is this fur?"

"It feels like fur," he agrees as he rolls me over and pushes me back. He buries his face against my mons. "God, I've missed you. I was beginning to think we'd never have sex again."

As he licks the slit separating my labia, I ask, "Is parenthood always like this?"

"Not for people who can afford really big houses and a nanny." His lips vibrate against my clit, tickling.

"Two nannies," I remind him then moan as he sucks my clit into his mouth. "God, oh God, I've missed *this*."

I enjoy oral—a lot—and as Garratt licks and sucks and bites, it seems like I am transported to a different realm. My entire body becomes languid, but also alive. My skin seems more sensitive. I want *touched*. All over. I encourage him to run his hands over my thighs. I hug myself, teasing my fingers up and down my arms. And when I can't take much more, I squeeze my breasts, pinch my nipples, stretch them out.

"God!"

Garrett knows exactly the right moment to slide his fingers inside of me, knows just how fast and how deep to pump me. He forces my orgasm to its highest pinnacle, then holds me there. I scream, anticipating the spiraling fall, but somehow…somehow…he holds me adrift, and just when the pleasure seems to take me to the brink of insanity, he allows me to fall into the spiraling chasm of *petite mort*.

* * * *

Two weeks later we are no closer to having nannies, but the children are in school and we are moved into the new house. I never dreamed it could happen so quickly, but as I lay in bed surrounded by moving boxes and even more exhausted than I thought I could ever become, I know I'm not dreaming.

"She has her own bed." Garrett grumbles about Athena-Sophia lying between us.

"Hektor says she's used to sleeping in the tent between several bodies. I think we're going to have to give her some time to get used to things."

"Put her in her bed or she'll never learn."

"*You* put her in her bed." I think every muscle in my body hurts even though I really didn't do anything. The movers did almost everything. God, how can I be this tired?

It seems like a dream as I listen to Garrett, trying to get the baby out of our bed into her own. She fights to get out of his arms, reaching for me. "Non, non, non!"

"Athena-Sophia, you learned a new word!" Garrett praises her. I crack open an eyelid in time to see her smile beatifically as he carries her from the room explaining, "You are such a big girl. You can sleep in your brand new big girl bed tonight."

Her screams carry through the walls and a few moments later

Garrett carries her back into the bedroom. Her bottom lip is pouted out. *"Non! Je suis un bébé!"*

"She speaks French," Garrett informs me.

Evidently.

Athena-Sophia pats her chest. *"Atso est un bébé."*

"Atso?" Garrett asks.

Athena-Sophia beams and pats her chest. "Atso."

From the other side of the bed Olympia and Nikkos pop up. "Can we sleep in here too?"

Garrett does his best to glare as all three children wiggle under the covers. "You know what this means?

"We may never have S-E-X again?"

"Exactly." He growls, turns out the lights and crawls back into bed. "We really need a nanny."

"Two nannies!" I agree, knowing that there would be no way one woman would ever agree to the responsibility of six children.

Unexpectedly Garrett's cellphone rings. It isn't late, at least not that late, only nine or so, but *still*. I'm party to a one-sided conversation which leads me to believe he's needed at the club. "I can't possibly leave right now. What happened?"

I sit up, turning on my bedside lamp when he leaves the bed. Pacing, he runs his hand through his hair. I lose track of the conversation when he leaves the bedroom and goes into the walk-in closet. He returns with a suitcase. "I'll catch the next plane."

What? Plane? My heart skips a beat as my thoughts turn dark. *God. Thomas. Please let Thomas be okay.*

Garrett looks from me to the kids. "We have a new problem."

I hold my breath not wanting to know. I don't want to know

anything. I rub the spot on my abdomen where it's tender from one or both of the babies kicking me. I close my eyes when Olympia hugs me tightly. She's old enough to know something's wrong. I return her hug and kiss her temple, remembering what it feels like to be young and scared and unsure about what the future will hold. Not even knowing the problem, I whisper, "It's going to be okay."

I meet Garrett's gaze, praying hard that Thomas is still alive, and am thrilled when he tells me, "My mom needs me."

I've never been so relieved. Cincinnati I can handle. Thomas hurt or worse, I'm not going to be able to deal with. I kiss Olympia again, hugging her closer. "Go to sleep, sweetheart. Nothing *we* need to worry ourselves over."

When I return my gaze to Garrett I know my nonchalance has hit a wrong nerve with him. What does he expect? I can't worry about one more thing. Whatever is wrong in Cincinnati it has absolutely nothing to do with us or our life here.

"This is what is hardest: to close the open hand because one loves."
Friedrich Nietzsche

CHAPTER 18

GARRETT

Cincinnati, Ohio

Standing on my parents' front porch with a white–knuckled grip on my luggage, this is not the homecoming I imagined. I hang my head, not really knowing what I'm walking into.

I've spent the entire flight, thinking about Kitten. I can't believe I left her at home, with Thomas's four children, and potentially going into labor at any time. I don't care what Dr. Wang has to say on the matter. Few women carry twins to full term and that has me so worried I can't see straight.

I begged her to come with me.

I can't show up on your parents' doorstep eight months pregnant with four spare kids in tow.

She was right, of course. Now isn't the right time, not with things the way they are, but will there be a better time? How will I know when that time is? It's not like I can keep my family a secret forever…

Well, I could, what's one more secret?

The problem is that for the first time in my life I want to share my happiness. The happiness without the chaos. Damn it, Thomas. Will the drama ever end? Eva. Nikos. Now Lattie.

Seriously, when is enough *enough*?

I imagine Celia having the same thoughts right now…about me. I left her with four children straddling two residences. I wish the moving truck hadn't already taken all of our furniture to the new house. I told her to leave the unpacking until I get back to help her. She sure doesn't need to be doing anything more than she's doing.

I decide with sudden clarity that I want to marry her, suburbia and picket fences aside. Forget normal. I want what I have with Celia right now. She is my family. And Thomas. And the children, regardless of how many children. It isn't insanity. It's our life. It's the way it's supposed to be.

I remember all the times I went to Thomas's and I was so envious of his children, of his life. Now he's sharing it with me and before I got on the plane for Cincinnati, I somehow saw it as a burden. No sleep, no sex, no *playtime…*

Those things can be arranged. Our life won't be as spontaneous as before but I have few memories that rival the strength of Celia, sitting on the floor drawing pictures with four children each vying to sit closer her. Lifting my hand to ring the doorbell, I realize it took coming home again to make me see reality. The last time I was home I thought I had to be *vanilla* to have a family. I'm an idiot.

The door opens without my having pressed the button.

"Johnathon! What a nice surprise," my dad greets me, leaving me confused. He shouts over his shoulder, "Honey, Johnathon's here! Did you know he was coming?"

I stand gaping in the threshold as I watch my father turn around and walk back through the house. I step inside and drop my bag before closing the door. My mother comes out of the kitchen, wiping her hands on a towel. She had said a family emergency. I don't know what I thought, but this wasn't it.

"You saw your father."

There is a distance between us, not that I expected her to rush cross the room and pull me into her arms, but some warmth. The dark circles under her eyes tell me she is exhausted. "He called me Johnathon."

She nods. "I always thought you bore a resemblance to his brother."

"Uncle Jack?"

"Who else?" She shakes her head and turns away.

I follow her into the living room and find her sitting on the sofa, she's flipping through a photo album. She pats the cushion beside her and I sit, looking at the page she opened to. Although the photos are old they have been preserved beautifully. I seem to remember a year awhile back that Mom went through a scrapbooking phase.

She points at a photo of a man in his late thirties, a man I seem to bear an uncanny resemblance to. "This is your Uncle Jack. I think this photo was taken a few years before he died. Do you even remember him? God, you were so young. A baby."

"I was nine or ten when he died. I remember him." I sigh heavily, the quick trip down memory lane not detracting from the greater issue. "How long has Dad been exhibiting signs of dementia?"

She looks away.

"Mom?"

"He hasn't been a hundred percent for years, but it's recently gotten *noticeable*. He's had to leave his practice."

"And when were you going to tell me?" My voice is raised, earning me a harsh look.

"What was there to say? Why would I worry you?"

"Next time worry me." I take her hand and find her trembling. "What do the doctors say?"

"The neurologist hasn't given us any clear answers. He's ruled out a tumor, considered Alzheimer's, but is concerned by how rapidly your father is declining." Her voice cracks, and I realize just how worried she is. She doesn't cry, and when I try to pull her closer she doesn't let me. Lifting her chin, she gives me the look, demanding, "When were *you* going to tell me you got *that* woman knocked up?"

I don't deny Celia is carrying my child as I straighten stiffly, rankled by her tone.

"Don't look so surprised that I know. You are my only son and I do keep track of you, even if I don't appreciate the lengths I have to go to in order to spy on you. I was so excited when your *business* added a blog to its website."

I cringe, considering Lewd Larry's sexually explicit lifestyle unambiguous blog.

"She's very pregnant, according to the pictures that posted last week. I was somewhat surprised you agreed to come. She must be due any day now. Unless the child isn't yours."

And there's the rub.

"There's that other man. What do they call him? Lord Fyre? If you ask me, he looks fairly disreputable. Not that you're asking my opinion of course and I wouldn't give it even if you did, but I just don't understand how you could lower your standards so far."

"I didn't come here to discuss my life, my lovers, or the child Celia's expecting." I don't mention twins. It's none of her damn business at the moment. I'm tired of the condemnation. "I'm here because you said there's an emergency."

My father comes into the room suddenly. He is no longer smiling, and I realize it is because he is having a moment of clarity. I stand, facing him as he shouts, "You aren't welcome here."

"Oliver!" my mother chastises.

"You knew he was coming? You welcomed him into our home?"

She takes him by the elbow and steers him to the back of the house. I assume his "boy's room" is still there. Big screen television. Poker table. Pool table. Well stocked bar. The only room in the house she allows him to smoke cigars in.

I sit down on the sofa with a hard thump. *He hates me.* I knew he did, but he's never shown me such vehemence before. My mother isn't gone for long, and she returns alone.

"Thank God he's easily distracted. Like a child. That's the real blessing. It would kill him if he realized he was afflicted."

"I didn't expect—" The words get stuck in my throat. "I should go."

"No. He isn't himself, I've already explained that. Part of the issues we're dealing with is huge swings in emotion. Irrational emotion."

"Don't patronize me, Mother. He hated me before the changes in his medical status. I'd like the phone numbers of all of his physicians. I can be as much help to you from a hotel room as here. For that matter, I could have talked to his doctors from San Francisco and advised you of my opinion *from there.*"

She sits beside me and takes my hand. "He loves you. He hated what he saw as a horrible waste of a medical career."

"He hated that I'm homosexual."

"Are you? Homosexual?"

I look her in the eye. "I don't consider it much but I suppose if you must supply a label, I am bisexual since I have both male and female lovers."

"Lovers? Or just Lord Fyre and Kitten? I read somewhere that you're a committed ménage?"

I shake my head. *I'm erasing my online life as soon as I get back to San Francisco.* "Don't change the subject. We were talking about me getting in touch with his doctors."

"I don't need help with your father's medical condition. I know how to handle doctors after being married to one for forty-two years. Your father has bankrupted us."

"What?" I stand, shocked, confused.

Mother stands too, wringing her hands. "I wouldn't have called but I didn't know what to do."

I wait for the punch line. I look around the room, waiting for secret guests to jump out and shout "Surprise" even though my fortieth birthday isn't for another two months.

"From what I've learned, he donated most of our savings to the Republican presidential campaign and our stocks to a dozen different charities. I need to sell the house." She paces the length of the room, gesturing nervously with her hands. "We should have downsized years ago."

"You love this house."

She shrugs. "It's just a house."

I catch her on her next turn, pulling her into my arms. "You didn't have me come here to help you put the house on the market. Or because Dad is sick."

She breaks down, clinging to me, sobbing. I don't know when I've ever seen my mother cry. "What is going on?"

"I can't do *this*. I haven't been in love with your father for thirty years. He hasn't been *here*. He spent his best years with a woman named Jane Black. He never knew I knew about her, but I did, every secret meeting, the hotels, the expensive gifts he bought her...and now…now that he's sick and we're broke…she doesn't want him! Well, I'll be damned if I'm going to be stuck with him." She steps back, wrapping herself in her arms, and the look she gives me convinces me when her words might have failed. "I've filed for a divorce but because of his current medical state, he needs a proxy. I need you to become his power of attorney and take over the management of any remaining assets, arrange for his future caretaking needs, and represent him in the divorce."

My mouth opens and closes. I don't know what to say. *Fuck.*

"I know this is a lot to lay on you all at once. I'm sorry." She pats my arm. "You know your way to your room."

I'm not comfortable with that, not with my father's hatred and unstable mental status. I'd like to survive to see another morning. "I've already arranged a hotel."

She nods and walks away. No argument. No further discussion. Through the walls I hear her trying to coax my father to bed. "Is *he* gone?"

"Yes, dear. We're alone."

An hour later, my head is spinning. I feel like I've fallen down a rabbit's hole into some mad alternate universe. My mother wants a divorce? *My mother?* I can't believe she'd really abandon him without any thought to a caregiver. By becoming his proxy, am I expected to become his caregiver or arrange for his care? We haven't been close, not for more than fifteen years. *He hates me.* I don't hate him, but I certainly don't want to be responsible for him. God, that sounds horrible. The man gave me life and yet I would turn my back on him? No, I can't turn my back, but I can make my mother see reason.

Back at the hotel I call Celia. "I'm in the Queen City."

"How are your parents? What was the emergency? God, I've been so worried."

"Sh-h, don't worry. I don't want you losing a second's sleep. It's just as I imagined, my mother overreacting. My father needs some tests done and he needs persuading. Doctors really do make the worst patients." My reassurances sound false to my own ears, and I wonder if she's buying my nonchalance. I hope so—I'm not ready to divulge any of the conversation I just had with my mother—especially over the phone. "How are things there?"

She sighs heavily and I expect the worst. "I'm going to be the worst parent ever in the history of parents."

"I doubt that."

Laughing, I lay on the bed, happy to be vertical. Listening to her tell me about her day and the horrors of baby drool, snotty noses and diaper changes, I wish I was there with her.

Suddenly her voice brightens. "Atso calls me Ce-La."

"If you don't know where you are going, any road will get you there."

Lewis Carroll

CHAPTER 19

KITTEN

The children are happy as I drive them to school. It's a relief, no tears, no screaming. I find myself smiling and humming to a song on the radio. I never believed I could do it, I never thought I could manage twins, being a mommy, but I'm doing okay as an aunt. *God, what a beautiful day.*

Garrett is never going to believe the progress I've made.

Miles of sunshine later, I glance into the rearview mirror and notice a dark car, which wouldn't be so unusual except it seems I saw the car earlier—while we were still in the city. What's the chances a car would drive the same roads from San Francisco to Lakeside? The hair on the back of my neck prickles as I assure myself lots of cars drive from San Francisco to Lakeside every day. Still, I'm glad when I pull into the school's roundabout and checking again see the car I believed was following me kept driving past the school's entrance. I'm sure I was just imagining things, but as Hektor and Olympia climb out, I'm nervous. I suddenly don't want them to go to school today. They are smiling, laughing. The sun is still shining. The only difference is *me*.

Maybe this too is hormone related. Lord knows I've acted pretty crazy through most of the pregnancy. I try to shake off the worry, the fear. I'm being silly.

Driving through the school parking lot, I adjust the rearview mirror to look into the back seat at Nikkos and Atso. They are both waving their sippy cups in the air to some mad imaginary tune. I laugh and readjust the mirror just before I pull back out into traffic. A second later my humor is gone when I glance into the rearview mirror and I am left gripping the steering wheel in white-knuckled terror. *It's the same car.*

I pull over to the curb, park in front of a row of chic boutiques and breathe a sigh of relief when the dark car keeps driving, passing me. It's paranoid as hell but I decide to stay in Lakeside instead of driving all the way back to the city.

As I unbuckle the babies and take them inside a coffee shop, I tell myself it's because I've been wanting to check out all the cute, artsy boutiques in town and not because of the dark sedan. The heavy fragrance of fresh roasted coffee beans almost helps me relax, and as much as I'd love a cup of coffee, I order juice all around. We sit at a sunny window seat so that I can keep my eyes on the passing cars. I know I shouldn't bother Master, but I pop my headset on and dial, needing to talk. He answers before I can change my mind and hang up.

"Hello?" He sounds stressed.

"I shouldn't have called." As I shuffle drinks and pieces of muffin I'm glad I have my hands free.

"Is something wrong? The babies?"

"No, no. I'm fine. The babies are fine. I just needed to hear your voice. I'm scared. I think I'm being followed."

"Followed? What are you talking about?"

I tell him about the car but he doesn't want to hear it, or maybe I really do sound as insane as I think I do and he's worried about my mind and trying to give me assurances so that I don't do anything stupid. My God, am I going to do something stupid? What would I do? I realize he's talking and I'm not paying attention.

"It's going to be okay. I know you're worried about Thomas and the trouble he's facing. God, this is the worst timing in the world for me to be away."

I hear regret in his voice and know he'd rather be here then there. "Are your parents okay?"

"They will be. Don't worry about them, or me. Is Enrique doing enough?"

"Enrique is wonderful," I assure him.

He sounds wistful when he says, "I wish we'd have gotten the nannies arranged before I had to leave," making me wish I hadn't called. I don't know what's going on with his parents, but he doesn't need to be worrying about me right now.

I shake my head, even though he can't see. Nikkos starts to get fussy, so I make faces at him and make him giggle. "Just as well you didn't. I think we should wait. I don't want to rush into adding even more new people into their life. Let's help them feel safe and secure. There's plenty of time for nannies."

It's obvious the babies are ready to go, and so I throw trash away and pack everything up. I keep talking to Garrett as I stroll up the street, Atso on my hip, holding Nikkos's hand. I still have four hours until school lets out for the day. A chic baby boutique catches my eye, and I wander in. I could spend hours looking at cute outfits and nursery decorations. "Oh, Garrett, you should see this."

"You sound different."

I shrug, realizing I feel different. I should be hysterical or catatonic with both Thomas and Master away but I'm not, I'm doing okay.

"Still the same Celia," I say and then I realize what I said. Celia, not Kitten. Citing a fussy baby, I hurriedly end the call then apologize to Atso for involving her in my lie. I kiss her pink nose and she grins. "You are the happiest baby."

"Happy," she repeats, and I am glad we are crossing the language barrier.

I look down at Nikkos. He's so quiet compared to the others. Aside from the death-grip he has on my hand, I could forget he is there. Squatting, I hug him to me with my free arm. "You are a happy boy, aren't you?"

He nods against my neck, and I hold him tighter. I hope he can stay happy. What happens if Thomas doesn't return with their mother? I fight back tears.

"Looks like you have your hands full."

I jerk, still on edge, but look up to find a pleasant enough looking saleswoman. Lumbering back to my feet, I agree, "Yes."

"When are you due?"

I let out a sigh. "A few weeks."

She laughs. "I imagine, not soon enough for you?"

I nod, not admitting that with my present circumstances I wish they would just stay inside indefinitely.

"Are you looking for anything in particular?"

"A little bit of everything," I admit, realizing that even though I am due in a few weeks I haven't really bought anything for the babies to come home to. "Newborn sleepers and—" Looking at Atso and Nikkos in their desert garb, I realize they need American clothes. "—do you have anything in their size?"

Suspecting a big commission, the clerk goes to work, throwing together outfits for Atso and Nikkos while I shop for sleepers and cute little infant head and hand warmers. I take a huge pile to the checkout counter, and then spy the bigger kids section. It hardly seems fair to return home with something for everyone except Hektor and Olympia, even though they did just get new school uniforms. Impulsively, I grab several summer dresses for Olympia and some shorts and t-shirts for Hektor.

Through the boutique window, I see the same dark car driving past.

Shaking, I present my credit card and am rewarded with a fast transaction. After the woman's helpfulness I know I seem exceedingly rude as I rush away from the counter and herald the kids out of the store. The car is parked at the other end of the block, making me wish I hadn't walked so far. *Idiot. I'm such an idiot. This is not my imagination!*

I toss shopping bags in the trunk, strap kids into car seats, and hurry back toward the school. Halfway there, I call the principal's office and tell them there's been an emergency and I'd like the children brought to the front door so I can pick them up early.

The secretary informs me I have to come in and sign them out.

Frustrated, I start to lose it a little and imagine she thinks I've lost my mind. "I cannot take the time to come into the office and sign them out! Do you understand that I said it's an emergency?"

I feel like a lunatic, but when I pull up to the curb I am relieved to see the children waiting with the principal. He walks them to the car as I'm climbing out. "I'm sorry. I know this isn't standard procedure."

"Is there anything I can do?"

I meet his gaze. "Pray."

I secure seat belts and climb back behind the wheel with no plan. As I leave the parking lot I memorize every car, and as I get closer to the house I try to pay specific attention to each person…a workman on telephone pole, a woman walking a dog, a man sitting in a car cross the road, reading a newspaper. This is a new neighborhood, each one of these people might actually be perfectly in place but even though Garrett's assurances made perfect sense I don't feel like I'm being ridiculous now.

Maybe I am transferring my concerns about Thomas's safety into baseless fears, but I'd rather be safe than sorry. Thomas would want me to pay attention to what my gut is telling me.

I drive past the house. "Hey kids, wanna go to the beach?"

Cheers come from the backseat.

I call Enrique and give him a list of groceries to bring to us.

Looping around, I drive to Thomas's Sea Cliff Road property. The house is familiar since I spent almost three months here with Thomas. I feel safe here. Maybe because it's only two levels instead of four—that's a lot fewer rooms to hear noises from—but more I think it is because it is Thomas's house.

Strangely, as I prepare dinner from a hodge-podge of pantry finds and the children watch cartoons on the television, I begin to feel a certain *rightness*, like this is what I've been waiting for all along. Why did it take Thomas's house to make me feel *at home*?

I don't want to consider it, but I do.

I try to not think about the day Garrett asked me to marry him and *I couldn't*, or the day I asked Garrett to marry me and *he couldn't*. Or that I whispered to Thomas that I felt already married to him. I can't help that my soul feels drawn to his.

Settling the children around the dinner table, I imagine Thomas sitting at the head of the table. He would be comfortable there, surrounded by his family, but try as I might, I can't see Garrett taking on the role. I can envision him as Uncle Gar, making hasty entrances bearing hugs and gifts, and even hastier exits, always in a rush to get back to his real world.

Our real world, right? I *am* Kitten.

Ding-dong. When the deep-toned doorbell rings, I almost jump out of my skin. I tell the children, "Stay in your seats. Don't move."

Heart pounding, I cautiously look through the peephole. *Enrique.* Opening the door to let him in, I see his arms are laden with bags of groceries, but I don't assist him. Noticing the same black car from earlier, the one that followed me to the school and then into town, parked along the curb, I jerk him inside by his sleeve.

"Why ju not come home to da new house?"

I slam the door but keep an eye on the car through a narrow window. I'm truly terrified when a man steps out. I try to remember every detail. He is wearing sunglasses and a ball cap. It's dusk and everything is shaded, I couldn't identify him if I had to. I write down the details about the car he is driving but can't see a license plate number. I notice another vehicle that's been parked out front too long, a white, late model van with *Huey's Carpet Installation* written on the side.

"Did you notice that van out front?"

"Ju are scaring me."

"I'm scaring myself," I admit as I google *Huey's Carpet Installation.* Nothing. Not a single match. "If he was legitimate, wouldn't his information pop up on my screen?"

Looking over my shoulder at the screen, Enrique shrugs.

Calling 911 seems out of the question. I tell Enrique, "You should go back to the house."

"I'm not leaving ju here alone."

Meeting his gaze, I try to convince him. "Please go. I'll be fine."

He stands his ground, and I leave him to gather the children off to bed. It seems early but they don't argue. We're all nervous and even though I'm doing my best to hide it, the children sense my fear. I can see it in their eyes.

* * * *

At midnight, I risk looking outside. Two men sit in a car, seeming so clichéd FBI I almost laugh except I can't find the humor. The same woman walks by with her dog. I try to remember details from earlier and decide it could be a different woman, maybe even a different dog, but as she glances up to the house, I know I'm not being paranoid. *She is watching us.*

Panicky, I ramble through the kitchen, opening every cabinet, testing each appliance, even opening the stove, turning all the dials. I search each bathroom for anything out of the ordinary. Nothing. What did I expect? A secret panel?

I walk back to the bedroom. *This is Thomas's house. He wouldn't live in a house that didn't have special security measures. Think.* The bedroom is a huge room, but when I pace off the inside room against the number of paces down the hallway, I end up two feet short.

Back inside the bedroom, I tap the wall behind the bed. It sounds hollow but there's no hidden levers on the headboard. No remote control. Nothing. Lying on Thomas's side of the bed, I inhale a deep breath, and exhale, trying to think like he would. Reaching down, I feel under the bed, running my hands along the underside of the frame. *There!* Two buttons. *Shit, shit, shit.* Which button? "Here goes."

I push the first button, and the wall beside the bed opens. I leap out of the bed and find a small arsenal.

"Holy mother of God," I mutter under my breath. At the same moment Enrique comes into the room and echoes the sentiment.

"I told you to go away. Go home."

He comes up to stand beside me. "What are you doing now?"

I look at Enrique because I've never, ever heard him speak without his thick accent. I pick up a small caliber and tuck it into my waistband. "I have no idea, but I'm going to be armed."

"No, no, no." He reaches for the gun. "This is too dangerous."

"The safety's on."

Grabbing two boxes of ammunition and two handguns, I lay them on the bed.

"You're going to get you and Thomas's children killed. That's what you're going to do."

Racing down the hall to the garage, I find the family cars, an Audi SUV and a BMW wagon with three car seats in the back and although it looks sporty, I assume the wagon was Lattie's. I'm so used to seeing Thomas either behind the wheel of a sports car or on a motorcycle, the cars here remind me he also has another life—as a family man.

Enrique steps down into the garage with me and whistles. "Q-Five."

"Does that mean something?"

"Fast, super charged. Off-road, up mountains, this baby is dezined for speed and maneuverability."

I nod, not knowing what I'm thinking but thinking hard. Enrique opens the door and looks inside, inhaling deeply. "Leather."

"You said fast. If you were going to pick a getaway car, which one would you choose?"

"Getaway car? What are you talking about? You're scaring me."

"Garrett doesn't want to believe that we are being followed or watched, and that whatever is happening is taking place in Africa, but I know in my gut that we are and I don't like it. I don't know if the people out there are here to protect me or kidnap the children or kill us all in our beds while we sleep, but I don't want to stick around to find out."

My gut tells me I have to get the kids off the grid, and I hurry back into the house for the shopping bags of clothes I bought earlier. They are by the front door where I dropped them because I was in a hurry to start dinner and try to put my fears out of my mind.

I toss the bags into the trunk of the Audi SUV and then start transferring car seats from the large BMW van to the smaller vehicle. I'm one short, they didn't have Atso when they lived here. "Enrique, get Atso's car seat out of my car in the driveway. Use the side door."

He doesn't question, and he's back in a flash.

"You have to help me if I'm going to make this work," I tell him as I buckle the final seat into place.

Eyes wide, he nods. Together we load the car with Atso's diaper bag, the snacks and the bottles of water and juice I had Enrique bring us in preparation for a few days at the beach, and a quickly packed bag from what I could find in Lattie's closet for myself—honestly, not many of her things would fit me in my present state, but at the back of her closet I'd hit paydirt, finding several loose-fitting caftans and stretchy pants that I could wear pulled up only to where my big belly starts.

It looks like we're going on a long trip. I can't think about that—the long or short of it—I only know I have to escape this house right now. "You are going to take the BMW and peel out. Head toward Mexico. I am going to head the opposite way. They can't follow both of us."

"This is a stupid plan."

"I don't have a better one." He is close on my heel as I head back into the house. I empty my purse of everything that identifies me as other than Blair Harrington. Being more paranoid than I've ever been in my life, I leave both of my cellphones laying on the table, fearful whoever is following me might use them to track us. "Help me get the kids loaded."

"This is insane."

Hurrying through the house, I tell him, "If I have to tie you up and gag you I will. Is that what you'd prefer?"

He looks truly torn. "Where will you go?"

"I can't tell you. Someplace safe. And when the dust settles and we can all live happily ever after again, I'll come back."

"Have you forgotten you are pregnant?"

"I know."

"You are talking about dragging four children God knows where—"

"Yes, I am. Look, I can't sit around here…waiting for the worst to happen."

I wake up Hektor and ask him to get Atso and buckle her in her car seat. Picking up Nikkos, I pray he won't wake and start crying. Thankfully his head rolls against my shoulder like a drunken man's. He is out.

Gently as possible, I awaken Olympia. "Wake up, sweet girl. We're going for a ride."

"To see Daddy?"

"Not yet, but soon you will see Daddy."

I buckle Nikkos and Olympia into their seats. On the other side of the car Hektor buckles in Atso.

Behind me, Enrique begs, "At least call Garrett."

Frustrated, I turn toward him. "I did but he's busy dealing with his own emergency. He thinks I'm imagining things and if my fears do materialize, I can't wait for either of my men to rescue me." Looking over the roof of the car, I tell Hektor, "Get into the front seat and fasten your belt."

Thankfully, the boy doesn't argue with me. Should I be concerned the children are taking my midnight madness in stride? Climbing behind the wheel, I try really hard to convince myself that I'm not overreacting. I glance at Hektor, and the look he returns is stoic.

"Is this an emergency Aunt Celia?"

I shake my head robotically, not wanting to frighten him or the others.

"Because if it is, we have to follow the rules."

"The rules?" I ask dumbly as I turn in my seat to double check each of the children's car seats. I try to not think about the fact that my gut instinct was to choose this car for speed instead of the wagon.

"We have to follow the emergency evacuation plan. We've practiced it lots, like a fire drill at school but for home."

Of course, my Thomas would have trained his children to escape in case of an emergency. I should have just asked the son if there were guns in the house. I would have probably saved some time, except I look at Hektor and see a little boy. He shouldn't know about guns and escape plans.

"I'll be right back," he says, leaving the car.

"Hektor! No!" I watch him hurry back through the garage door and into the house. "Enrique, stop him! We have to go now!"

But I needn't have worried; Hektor is back before Enrique can even chase him. He returns carrying a duffle bag and four child-size backpacks. He climbs in and I help him maneuver the bags in the rear floorboard. He explains, "We can't leave without our Go Bags."

"Go bags," I repeat.

He presses a lever overhead, opening the sunglass holder and removes a remote control. He tells me, "Push the red button."

I do. Nothing happens. I was expecting the garage door to go up.

"Count to twenty," he says, as if repeating it from memory and starts counting aloud with, "Two...three...four..."

I keep the count going in my head...*eighteen...nineteen...twenty.*

"Now what?"

"Is it still an emergency?"

"Yes! Hektor. What do I do now?"

Swallowing hard, he opens the glove box and pushes a button on the garage door opener he finds inside. He braces himself, squinting his eyes closed. "Start the car and as soon as the door is up push the black button and floor it."

"What happens when I press the black button?"

"I don't know, it's what Papa told Mama to do."

I push the black button and go, burning rubber out of the driveway and onto the residential street. I look in the rearview mirror to see that Enrique did what I told him to. Following in the BMW, he turns at the first intersection that will lead him to the interstate but is immediately blocked off, surrounded by black SUVs.

Shit, oh shit. Did I just send Enrique to his death? I accelerate, expecting a pursuit and not knowing what to do to help Enrique. *This was a stupid plan.*

Beside me, Hektor still has his eyes tightly closed.

Keeping my eyes on my rearview mirror, it appears no one is following us. I sigh with relief as I pause at a stop sign, but then from nowhere two black SUVs appear, barreling toward us. I push the accelerator to the floor, leaving behind more rubber...and then all hell breaks loose behind me. The house explodes. Four smaller explosions follow, taking out each of the nearest fire hydrants.

The closest SUV dodges falling debris. The second vehicle isn't so lucky, a chunk of falling metal hits its hood, stopping it cold.

"Oh! Shit! Oh no!" *I blew up Thomas's house!* I drive like a maniac, zigzagging through residential streets until I am certain no one is following us. The streets are deserted, except for the fire engines and police cars flying in the opposite direction. I keep driving away from the house. "Now what?"

Calmly, Hektor opens the glove box and takes out a GPS. He plugs the adapter into a cigarette lighter and scrolls through a list of *favorites*. I try to see the choices but the words make no sense, the letters seem combined nonsensically.

He selects one seemingly at random.

"Where are we going?"

He shrugs.

"What were the choices?"

"I just picked the month from the list."

I nod, sure. Pick a month, any month. "You picked May, right?"

He giggles beside me. "Yes, Aunt Celia."

The GPS leads me out of San Francisco

"You are a seven-year-old boy, right?"

For some reason my question makes him giggle.

"So, your dad programmed the GPS?"

"Yes."

I breathe a sigh of relief, because he'll know where we're at...even if I still don't know where I'm going.

As I follow Interstate Eighty, I figure out we're headed toward Nevada. I don't know if that's better or worse than where I'd have chosen if left to my own devices. Four hours later on a long stretch of Interstate Fifty, I know I wouldn't have chosen *this* road. There doesn't seem to be another person anywhere. No cars, no houses. No artificial light sources at all, except for my headlights. I feel like a sitting duck.

We're out in the open, and although it's still hours until daylight I don't feel the cover of mere darkness is enough. The GPS reveals we still have four hours until we reach our destination.

All of the children are asleep except the ones inside my belly, and I think they have decided it's time for a game of soccer. I hold the tender spot under my ribs, wishing the twins would at least give me a break from their constant kicking.

At eight-fifteen we reach the town of Ely. After a quick fuel stop I make a hard left off-road toward the mountains just as the kids are waking up. Hektor is a huge help, doling out juice boxes and snacks from their Go Bags in answer to their cries of "I'm hungry," and "I'm thirsty." I feel horrible for thrusting so much responsibility onto him and have to keep reminding myself he is only seven.

Forty minutes later, I am sure we are lost. We are surrounded by mountains and rocky fields that seem hardly capable of sustaining the cows grazing there. I haven't seen a single vehicle or person since we left town. We've been off-road for twenty minutes, steadily climbing a rough, rocky route. Suddenly, the GPS announces, "You have arrived at your destination."

I stop the car in the shade of a gray limestone formation, idling, not bothering to get out because there isn't anything to see. Dirt. Scrub. A few unidentifiable trees. I don't know what I expected but rough camping in the desert wasn't on the list. Looking closer at the pile of rocky terrain next to us, it starts to take shape. I put the car into park, climb out and walk around the hill, realizing as soon as I reach the other side that it is an adobe-earth house half-buried into a hillside. I breathe a huge sigh of relief.

An unlocked iron gate leads into a front courtyard, surrounded by a low stone wall. A gnarly olive tree looks right at home with its gray-green foliage, tucked as it is between stone wall and fountain. The fountain is dry and obviously hasn't been used in years.

Not knowing what to expect, I knock on the front door, though it's fairly obvious no one is here or has been here in a very long time.

Hektor joins me carrying his littlest sister. "She's wet."

Atso reaches for me, and as I take her I realize she's soaking wet. "Oh!"

Prepared, Hektor hands me the diaper bag and together we manage to get her changed without having to lay her on the rocky ground to do it.

"Are we staying here?"

"Yes. I just don't know how to get inside."

Hektor points to a combination lock similar to the one at Sea Cliff Road. I try Sea Cliff's combination and it works. "Well, that doesn't seem very safe. *Your father* should have them programmed with different numbers."

Hektor laughs at my censuring tone as we go back to the car to get the other children. It doesn't hit me until we're settled inside the house that I don't know if Thomas is okay or not. We haven't heard from him. I am hiding out in the middle of the desert with four small children, waiting for him to come and save the day, but what if he never shows up?

And we only have enough food for a few days.

And I don't have a cellphone.

What was I thinking?

* * * *

"I'm a damn good shot," Hektor announces.

"Watch your mouth!" I look up to see that he is unpacking the bag I loaded with guns and ammo. "And put that down!"

I hurry across the room and put all the weapons back into the bag. Hektor looks like he is going to cry.

Pulling him against me, I hug him. "I'm sorry I yelled. I don't want you cursing, and I don't want you to touch these guns. I shouldn't have brought guns. I don't know what I was thinking."

He hugs me tightly. "I want to protect you. I will not let anyone put a bullet in your head like they did my grandfather."

I sit in a chair and take his hands in mine. "Oh, Hektor. This has been so hard on you."

"My mother is dead."

"No. Your father has gone to rescue your mother."

He shakes his head and walks away, leaving me overcome with emotion. The boy obviously believes his mother isn't coming home. *God damn it, Thomas. You should be here with us. What is taking you so long?*

I can't fault the boy for his fears. I'm worried too. I never dreamed Thomas would be gone so long. Or Garrett. If I hadn't spoken with him yesterday I might be worried something had happened to Garrett too, but I did, and I can't afford to let my imagination make me start thinking the worst.

Thinking quickly, I rally spirits with a game. "Let's search the house."

"What are we looking for?"

"Anything. Everything. Let's discover its secrets."

It's a very small house. There is a main room that doubles as living room and dining area, a small kitchen with a wood fueled stove, two bedrooms, one with a full bed, one with bunk beds, and a shared bathroom.

I sit on the lowest bed, ready to cry. Staying here seems absolutely impossible. Maybe if it was just me...but kids need *stuff*. As I watch the four of them investigate each nook and cranny with wonder I realize they might be better equipped for this adventure than I am. Hektor discovers a door in the floor. A quick look reveals a below ground cistern. There is no electricity and no refrigeration, leaving us to rely on kerosene, battery operated lanterns, and a few candles.

Outside I find an electrical panel, generators, batteries, and cables leading to solar panels. Inside, there is no refrigerator. Why? I do find an ice chest. And an ancient web and aluminum lawn chaise which I drag from the cellar to the front courtyard. Sitting in the sun always makes the most dire of circumstances seem not quite so bad.

Time ticks by very slowly in a desert, and it's too quiet. Aside from the delighted squeals of the children chasing small lizards around the courtyard for entertainment, we are surrounded by a most strange silence. Even the light breeze that comes through mid-day offers only a soft stirring of the leaves. After four hours I'm going stark raving mad. Worried about what happens after nightfall, I'm not entirely certain we can stay. I don't know when I've ever been so isolated. Are there bears here? Coyotes? Rattlesnakes? *Crap. I don't know anything about Nevada.*

I won't allow the children to explore beyond the stone wall.

After taking stock of our dwindling supplies—kids eat a lot—it appears a trip back into the small town of Ely seems paramount to our being able to stay here. I wish I'd have thought of that while I was pumping gas, but then I had no idea where I was going.

Honestly, we could get by for a few days but I tell myself we *need stuff*, and we do. If nothing else, for my own sanity I need to feel prepared for anything and right now I don't. Once in town I realize my shopable list is fairly short: rice, beans, canned goods, apples, bananas and granola not because they don't have more to offer, but because without refrigeration, I seem at a loss. I make up for lack of variety with vast bottles of juice then as an afterthought add olive oil, salt, and some bottles of spice. Just because I'll be making simple meals, doesn't mean they have to taste bad. For me, I add herbal tea because my nerves are shot. Several different types of crackers, cereal, powdered milk and peanut butter are added to the cart at the last minute.

We hurry in and out, but still, a pregnant woman with four kids in tow gets noticed. I regret drawing attention to ourselves, but also know I couldn't have left the children in the wilderness. I thought we were scot-free, but then the checkout girl asked, "New to these parts?"

Why do people in small towns have to be so damn friendly?

"Just passing through," I lie, smiling widely. "Going home to be with my family. You know, for when the baby comes."

She nods, still scanning items, and pops her gum. "You'll need some help."

I laugh, lying through my teeth, "Between my mom, two aunts, and three sisters, I'll have plenty of help."

She laughs too, handing me my change. "Well, good luck!"

I force myself to walk slowly and nonchalantly to the car, and then drive the wrong direction on Interstate Fifty for ten miles to make certain I'm not being followed before doubling back. By the time I get to the safety of the adobe, I'm a nervous wreck. Sitting in the chaise, I spend the rest of the late afternoon watching the surrounding hills. I don't know what I expect, the closest people are almost an hour's drive away and no one followed us from town, but still I watch for any movement.

Thankfully, the kid's internal clocks seem set with the sun and they are all sound sleep by dusk. After driving all night and a stress-filled day I am more than ready to fall asleep, but anxiety keeps me on edge and awake.

I take a shower and change into one of Lattie's caftans. It's silk and flows around my ankles, making me feel pretty and feminine despite my girth. Making a cup of tea, I take it with me out into the courtyard.

The chaise is a comfort, supporting my weight in a way furniture doesn't. Sipping my tea, I realize again just how alone we are out here. As the stars come out against the black night sky, there isn't a single other light for as far as I can see. I feel like I'm floating in space. It's an utterly peaceful feeling. Still, I'm watchful and don't fall asleep.

Strangely, the howl of coyotes is a comfort. Their soft yips back and forth are a conversation. I don't think they'd be making such a racket if there were any other humans near, maybe I'm wrong about that but for a while it brings me peace. It doesn't last. By dawn I feel as if a leaden mantle cloaks me. I've felt this way before, much like the physical and emotional letdown following a death. I experienced this feeling when my mother died, and to some extent when my father died, except no one has died now. Wrapped in an agony I don't understand, I allow myself to cry.

I know it was important to leave the cellphones behind, but having no way to call out I'm afraid. I need to hear Garrett and Thomas's voices. Apprehension greater than I have ever known tells me that Garrett is the one in danger, and it makes me angry that he scoffed my fears. I can't stand the thought of him being in jeopardy, and it's taken all night for me to realize paranoia didn't put me here, real menace did, and Garrett has to be warned he could very well be in peril too. I feel stupid for not considering it before. I have to drive back into town and find a pay phone.

I debate with myself about whether I will tell him where I am and finally decide I'm not going to. I trust him, but I don't trust whoever was following me and the children, and now that we're safe, hidden, I can't risk being found.

Thomas charged me with the care of his children until he returns, not Garrett, and I feel the weight of the responsibility.

What if Thomas never comes?

"No, no, no. I refuse to think that."

Inside, I hear the children rising and hurry to wipe away the evidence of my sadness. Standing, a sharp pain tears through my groin. *God, no, not this, not now.*

"You know how often the turning down this street or that, the accepting or rejecting of an invitation, may deflect the whole current of our lives into some other channel. Are we mere leaves, fluttered hither and thither by the wind, or are we rather, with every conviction that we are free agents, carried steadily along to a definite and pre-determined end?"

Sir Arthur Conan Doyle, *The Stark Munro Letters*

CHAPTER 20

GARRETT

"Your father's brain is shrinking at an alarming rate."

Doctor Graham, my father's neurologist, lays out the most recent brain scans as evidence. Pointing with his fountain pen into the empty spaces between skull and brain matter in an assumption that I have no idea what I'm looking at. I appreciate the fact that he is trying to help me to understand why the medications he has prescribed aren't providing my father any relief from his symptoms.

"How long does he have?"

The doctor is taken aback by my question but answers, "Months—at this current rate of decline—weeks."

Stunned but not surprised, I nod and leave his office. This isn't the news I wanted to take to my mother, but she needs to know. There is much she needs to prepare for.

My mind is distracted as I leave the Physician's Center but not so distracted that I don't notice a dark sedan tailing me. I tell myself I have an overactive imagination fueled by Celia's nonsensical fears, but as I make two unnecessary turns and both are shadowed I know I shouldn't have dismissed her qualms so lightly.

I don't meet my mother at her attorney's office. Even though I'm running late I keep driving, jumping onto I-275, then driving fast, too fast, waiting until the last possible second to cross three lanes to whip onto the I-71 exchange that will take me into the city. The sedan flies past the exit unable to negotiate the turn.

I sigh, but not with relief. Fear leaves me cold as I try Celia's cell and she doesn't answer. I call the landline phone at the new house, but it goes straight to voicemail. I dial Enrique, both his cell and his number at the penthouse only to get voicemail at each. I call the club, speaking first with my secretary and then with George, neither of which have seen or spoken with Celia. What did I expect, her to drag four children to Lewd Larry's?

I call Jackie but she hasn't spoken with Celia for several days. "Have you tried?"

"What?" She sounds distracted and confused by the question.

"Have you tried calling Celia and she didn't answer or have you just not bothered calling for a few days?"

"I've been busy. Why? What's wrong?"

"I'm in Cincinnati, and she isn't answering the phone."

"What are you doing in Cincinnati?" Her voice is shrill. I don't have time to explain so I hang up on her and try Celia's cell again. A sickening feeling fills my gut as I ditch Mom's car and take a city bus across town. Riding, I try to piece what I know together to make sense. Who would be following me and Celia?

Exiting the bus and catching a taxi, I ride back to Indian Hills and my mother's attorney's office. She is waiting impatiently in the lobby. "Where's my car?"

"Downtown. I parked it in a garage downtown." I hand her the parking stub so that she can locate it. "I need to get back to San Francisco."

"What?" she demands. "You can't leave now. "

I steer her out of the main lobby into a small waiting area that is made private only by the distinction we are the only ones using it. A wall of palms separate us from the reception area. I take my mother's hands and with no delicacy tell her, "You don't *need* a divorce. I doubt Dad lives long enough to make it to the court date."

She pales.

"When you speak to the lawyer, explain the situation. Your husband is dying, rapidly."

"Don't be ridiculous. You saw him this morning. He's irritable, cranky as an old bear."

"The neurologist hasn't given you all the facts you needed. As Dad's brain continues to atrophy he will lose body functions. His major organs, control of his muscles. He will reach a point where his heart and lungs stop."

She stares at me, not wanting to believe me.

"Your lawyer will explain everything that needs to be done."

My mother gapes at me. "You're really leaving me to deal with this?"

"Yes, Mother. My *family* needs me."

"There is a tide in the affairs of men, which taken at the flood, leads on to fortune. Omitted, all the voyage of their life is bound in shallows and in miseries. On such a full sea are we now afloat. And we must take the current when it serves, or lose our ventures."

William Shakespeare, *Julius Caesar*

CHAPTER 21

THOMAS

We are taken to a privatized military base in the desert—not as prisoners—as allies. The building is a single story mud brick as long as a city block, and as deep. We are taken through a maze of corridors, and the room we end up in is no more than a carved out cave. Dirt floors, bare light bulbs, roughly hung, and lack of windows take me mentally back to assignments I wish I'd never been part of. Outmanned and outgunned, my entire team is on edge, waiting. Maybe I've been in similar circumstances so many times in the past, I'm immune to the threat, not the danger. I no longer react to pompous assholes carrying bigger guns than mine. I'm armed, well armed, and as long as I have my guns, knives, and body armor, I'm okay with their show. Puffed chests, pumped biceps, and crude jokes aside, I know we're equals even if they want me, us, to believe differently. Now, if anyone tries to take away my weapons that ups the ante and I might have to prove who has the better trained team.

It helps that I know most of the soldiers escorting us, recognizing them as *Glorianna's* men. Still, I'm surprised when she arrives on site.

As far as I knew she was still in Washington DC playing her role as Republican presidential hopeful, but the woman standing in front of me is a far cry from Senator Abigail Wainwright-Fuller. Glorianna is tough as nails, battle ready. Glorianna has the ability to scare me. She stalks toward Nikos, pushing up his chin with two fingers. Narrowing her gaze, she says icily, "Your locator says you are safe and sound in the United States. Imagine finding you *here.*"

He turns around, showing her the back of his neck. It is jaggedly scarred, well healed. He probably hasn't been implanted since his first day at Lewd Larry's. He explains, "Bar fight. Got hit over the head. Must have popped out." Shrugging, he turns back around, meeting her gaze with sincerity and the bit of cocky arrogance that makes my brother so charming to women and so threatening to men. "Sorry."

"We'll discuss this later," she promises icily, but I recognize the look in her eyes as pure lust. My brother's first mistake: challenging her. His second: catching her eye.

Careful, brother. I hope he understands the look I give him when she turns her back on us to address the entire group. It doesn't pass my notice she intentionally avoided *my* gaze, and for some reason that bothers me. "There's been an incident. What we thought was an isolated territorial event in Sudan has proven to be much more. There have been four assassinations and a dozen kidnappings across the world, which at first glance have absolutely no connection. However, on closer inspection have proven to be a direct attack on the Guardians."

She opens an envelope and scatters photos across a table for dramatic effect.

"You may not recognize all or any of the faces, but let me assure you these people are important to everyone standing in this room."

My heart skips a beat and I am overwhelmed with dread, seeing that both Celia and Garrett's photos are among the scattered.

She pins a photo to a tan cork board. "The first assassinated was Charles François Charbonneau, an arms dealer, though had this woman—" She hangs Lattie's photo directly beneath his. "—not been kidnapped, the assassination itself would not have warranted the Guardians involvement. However, she was, which drew one of our top agents into the intrigue." She meets my gaze before hanging my photo directly beneath Lattie's.

The muscles in my jaw tighten as I nervously wait for her to drop the other shoe, but she leaves Garrett and Celia's photos on the table in favor of picking up the photo of a man I don't recognize.

"The second assassination was a man of little to no importance, a banker in Israel, and the child kidnapped, his daughter, might have only been a coincidence, but garnered the Guardians full attention when it was realized these two were directly related to this woman." She hangs photos of the banker, the young girl, and the female, a mossad agent I once completed an assignment with.

"The third assassination was of global consequence, Charles Linquest, king of Sweden. The second and third kidnappings were two brothers, Charles and Randolf Linquist. Charles is heir apparent to Sweden's throne."

She attaches the three photos to the board, father above, sons below, and beneath the sons, she pins Eva's photo, a lover from my past.

"The fourth assassination was Senator Duluth of Kansas. His wife and children are safe. Fast actions on their own part prevented the attempted kidnapping."

She hangs the photo of the senator and beneath it his wife and children. And lower, Claude, a man standing in the room. The likeness he bares to the senator leads me to believe it is his father.

"Are we noting a trend?" She taps each face on the bottom row of photos. "Agent, agent, agent, agent. We are only as strong as our weakest agent, and as of this moment our four strongest agents are emotionally compromised. And why?"

She glares at us.

"What is the first thing we learn when we become a Guardian? No emotional attachments. You do not have family. If you have a lover you must keep the fact in your mind at all times the person is expendable."

She paces the length of the room. "Who's next? That is what our enemy wants us to spend our time thinking and worrying about. We cannot gather every single father, mother, spouse, child or sibling into safe houses. We cannot protect your lovers."

She stops directly in front of me. "You took a wife, bore children."

She moves to Claude. "*You* went home. Tell me, what point was the elaborate cover story? Your death, your funeral? If you were so weak that you had to run home to Mommy and tell her you were alive?"

"She had a nervous breakdown," he argues in his defense.

She slaps his face and in the same moment one of her men, who until this point has merely been one among us, stabs a hypodermic in the back of his neck. Claude drops at her feet, and she doesn't give him a second glance as she walks around his body. It is fairly obvious he is dying, but no one makes a move to aide him.

She faces us, posture stiff. "Who are we?"

As a group we answer with a rally cry, "Guardians."

"We are at war, Guardians. Our enemy believes we will be drawn out. They don't really *know* us. If they did, they would know that these brothers are expendable." She taps the photos of Eva's brothers for effect. "This sister, this wife—" Her gaze locks with mine and I know Lattie has already been confirmed dead. "—expendable."

One of her men asks, "Do we know who *they* are?"

"No," she answers curtly. Moving to a laptop, she types. On a wide screen, photos flash large then move to thumbnail size before another large photo flashes and another thumbnail. When she has moved through the sequence there are thirty faces looking back at us, twenty-seven men and three women. "These are our known rivals, some powerful, some we have believed weak enough not to be any threat at all." There are ten agents present, including my brother and myself. She hands us each a manila envelope. "Within forty-eight hours I expect any and all threats to be eliminated."

No one is brave enough to ask what happens if none of those identified turn out to be at the root of our current problems.

She claps her hands. "Move out." She finally meets my gaze. "Except for you."

"I heard you were dead," I hear my brother say. He is hamming it up with one of the other agents as they leave the room. If he is troubled that he has been reactivated, he doesn't show it.

The agent he addressed answers, "As I did you," just before the door closes on their conversation.

"You don't think you're overreacting a bit?" *Someone will notice this.* Several of the thirty were high-profile dignitaries. I lay the manila envelope on the table beside the scattered photos.

She looks at me with boredom. "I'll know in forty-eight hours."

She grazes her hand over my shoulder, a touch meant to be reassuring that makes my blood run cold though there is no immediate threat of death. I remind myself that neither Henri nor Claude saw it coming either.

"I told you to stay home with your children." Glorianna moves fast, hugging me. She could have as easily killed me but she has no intention of that. I see that now. I feel like my chest might explode from within. Every emotion I've ever felt for her collides. Love. Hate. Empathy. Fear. I would sleep better tonight knowing she was dead, but I can't will myself to wrap my fingers around her throat. My guess is that she feels exactly the same way and so we will part, granting each other life. "You shouldn't be here."

I look at my feet. "I had to try to rescue my children's mother."

She lifts my chin and catches my gaze. "Even if it left them orphaned? With no protector?"

There is a threat underlying the question, and it dawns on me that I have been moronically reckless.

"Can I count on you to perform the tasks I've assigned you?"

"Can you tell me you have proof of Lattie's death? Will you give me assurances as to the safety of my children and my lovers?"

Pursing her lips, she looks old, bitter. "You're so damn greedy."

She crosses the space to open the door to a room that is little more than a closet, obviously used to store artillery. She walks over to one of the boxes in the pile and touches it with her hand. "I'm sorry for your loss."

She strides by me, leaving the room quickly. I don't want to go into the closet-size room, as much because I really don't want to look inside the small crate that is obviously too tiny to hold a body for fear of what I might find within the box as I fear entering a trap.

I can't leave without looking.

I cross the small space in two strides and use a metal bar to pry off the lid. There is a body bag inside and although it is folded onto itself to fit in the box, it obviously holds something. I unzip the bag and looking, immediately regret that I did so. As my field of vision blurs, I know I needed to see. I wouldn't have believed without visual confirmation. *Latisha is dead.*

As I reseal the box, Nikos comes up behind me and puts his hand on my shoulder. "Glorianna sent me. She didn't want you to be alone."

I swallow, unable to speak.

"Are you all right?"

"All that's here is her head."

"God, Ari, I'm sorry."

I grip the side of the box as a wave of dizziness washes through me. I thought I still had time to find her, to get her out alive. I never thought for a minute *this* would be the outcome. Obviously, we've had our differences over the last two years, but she was so passionate about life, so vibrant. I can't imagine a world without her in it. "I failed her."

"No. You didn't. She shouldn't have been *here*. Thank God you got your children out."

"Yes, thank God."

It bothers me that Glorianna's team reached my children before Pepé's team. The only way it could have happened as it did was if she already had men on the ground when she called me from the shower.

I don't understand.

I lift the small crate, planning to deliver Lattie's remains to her relatives, but Nikos keeps me from leaving the small chamber. "Are you carrying out her plans?"

Our gazes collide.

"I'm going to appear to, for now."

"Outnumbered, outgunned is it? You've become a coward?"

"I won't leave my children orphaned. Once I get my feet firmly back on US soil, I'll make what decisions I need to. For now, I cooperate." I push past him to go into the larger room.

"Are you sure your children *are* alive?"

I pause beside the long table where Glorianna left dozens of photos scattered. Setting the crate down, I pick up the photos of Celia and Garrett, and start pushing the other photos around, hoping I don't recognize any others, but I do. Nikkos. Hektor. Olympia. Athena-Sophia.

Beside me, my brother opens my manila envelope and looks through the information of the targets I was assigned. I don't have to ask what he's thinking, he's planning on completing his assignments *and mine* in the allotted time. I don't doubt that he can, I wish he wouldn't. I wanted a life free of the agency for his future, but his future is the least of my worries as I stride from the room to confront Glorianna. I wave the photos of Garrett, Celia and the children in front of her. "Tell me about these."

Her bodyguards move to intervene, but she waves them off.

"I planned to wait until we are on the plane back to the United States before discussing this."

"Perhaps you should tell me now." I palm my handgun but don't aim it at her and am rewarded with an AK-47 pressed up against my temple by her nearest guard.

Behind him I hear a click as Nikos, having my back, cocks his revolver.

"The plan was to round up the ones we believed were important to be placed under the protection of the Guardians."

"There were at least thirty photos on that table. You're going to provide protection for every family of every agent you feel is at threat?"

"That's ludicrous." She puts her hands on either side of my face and holds my gaze. "Only the ones we have already identified who are in *immediate danger*."

I drop my gun.

The soldier holding the AK-47 to my head steps away, removing the threat, but coldcocks Nikos with it as another soldier disarms him. I close my eyes against the unsaid in Glorianna's eyes. I know her too well. "Please, tell me they are safe."

"I can tell you we successfully airlifted Garrett out of Cincinnati at fourteen hundred hours."

Garrett was in Cincinnati?

"However, following an explosion at zero hundred hours, we lost visual on Celia and your children."

"An explosion," I repeat, opening my eyes.

"We have every reason to believe that Celia and your children are alive. No bodies were recovered, and two vehicles were reported fleeing the scene."

"The scene? Where was she?" Pulling away, I shake my head, trying to make sense of what she is telling me.

"The Guardians were preparing to extract her and your children from your Sea Cliff Road residence when the explosion occurred."

They'd have never seen the Guardians coming, which means someone else spooked them. Sea Cliff. If the house exploded it was because someone triggered the self-destruct. It's a complicated sequence, not something you can stumble on and get right accidentally, which means she was spooked enough for Hektor to tell her how to do it…and what to do next.

Two vehicles were reported fleeing the scene.

"Two vehicles?" I ask. "Celia was pursued?"

"The driver of the second vehicle was apprehended. He reported his name as Enrique, Garrett Lawrence's *houseboy*. Mr. Lawrence has confirmed his identity."

I'm more distressed that Garrett is under the protection of the Guardians than I am that Celia and the children are missing, what does that say about my trust level right now? On the ground, Nikos stirs.

Another soldier enters the cavern announcing, "We're ready to transport you to the airfield."

Glorianna is insistent. "We need to go. *Now.*"

"I came here to recover my wife. I won't go back to the States without returning her remains to her family."

She waves her hand dismissively. "We have errand boys for that. I need you to leave with me immediately."

A soldier takes my wife's remains and carries them to one of the armored vehicles waiting for us.

Nikos slaps me on the shoulder. "This is where we part ways."

"What?" I demand. "No. Fly back to the States *with us.*"

He smiles, tilting his head. I can tell by his expression that he isn't willing to spend the rest of his life on the run—that's what I'm looking at—and if I'm honest with myself, he's excited about getting back into the field. Ever since we started our training for the WODC, he always loved the danger, the excitement. I don't remark on the shiner his encounter with the butt end of the rifle left him.

He hugs me.

I whisper against his cheek, "I expect to hear from you. Phone, email, Facebook. I don't care how you stay in contact but you do it."

"I'll find you," he whispers back.

I watch him run to a waiting vehicle and have to laugh. He's like a kid running headlong into the surf. Now I'm especially glad for his company the last two weeks. It doesn't make up for the decade we had apart, but I at least know his head is screwed on straight. I wait until they've driven away before joining Glorianna inside the Humvee. As soon as I am settled we're in motion. I look out the window into the billowing cloud of sand created by the vehicle's tires. We ride in silence, the driver and another soldier in the front, me and Glorianna in the back. Not a word. At the airbase, both soldiers disembark with their weapons aimed and ready. Under their cover Glorianna and I run to the plane, very aware that we are in hostile territory.

Minutes later, we are in the air. Glorianna and I both speak at the same time.

"I can't—"

"I'm sorry—"

I gesture for her to speak first, because I know what I'm going to say is going to start an argument.

"I'm sorry for your loss."

"Thank you," I tell her, taking a deep breath. I still can't believe Lattie is gone. There will be a time to mourn, but now isn't it. I can't dare let my guard down here.

"We're doing everything we can to locate Celia and your children."

I remember who I'm dealing with and too late I realize I haven't reacted to Celia and the children being missing. I think she already suspects that I know exactly where they are—and I do—if everything went according to plan. "I can't go back to being Lex Karros. I can't abandon my children now."

She nods and I expect her to say something—argue with me—but she bides her time, leaving a crater of empty silence between us.

"Will you please say something?"

"Are you going to tell me where to send the recovery team to so that we can protect Celia and your children?"

I rub my face, the hours and days catching up to me. *How do I politely decline her protection?*

She says lightly, "Before we part company so that you can get to work, I need you to make a final appearance as Lex Karrros. Stand at my side while I withdraw my bid for candidacy."

I stare at her blankly.

"I thought I could wear two caps, but the truth is I would rather protect global concerns than try to make a stronger US. And if all of this was some divine act to force me to see the error of my ways, then I've chosen, and if it is to divide us and break the Guardians, then I need to focus all of my passion toward saving *us*."

Face to face with her fervor, I don't envy her antagonist.

"So after I stand at your side for this final performance, and assassinate the three targets in this envelope, do I get my life back?"

She shrugs. "Which life? Who do you want to be? I can't go back to being Senator Abigail Wainwright-Fuller, you can't go back to being Lex Karros but neither can you go back to being Thomas Stephanopoulos. I *will* continue to be the director of The Guardians but by your tone, I assume you want to be free of us." I meet her gaze but move far enough away to avoid further casual touch. She tsks under her breath. "We've been through so much together and still you don't trust me?"

I guess she could take my silence either way.

She cocks one eyebrow, weighing me, measuring me. "If I allow you to walk away, will you enjoy a quiet retirement? Or will you become my worst nightmare? I don't think the world is ready for you as a rogue agent, fighting only the injustices you choose to fight. That's why our kind are never allowed to be completely free. We can't be trusted, not really. My lover tonight, my murderer tomorrow, isn't that how it goes?"

"I could say the same about you."

"But I have already stated my intentions. I am a Guardian."

"I intend to retire. One hundred percent. My loyalty is solely to my family now."

"Family." She scoffs. "People like us cannot have families."

"Yet you gave me your word and I fulfilled my part." If she hears the threat in my voice, she doesn't comment on it. The remainder of the flight, all fourteen hours of it, we spend in silence. I've never been so happy for a plane to touch down.

We are met on the tarmac by her personal secretary and Zita.

She takes the dog, her voice changing immediately to Senator Abigail Wainwright-Fuller's voice. "Baby! My beautiful! Did you miss Mama? Oh God, I missed Zita! No more business trips without my baby, I promise."

The little dog licks her face, happily, believing her promises with blind devotion.

* * * *

Her speech before a standing room only crowd is short, sweet and to the point. The crowd reacts with great disappointment and sadness. America loved their Republican Princess and I have no doubt she'd have taken easy street to the White House.

A mob of paparazzi witness our climbing into an SUV, they do not witness our smoke and mirrors exit just before our vehicle explodes, and our deaths are covered on the evening news. They are also not privy to Glorianna's complete and utter emotional meltdown when she discovers her beloved Bolognese is missing.

With mascara-stained tears running down her face, she sobs. "Zita! Oh God, Zita! If anyone hurts you, they will pray for death!" She turns to me, clutching my shirt. "Find my Zita. Please!"

She crumbles into an incapacitated ball of emotion. *Fuck. Now what?*

Indeed. What. Thinking fast I make phone calls and create contingency plans on the fly. Several hours later, barely recovered, Glorianna takes me with her to the mid-range hotel where I am assured Garrett has been kept *safe*. I am not allowed to see him. Instead, we join a meeting already in progress, an update on the current level of threat.

An unidentified speaker is briefing the group. "Six assassinations have been reported and more than a dozen additional kidnappings."

As photos flash over the large screen, I hold my breath, hoping Celia and my children are not part of the official report.

"As much as I hate to have my fears confirmed, ladies and gentlemen, we are under attack. As of this moment we are at our highest level of alert, and we are at war."

I back away, reining in my inner soldier that rallies to the battle cry. I have to protect my children, my family. *This is not cowardice.* What of my duty?

Duty!

Damn it! Duty to whom?

Glorianna shakes my hand after shaking a dozen others. She could as easily be thanking me for my pledge to stay with the fight to the very end as passing me the room key for where Garrett is being kept. Our gazes collide a final time, and all I see reflected in hers is regret. Her anger and sadness have been replaced by something colder and bitterer. "Have you ever felt the joy and peace that can only be found in unconditional love and devotion?"

My children's faces all come to mind, as does Celia's kneeled form at my feet. I know it isn't the answer she wants to hear because she'd rather believe such love isn't possible but I whisper, "Yes," just the same.

Her face starts to crumble but she reins in her emotion. "They took my dog. My precious baby girl."

"I'm sorry."

"Protect those you love, my darling. *They* aren't expendable."

A woman enters the conference room, uninvited and is immediately surrounded, fear and suspicion creating chaos from nothing.

"She's fine," I call out, waving her toward me. "She's with me."

"Who is *she*?" Glorianna demands. "Why is she here?"

The young, dark-haired woman nervously approaches. "You called *My Darling Angels*?"

"Yes. You received payment?"

She nods and reaches into her tote, I still her hand. Turning to Glorianna, I stroke her cheek. "I know how important Zita was to you, and she wasn't expendable either. And while I pray you recover her, I also hope you will find room in your heart for a special boy that needs a home."

As if on cue the woman lifts a small puppy from her bag. He is a ball of black curls and wide dark eyes. "I'm sorry, we didn't have any Bolognese available, but this Bolonka is very precious."

He is small enough he could fit into a tea cup.

"Oh! There's been a mistake," Glorianna argues, stepping back as if she's been struck.

I lift the small puppy to my shoulder. He barks and wags his tail. The other agents crowd closer, and it is evident that any distraction from the day's worries is a welcome one.

"Does he have a name?" Glorianna asks, reaching tentatively to pet him.

"Mischa."

I hand Glorianna the puppy. "Let him heal your heart while you continue your search for Zita."

"My baby girl is gone forever, you know, I know it. The damn bastards." The puppy licks Glorianna's cheek, and her countenance warms. "Aren't you just the sweetest boy? Mischa. I'm your new mommy, and I will never leave your side."

"When you realize how perfect everything is, you will tilt your head back and laugh at the sky."

Prince Gautama Siddharta, *founder of Buddhism, 563-483 B.C.*

CHAPTER 22

CELIA

I breathe through breakfast, hiding the throbbing ache that has made my lower back its home, and every five minutes the contraction that reminds me I am in labor. I dole out cereal, pour on some of the milk I made from powder, and distribute spoons, each action measured. I cannot allow the children to see my panic.

I pour myself a glass of juice and take it out to the courtyard. Looking up at the brilliant blue sky, I ask, "Is this your idea of a joke? I wanted a natural birth *with* a doula! I can't do this by myself!"

What if something goes wrong during the birth? What if something happens to me and I can't take care of the children? What if I die? God, we're in a wilderness, the children could never find their way to safety alone!

"Auntie Ce?"

I turn to find Hektor, my constant shadow. Gripping my belly and gritting my teeth behind a smile, I ask, "Is everything okay?"

He narrows his eyes, looking every inch his father. "The babies are coming, aren't they?"

I shake my head. "I'm hoping it's a false alarm. That happens sometimes."

He goes back into the house. Pushing into my back, I sit on the stone wall and start laughing hysterically. "This is beyond ridiculous!"

Watching cottony white clouds cross the sky, I try to recall what I learned at the Primal Birth Center about the stages of labor and try to fit what I know and what I'm feeling into some schedule. The pain isn't too bad, the contractions are still spaced far enough apart that I guesstimate I have *hours*. I would have plenty of time to drive into town and find a hospital—and once there, I would have to reveal who I am and who the children are. I don't know who was staking out the house or why but popping up on the grid seems like a horrible idea. I focus my thoughts to one: *I need you, Thomas! I need you.*

I breathe through another contraction, and then hurry to the bathroom. As I hurriedly get my pants down and sit in time, I remember reading that some women experience diarrhea at the onset of their labor but *oh my God*. I'm left worried about getting too far away from the bathroom as waves of cramps roll through my lower back.

I can't go to town.

I can't call for help.

I have to do this—alone.

Cleaning myself up, my only thought is how I am possibly going to manage an unassisted birth surrounded by four young children. Potentially, this experience could emotionally scar them for life—but then I remember a young woman from the Primal Birth Center—Karina. She was pregnant with her third child, her previous two children under the age of five, and as crazy as it sounded at the time she was giving her presentation, she planned for her two children to be at her side, helping her, when the time came for her to deliver.

Hearing a crash, I hurry to the kitchen to find a mess of uneaten cereal and milk on the floor. Grabbing a towel, I start cleaning it up. "What were you doing?"

"We were just putting our bowls in the sink. We wanted to help you," Olympia explains. "Nikkos dropped his."

I shake my head, wanting to yell and scream and cry with frustration. I don't but it becomes immediately obvious too that I am not Karina. I force myself to be calm as I push damp cereal back into the plastic bowl with a towel. "Thank you for being so helpful this morning."

Squatting beside me, Olympia asks softly, "Are the babies coming?"

I meet her gaze, finding wide orbs of wondrous anticipation. There isn't much point in lying about it. "Yes."

As soon as I admit the truth, I become calm. I fight back my tears and my panic. I take a deep breath, inhaling. Exhaling. Everything happens for a reason; I honestly believe that. When Jackie introduced me to the idea of Primal Birth and Garrett made it painfully clear that my only option was a hospital birth, I should have dropped it, but I didn't. I'd experienced such a profound resonance with the program, just reading the material, I couldn't let the idea go. Even knowing that attending the meetings irritated Garrett, my Master, I still went. That has to mean something.

If the basic idea behind the Primal Birth premise is that any woman can give birth unassisted—no midwife, no drugs, no pain—I've spent months preparing for this very moment.

"Everything's going to be fine. Having a baby is a normal part of life," I assure them. *Oh shit, oh shit, oh shit! I cannot panic.* As I stand, a fresh bout of diarrhea is the big distraction.

Sitting on the toilet with four wide-eyed children staring at me from the doorway, I am struck by the hilarity of the situation.

I'm really not sure what to do. *Should I boil water?* I shake my head. *Towels and blankets?* I shake my head again. I need to build my birthing nest. I hadn't given nesting much thought because without Garrett's cooperation, I knew I'd end up in a hospital, most likely drugged and forced into a Caesarian section.

"Oh yes, be careful what you pray for." I look at the ceiling, not as God-inspiring as the vast Nevada sky, but still looking up to that place above God is watching down on me from. "Very funny."

How many hours have I spent lying in the dark asking God to delivery me from just that fate? I laugh out loud, still sitting on the toilet, realizing the liquid hitting the water in the toilet isn't poo. My water broke.

"This is happening. This is really happening."

None of the children say anything as I manage to walk into the living room and then immediately turn to go right back into the bathroom, feeling like I *really* need to push. Instinctively, I realize it isn't diarrhea that wants to come out. I don't go into the bathroom, I sit the children on the sofa; all four of them side by side. "Don't move."

I feel horrible when Atso starts to cry and I can't comfort her but as I hurry to the bathroom and close the door, I realize it isn't an option.

Grabbing towels, I lay one on the floor and sit on it, my back against the wall. I keep a few more near me, not believing this is happening so fast. "This is not an acceptable birthing nest."

When another urge to push hits, I push. Heart racing, I don't scream even though I feel like I'm being ripped in two. Between pains—which isn't nearly long enough—I breathe. *What am I doing wrong? This is supposed to be pain free!*

I close my eyes and take myself mentally back to the Primal Birth Center. I hear the facilitator's voice: *You can rule your labor or you can allow your labor to control you.*

She's right, she's absolutely right. Fear is creating this pain.

When the next contraction rolls through me, I open myself to it and drift along with it. Within seconds I am floating on endorphins. I know how to do this.

I need to create *my nest* and start considering my options. The facilitator had shown us so many options, boxes lined with disposable absorbent pads, or for the more green conscious—everyone in my group was very green—a plastic kiddie pool lined with blankets and towels. I don't have either.

The sounds of panic from the other room escalates, and I throw open the bathroom door. I hear Atso screaming over all the other voices, crying, "Ommy, Ommy, Ommy."

I think she has regressed in reaction to the other children's panic, but as she runs across the room to grab hold of my legs I realize she is crying *for me.*

"Oh!" I try to not react at all versus over reacting. Looking toward the other three, I ask, "Do want to help Auntie Ce have her babies?"

All four children race forward, overwhelming me with their enthusiasm. I'm most worried about Hektor. He's a boy, yes, a little boy, but still…

"Do you understand what is going to happen?" I ask the two older children but find all four of them nodding their heads.

"Our mother had Athena-Sophia in the desert."

I don't know much about her delivery except that Thomas was there with her. *Lucky bitch.* "Yes, she did. Did she explain to you how women give birth?"

"We were with her," Olympia says shyly. "All of us and our aunts and our father."

I chuckle. "I could go for a few of your aunts being here right now."

"Or our father," Hektor adds, making a face.

Taking his hand, I pull him closer so that I can look him in the eye. "Is this okay? I don't want you to be embarrassed."

Lifting his chin he tells me, "I will help you in my father's absence. He told me that my brothers are inside of you."

Standing, the urge to push rears within me, and I know I need to move into a position where I can. I warn the children, "This might get messy, and I want you to know that if you need to leave the room you can."

I remember yet another option presented at the Primal Birth Center, an underwater birth. I was so moved by the video we were shown, the baby moving effortlessly from the womb into the world. I want to try it. I start to run water into the tub. "Auntie Ce is going to climb into the tub. I think the water will be helpful since I don't have any grown-ups here to help me."

I can't worry about the repercussions now. The boys are insistent on coming out. I test the water, making sure it is a comfortable lukewarm. Pulling the caftan over my head, I have a flash of embarrassment as I step into the tub but realize the children aren't reacting to my nudity. They are young. Very young. Maybe they haven't been taught false modesty yet. I carefully lower myself into the water, knowing I've made the right decision as soon as I settle. My entire body relaxes. I keep the water running until it covers my belly and breasts.

The water seems to intensify the contractions, but I accept the pain as it moves through my body. I put the children to work. "Olympia, I need you to get the bed ready for me. Add extra blankets. I want you to bring some extra towels in there too. I'm going to need to wrap the babies in something to keep them warm."

She starts to leave the room, anxious to help but I stop her. "Take Atso. She can help carry towels."

"Hektor, I need you to find a pair of shoelaces. Take Nikkos with you."

Excited to be helping, all of the children hurry from the room. I sigh, relieved to have a private moment. I take the time to examine myself, pushing two fingers into my vagina I try to gauge how dilated I am. It seems like an impossible task until a contraction pushes against my fingers and I realize I am feeling the top of one of the baby's head. I bend my knees to lift my hips, which is made easier in the water. Relaxing against the back of the tub, I float in the water. The baby's head presses against my fingers as I gently push. The contraction seems to carry the baby's head through the birthing canal. I'm stretching, I can feel my labia pulled taut. I breath in, breath out. The baby crowns.

Olympia returns with Atso and stops in her tracks, watching with awe.

I breathe in and out, feeling the contraction move my baby forward. Feeling with my fingers, I push against my stretched labia and feel the moment the head slides free. I breathe a sigh of relief, but know I'm nowhere close to done.

I can't believe how calm I am, how relaxed. I slide my hand under the baby's face, feeling the miracle of his transition from the world within my womb to the one outside. I'm glad I chose the water. It seems less jarring—for him and for me.

I push gently, feeling my baby's neck and shoulders slowly slide out. I grip him under his arms and the rest of the body slithers free quickly. I'm so surprised, all I can do is stare at him under the water, but then he opens his eyes and I pull him onto my stomach, cradling him close. He blinks, looking at me, and I remember I'm supposed to be checking his airway. Even though I can tell he's breathing, growing pinker, I use a hand towel to wipe his face. He doesn't like the roughness of the cloth and starts to cry. It's such a small sound, not a big throaty cry at all, which worries me, but as his body grows a deeper shade of pink from fingers to toes, I know he's going to be all right.

I hold him against my chest, tears streaming down my face. *God, oh God, thank you.* I suddenly realize he's still attached to me by his umbilical cord and the cord is still attached to the placenta. I remember something about not pulling the cord tight, to let it stay loose, but I have another baby that needs to come out. I might not have thought this through completely.

A pain hits that is worse than all the previous ones. "God!"

Pain, not the urge to push. Just pain, wrapping around me, shooting through me.

"God!" I scream.

Hektor comes to the door and seeing the bloody water, he starts to cry. He wasn't present for the gentle beauty of my first baby's birth. "Auntie Ce?"

"It's okay, it's okay!" I try to convince him, I try to convince myself. *Shit, oh shit!* The last thing I wanted was to scare the children. "Olympia, I need you to get into the tub with me."

I make room for her between my legs and she climbs in. She is still wearing her clothes, shorts and a t-shirt. "Sit down, I'm going to hand you the baby to hold. Keep his head supported above the water." I hand her the baby, and she cradles him close to her chest. "See the cord attaching me to the baby? It has to stay loose, so stay close to me."

Another pain hits and I hold in the scream, breathing through it. I push without the urge to do so and press high on the top of my belly, because it seems like the right thing to do, and then finally, with the next contraction there is the urge to push. I push and push and push.

Again. Push. Push. Push. I feel between my legs, expecting to feel the baby crown but instead realize a foot has pushed out of my body. "Oh God, please let this baby come out. Please."

Fighting panic, I move to a squat in the water. *Isn't that what the facilitator told us to do in the event of a breech? Why didn't I pay closer attention?*

Puuuushhhh!

Finally, there is a stretching sensation and I reach down, feeling both of the baby's legs present. I pull gently, feeling his torso and the umbilical cord. It isn't around his neck. Slowly and easily, I push. The baby's body coming out isn't nearly as dramatic the second time around, but it is a relief. A miracle as I hold his ankles and catch his body underwater. Pulling him to the surface, I wipe my second son's face free of mucus and am rewarded with a lusty wail. "I know *you* didn't want to come out."

Nestling him close, I hold him against my chest as I lower myself back into the water. I breathe through the contractions, which seem much weaker but manage to clear out the placenta in a gush of water and blood. I worry about the kids seeing the water turn red with blood and goo but there doesn't seem to be much I can do about it.

I count heads, Olympia, Nikkos and Atso are awe struck. Hektor is hidden behind the door.

"Do you have the shoelaces?"

Hektor comes into view and hands me the shoelaces with a shaking hand.

"I'm okay, sweetheart, but I need your help."

I never knew small children could look so relieved.

"Hektor? There is a pair of scissors in the kitchen. I want you to bring them to me. Remember how we carry scissors safely?" He nods and hurries into the kitchen. I call after him. "Don't run."

I cover myself up as much as I can with a towel while I wait for him to bring me the scissors. *I'm forgetting something.* I don't want to cut the umbilical cord. I'm nervous. I don't want to do it wrong. I try to remember everything I ever heard at the Primal Birth Center about an emergency birth and remember where to tie the laces, when to tie the laces, and when to cut.

Hektor returns with the scissors.

Should I wash the shoelaces first?

Should I boil them?

I suddenly remember that the umbilical cord has to stop pulsing and I make sure that it has before tying it into segments. Nervously, I take a deep breath and cut, not thinking, just doing it, fast, before I change my mind. Hektor watches, seeming to hold his breath. I cut the second cord.

Fuck, I should have boiled the laces. I close my eyes, say a prayer and hope for the best. I remember seeing some antibacterial gel and iodine in the pantry and hope that sanitizing after the fact is better than not sanitizing at all. *What did women do before modern medicine?* Garrett's voice in my head provides the answer. *They died of infection. Their babies died of infection.*

I hold my second born son to my breast, remembering that nursing slows bleeding in the mother and provides important antibodies to the infant. It is harder than I think it should be getting my nipple into his mouth. I never thought of my nipples being huge before, but his mouth is so small.

"What are we going to call him?" Cross-legged, Olympia sits as close to me as she can, her newborn brother held gently. Hektor, Nikkos, and Atso line up against the side of the tub, watching the baby nurse.

I shrug. We haven't discussed names. "I don't know."

"A baby needs a name," Hektor says wisely.

I nod, they do need names; I'm just not up to naming them. With the rush of adrenaline and endorphins fading, I'm left shaking and wrung out. I need to get us all out of the water and dried off.

I wait for Baby Boy Number Two to stop sucking and wrap him in a towel.

"Hold him?" I ask Hektor.

Hektor comes closer, and I hand him the baby. Smiling, a look of pure pride on his face, he holds him close.

I take Baby Boy Number One from Olympia and allow him to float in the warm water as he passes from her to me. I suppose it's normal to be so exhausted, isn't it? Leaning back against the tub, I close my eyes and, bringing my firstborn son to my breast, help him to start nursing. "Go ahead and climb out, darling. Dry off, change your clothes. I'm going to need you to hold the baby again."

Olympia does as she's told, hurrying from the room. She returns half-dried but in fresh, dry clothes.

I jerk awake, a baby still in my arms, four children sitting on the bathroom floor, watching and waiting. Waiting for what seems like the next question I need to answer. I appear to be all right, the babies are okay. We can't stay in the bathroom all day. I smile at Olympia, trying to be reassuring. "Get a dry towel and you can take this one from me."

She grabs a towel from the pile and holds out her arms. I hand her my son, and she bundles him tightly.

With her holding Baby Boy Number One and Hektor holding Baby Boy Number Two, I clamor out of the tub. It saps the remaining strength I have. "Can you take the babies into the bedroom and wait for me?"

With the two older children busy, I take a minute to pee, check my bleeding, and clean up a little more. I put a folded hand towel between my legs until I can figure out an appropriate substitution for a menstrual pad and pull the caftan back on. By the time I have scooped the placenta into a plastic trash bag and drained the tub, the thought of walking all the way into the bedroom is more than I want to consider, so I don't think about it. I force myself into the bedroom, Nikkos and Atso following behind me like little ducklings—if little ducklings could suck their thumbs.

After climbing into the bed and covering up, I hold out my arms for my newborns and cradle them into the V formed between my thighs. I know they aren't capable of rolling yet but it seems like a safe zone as long as I can keep the toddlers on either side of me. *How did I know they'd want in bed with me?* I get Nikkos tucked in on my left and Atso tucked in on my right. They both huddle as close to me as they can. It is almost suffocating, but I don't push them away. After all they've been through I understand their need to crowd as close to me as possible.

"Okay, we need a job list."

Hektor and Olympia perk up excitedly.

"Hektor, I need you to go in the kitchen and carefully pour me a glass of juice. Olympia, I want you to go into the living room and bring in the bag of new baby clothes."

God, I'm exhausted.

Olympia returns with the bag and helps me find the soft, knit newborn caps. I put one each baby's head. A smart girl she also brought me two disposable diapers—Atso's. They're huge but cutting them down to size, I make them work, swaddling the babies. I dress them in the long-sleeved sleep sacks that looked so tiny in the store, but which swallow them up. They both sleep through the diapering and dressing, their birth was hard work for all of us.

Olympia climbs onto the foot of the bed and sits between my ankles, watching the newborns intently. Hektor returns with a glass of juice and I happily take it, drinking it down in two swallows. When I hand him the glass back I ask him to bring me another. I also ask him to bring me my purse, which I know has some acetaminophen inside. He returns with both and I happily swallow four pills and drink the second glass of juice.

As an afterthought, I dig a marker out of my bag and write a one and a two on the heel of the appropriate babies' foot. Even though I have the presence of mind right this second to know which was born first, I can't guarantee myself I'll remember when I wake up.

"Can you close the front door and lock it?"

"I already did, Auntie Ce."

"Good boy, Hektor."

I watch him climb up onto the foot of the bed to sit with Olympia and know that fighting sleep is going to be impossible. I tell them, "No one gets out of this bed until I wake up, understood?"

"A dream you dream alone is only a dream. A dream you dream together is reality."

John Lennon

CHAPTER 23

THOMAS

No guard stands outside of Garrett's door, which makes me nervous. Why hasn't Garrett just walked away? I could be walking into a trap. *No one retires from this business. No one.* Weapon ready, I slide the electronic key and step inside fast.

"It's about bloody time."

As my eyes adjust to the lack of light, I find Garrett sitting in the corner.

"Where the fuck have you been? Where's Celia and the children? And why am I being held prisoner?"

I put my fingers to my lips, a gesture for him to be quiet. His room has been bugged by the Guardians, I have no doubt about that. My concern is who else might be listening. I motion for him to come to me as I say loudly into the room, "All of your questions are justified, and I promise I'll answer all of them in time."

He crosses his arms stubbornly and doesn't move from his seat, and I don't turn on the lights.

Taking a butterfly knife from my pocket I cut the tracking chip out of the back of my neck and toss it onto the bed. Going into the bathroom I grab a washcloth and hold it to the wound while I clean my knife. I want a shower, desperately. From desert to DC on no sleep, and only caffeine and adrenaline keeping me going, the days without sleep are catching up with me fast.

It has been two full days since I recovered Lattie's remains, and it is still hard to believe that she is dead. *I have to tell my children their mother isn't coming back.* I scrub my face with soap and water, wishing I could go back in time.

Returning to the bedroom, I motion again for Garrett and when he doesn't come to me, I leave him sitting in the dark room alone. He catches up soon enough, finding me two-thirds of the way down the hallway. I duck into the stairs. I really hope Glorianna was on the level, letting me walk away free and clear. I doubt it, but I hope it just the same.

"I'm pissed at you," Garrett informs me.

I hurry down the two flights to the ground level, and he follows close but is left winded.

"Me too," I tell him, pausing on a landing.

"You're pissed at me? I didn't do anything!"

I turn on him, shoving him against a concrete wall. "You left Celia and my children alone. Unprotected."

He looks ashamed, offering sheepishly, "My parents needed me. What was your excuse? The wife who abandoned you? You sure took your sweet time coming home."

I shove him again. "Lattie's dead."

His eyes go wide, and he opens his mouth and closes it twice before managing to say, "God, I'm sorry."

I nod. "Me too. She was a sweet girl, and for a while, a good wife."

I run down the last flight of stairs and exit through a service door into a back alley. I walk to the end of the block, trying to get my bearings. I don't trust anyone in the vicinity, not even the taxi drivers or transit workers. Anyone could be Glorianna's people.

The wind howls, pushing against us, as I start walking toward a destination. Looking up at the sky, I see dark clouds gathering. I pray for a storm to disappear into.

Garrett follows behind me, quiet, too quiet. I wish he'd have kept yelling at me. I veer off the main road, preferring dark alleys. Garrett walks faster, bumping into me. "Does this seem safe to you?"

"Get used to the shadows, Garrett, and trust me when I say, I'm the most dangerous man you'll ever meet in the dark."

He trails close and silent. At the end of one alley where another begins, a fire inside a trash can burns brightly, drawing me like a beacon. Three men stand near it, though the night is warm, not cold. They're singing a capella until we get close enough to appear threatening. I pull a hundred dollar bill out of my pocket and hold it out. Nodding toward two of them I say, "Your jacket, and his."

The two men share a look and shirk out of their outerwear, one an Oriole's hoodie, the other a ragged leather. I gesture for Garrett to take the garments.

"And your hats," I say.

The closer man grabs the hundred as he hands me his knit cap. The second man hesitates. "I really like this cap, I've had it a long time."

It's a dingy gray skipper's yacht hat.

"I can appreciate that, man. It's a great hat." I take off my suit coat, flashing the tag that says Armani, and pull a second hundred from my pocket. "For your loss."

Hesitating, greed makes him hold out for more, but as our gazes clash he sees something in mine that makes him take my offer.

I stay facing them as I back down the alley, not even reassured when they go back to singing. When we reach the main road I press my back against the brick wall of a building. I pull on the knit cap and the Orioles sweatshirt, keeping the hood over my head.

"Put on the hat and the leather coat."

"You do realize how bad these clothes stink?"

I don't sugarcoat it for him. "You can shower after I get you out of town alive."

We finally reach the bus station, but we're not here for a ticket. Keeping my back to the security cameras and my head down, I head straight for the public lockers. Mine is three rows deep, not observable by any camera. I open it and praying no one comes near enough to see us, start stripping off the hoodie, knit cap, and shirt I've been wearing since the press conference. I pull on a black tank top I had stashed in the locker.

Garrett reaches up to peel the blood soaked washcloth off my neck. "That needs stitches."

"I'll live without stitches. I might not have survived being tracked."

He doesn't question the tracking device, or why I wasn't concerned before, and why I am now. "You've hit a vein, you're still bleeding."

I pull a quick-clot packet out of the locker and push some of the powder into the wound before shedding my slacks and pulling on a pair of faded and torn blue jeans. "Were you injected with anything?"

"No!"

"Are you certain? Was there any moment you lost consciousness and someone could have injected you without you knowing it?"

"I haven't slept a wink since I was picked up and brought here."

"Are you wearing the same clothes?"

"Yes. What's with the twenty questions?"

"I don't want anyone to know where I'm headed when I leave here. Take off your clothes. Everything. I'm not taking any chances." I step into black combat boots. While Garrett is stripping, I restock my weapons: shurikens, three knives, and two revolvers, several clips. I hide most of my weaponry with a loose black and gray Hawaiian shirt, buttoning only the two center buttons.

I toss Garrett a t-shirt, some sweats, and a pair of running shoes. The shoes will be too big, but he doesn't complain.

We exit the building as we entered, back to all the cameras, head ducked low. I'm pleased to see Garrett is following my lead and shadowing my moves. Three blocks from the garage but eight alleys later, I lead him into a high-rent, high-security parking garage. We drive out in a BMW X5M.

Garrett peels off the knit cap and tosses it out the window.

"Feel better?" I ask.

"No, we both probably have lice now. Are you going to tell me what in the hell is going on?"

"Not yet."

"At least tell me Celia is safe?"

I give him a look that shuts him up. I cannot bear to think about Celia and the children not being safe, and as much as I want to reach them as quickly as humanly possible, I can't lose my head. I'm not sure but I'm guessing Ely, Nevada is about a thirty hour drive, maybe more. I won't risk flying even though a week ago I would have trusted a dozen pilots. Tonight I trust no one.

General's Highway is almost deserted as I head out of town, except for the city cops. I drive past four cruisers in two blocks. Beside me, Garrett is pulled into himself. Angry? Frustrated? Confused?

"What were you told by the people who brought you to Washington, DC?"

"Nothing. They showed me a picture of Enrique, demanding to know who he was, and then they showed me photos of you and Celia and said if I wanted to see either of you again, I should come with them."

"Subtle. How did you know they weren't the bad guys?"

"Black suit, sunglasses, earpieces. I thought they were FBI or CIA. Turns out they were Secret Service. God, what does my mother think? I just left her in the lobby of an office building."

I sigh heavily.

"Just tell me. All of it. The worst of it. Not knowing what in the hell is going on is far worse than the truth."

I merge onto I-97, still obeying all the speed laws. I don't want to draw anyone's attention tonight. "The truth is there are a lot of people looking for me, and anyone who is close to me is now a target. You. Celia. My children."

"You're on the run, meaning *we're all* on the run." He shakes his head, his jaw tightening. "Your brother brought this on us, didn't he?"

I give him a long look, trying to figure out how he made that leap in logic, but then life hasn't been the same since Nikos showed up on our door, so it is no great leap from there to here. "No. He doesn't have anything to do with this. I made a mistake. I let down my guard, I got lax, I let people into my life, and now the people I have allowed to get close to me will pay the price."

"What does that mean—exactly?"

"It means you can't go home. Until the dust settles, you wouldn't be safe."

"I can't go home?" He snorts. "I'm not going to let some thugs keep me away from my life—that's insane. This is your life, your problems, not mine."

I pull off onto the shoulder, realizing this frustration has been building for a while, over a year. Probably since the first day we became a ménage because my comings and goings became more evident. I turn in my seat so that I'm facing him. "Even if we go our separate ways right this minute you can't go home. I drop you off on a corner, give you a phone number to call, and you will be picked up and given a new identity."

"A new identity?" He looks at me like I've lost my mind, unbuckles his seat belt, and opens the car door. "Fuck *that*."

I grab his arm. "You won't live twenty-four hours without protection. You have to choose now—a new life with me in it or a new life away from me—either way you can't go back to San Francisco. You can't go back to Ohio. You can't go back to being Garrett Lawrence."

The rain that has been threatening all night suddenly lets loose with big, plump drops hitting the windshield.

He jerks away from my grasp. "You said the dust will settle."

"It will. One way or another. Either the threat will be annihilated or my enemies win the big battle and the organization I've worked for will be destroyed. This isn't about me and you and Celia, Lattie and my children, or my brother. We're just the pawns as two factions struggle for control. Their strategy is to destroy the Guardians from within by making every agent weak."

"So you take me someplace safe and then you disappear to fight a war?"

I shake my head. "I'm no good for this fight. I quit. My only loyalty now is to my children and the ménage."

Lightning streaks the sky, and the rain pours down. He closes the door and buckles his belt, but doesn't look at me. I wonder if his decision to stay is solely based on the weather. I whisper, "Garrett, I'm sorry."

He closes his eyes and crosses his arms, shutting me out, but at least he's still in the car. I pull back out onto the highway and start driving. Even with the windshield wipers on full power, it is hard to see. If anyone was following me, they'll have a harder time of it now.

Garrett doesn't say anything for the eight hours it takes to leave Maryland behind and cross Pennsylvania, Ohio, and Indiana. I think he slept through most of the storm. There are few things more powerful than an early summer storm in the Midwest. High wind, rain, hail—I kept expecting to see a tornado on the horizon—but then the sun broke the horizon to bright blue skies.

"Do you want me to drive? You have to be exhausted."

I don't tell him that exhausted was three days ago. I exit as we cross into Illinois. "I'm all right. I'm going to refuel and get some food though. Hungry?"

He perks up as I pull into a multi-use fuel stop that promises petrol and a home-cooked meal.

"I could eat."

The restaurant is a typical interstate-dive, eggs, potatoes, and meat all prepared on the same grill on a slick of lard, my arteries' worst nightmare. As I bite into the crisp bacon, my taste buds do a happy dance. *God, when was my last meal?*

Between us we put away six eggs, three orders of bacon, an order of sausage, two orders of home fries, four biscuits, a bowl of gravy, and a serving of grits.

"Fuck me." Garrett says it, I'm thinking it. There's no way I'm going to stay awake to drive now. Eating was the worst thing I could have done.

I pay with cash.

"I will drive," he says as we approach the car, and I'm too tired to argue.

"I'm going to have to take you up on that but if you feel like anyone is following us, wake me up. Don't speed. We can't afford to draw any attention to ourselves."

We both climb in and buckle, he starts the car. "Where am I going?"

"Stay on Interstate Eighty West."

"For how long?"

Fifteen, maybe sixteen hours, but he doesn't need to know that. It's a little after nine, four hours sleep and I'll be good to go. "Wake me up when you stop to refuel."

It seems like I just closed my eyes when he wakes me up. "We're refueled. Stay on Eighty?"

"Yes," I answer, or maybe I just dream I answered. I may have dreamed the fuel stop completely because he shakes me awake. "We're refueled. Stay on Eighty?"

I rub my eyes and sit up, blinking at the clock. It reads nine thirty and it's dark outside. "Fuck. Where are we?"

"Wyoming, maybe? I remember Iowa and Nebraska. I know we entered Wyoming, I don't think we left it yet."

I rub my face, my five o'clock shadow is heavy and rough against my palms. The beginnings of the full beard I plan to have. "I'll drive. I just have to piss first."

I don't bother getting the key from the attendant, I empty my bladder into the grass behind the building. Walking back to the car I'm irritated at myself for sleeping so long, so deeply. *Anything could have happened.* Inside the car, Garrett is surrounded by snack food, a bag of granola, chips, candy bars, cola, bottles of water.

"Tell me you paid cash?"

"I did." He offers me the bag of granola.

"No, thanks," I say, realizing I'm dying of thirst. "Is there any juice?" He tosses me an icy orange juice. After several gulps I manage to say, "Thanks."

"We're not going to California?"

"No."

"You aren't going to tell me where we're going though, are you, even if we played twenty questions? Will you at least tell me Celia is safe? Are we going to see her again? Did those spooks try to make her the same deal they made me?"

I wish I could reassure him, but all I know for certain is that the Guardians don't have her. My eyelids are heavy, even after sleeping all day, and I realize it is because my heart is heavy. I can't bear to think of anything except Celia and my children being hidden safely in the Nevada wilderness. Any doubt that she might not be there would kill me, because if she isn't I have no idea where to even begin looking. "I'm driving to where I think Celia and the children are hiding. Just hope she's there when we get there."

He looks as exhausted as I feel, haggard.

I lean toward him. "Can I kiss you?"

"Shouldn't we be driving as fast as we can? Aren't all these delays dangerous? What if she was there but leaves because she gets tired of waiting?"

"If she's at the safe house, she won't leave. Hektor won't let her.

He knows the rules."

"The rules?"

I glance through the windshield to see the gas station attendant is watching us. I start the car and pull away from the pumps, wishing I hadn't asked him if I could kiss him. It was too soon. He just needs time. "I'll explain everything while we drive, okay?"

He nods, his face crumbling. "You realize this is too much, don't you? How do you do this? How many times have you started over? New name, new identity? How many lovers have you abandoned? And why are you keeping the ménage together this time? You could have walked away. That's what the whole thing was about back there in DC, wasn't it? You were supposed to walk away. So why offer me a new identity? Why not just let me go home and if the bad guys got me, killed me, who cares? I'd have just been collateral damage in some greater plan."

I drive onto the access road, and then onto the interstate. How do I explain to him that Glorianna knew the current threat to her organization would be nothing compared to my wrath if anything happened to Garrett, Celia, or my children? She has to be worried what the repercussions to Lattie's death will be. She also knows that my mind is distracted from revenge as long as I'm trying to get my other loved ones safely hidden away. It takes time and energy to hide, to regain some level of safety and security. As it stands, she probably thinks she won't have to worry about any threat from me for years. If ever. She also has my brother now. She knows I won't risk his life doing anything stupid, *and* she plans to recruit my children. She doesn't need to know that will only happen over my dead body.

"Is any of this ever going to make sense to me?" he asks.

I look at him, shaking my head. "I hope not. I don't want you to be in so deep that you ever understand."

He slides his hand up my thigh, squeezing. It isn't a kiss, but his touch is a comfort. I cover his hand with mine and can feel him trembling.

"Can you possibly understand how pissed off I am?"

I shake my head, keeping my eyes on the road.

"You expect me to give it all up—everything that I am. My life. My business. My dreams." He snaps his fingers. "Just like that?"

I don't know what to say.

"Stop the car!"

I look at him, not understanding. I know he's mad, but surely to God he doesn't want out now.

"Please," he asks more rationally.

I take an exit instead of pulling onto the shoulder and follow the signs less than a mile to a state park entrance. The sign reads *Green River,* but it's dark so I have no idea if there is a river in the distance. We're surrounded by trees, and against the dark sky it is possible to make out some towering rock formations. I'm positive by the light of day it would be a beautiful place to come. I unbuckle, turning in my seat to look at him. "I understand if you never want to see me again, but please don't leave without saying goodbye to Celia."

"I don't want to say goodbye to you or Celia. I need you to remind me why I'm staying. What is it about you that makes my blood sing in my veins? When I was sitting in that damn hotel room, waiting for you to show up or not, I thought I would rather die than never see you again. That isn't a sane thought."

I start to interrupt but I don't, I let him talk.

"I love being Kitten's Master, it fulfills a need, and I do love her, deeply, but I know myself well enough to know that if it was just me and her, we wouldn't work long term. I'm not Master enough for her, and she's not male enough for me. It was hard enough to stay monogamous with Tony, and I loved him, with my heart, my soul, my entire being. At night, I would lay awake, remembering *you*."

I want to hold him, but he has to make the first move.

"I hate you." He glares at me. "You've taken away everything and still, I want you. Being in this car with you, not touching you, is killing me, but I don't want you to touch me because I'm addicted to you."

Tears glisten in his eyes. As a tear escapes, sliding down his cheek, I catch it with my thumb and he pushes his face into my palm.

He sobs against my hand. "Tell me you're worth it."

I lift his face, touching my lips to his. "I love you. I don't want you to go away. Destroying your old life only has meaning if the three of us are able to build something new and better from the wreckage."

"Kiss me like you mean it. Kiss me like you're promising me that you will never leave us alone again."

I kiss him, hard, raping his mouth with my tongue and my teeth. If he's addicted to me, I'm just as addicted to him. The times when we are alone together, creating scenes together, are awesome times. As Lord Ice, he brings out in me emotion I have never allowed myself to experience with another person. I'm surprised when he pulls away and steps out of the car.

I don't follow him, not right away. I trail him with my gaze, watching him cross the parking lot and enter a grove of trees. Cursing, I climb out of the car and follow. I find him sitting on top of a weathered, wood picnic table. As I approach, he strips out of his t-shirt. He kicks off his shoes, and it is fairly obvious where this is going to lead.

When I step into the space between his knees, he wraps his hand around the nape of my neck and pulls me forward forcibly. Our gazes collide as our lips meet in a deep kiss. There isn't anything slow or soft about it as he takes what he wants from my mouth, teeth biting, colliding, our tongues having intercourse in the depths of each other's mouths. He leaves me breathless and needy. As much as I'd like to push his shoulders down against the tabletop and climb over him, straddling his face, I don't.

I pull down the elastic waistband of his sweatpants, exposing his cock and balls. He's hard as a rock, pointed skyward. I lower my mouth and suck him in deep. I slide my mouth up and down, sucking hard, biting softly.

He lays but manages to keep watching me suck his dick.

I use him with my mouth roughly, bringing his need to a sharp point fast, too fast. I don't give him time to hold back and leave him hanging onto me. Coming, he sits up cradling over my head, holding onto my shoulders.

I keep sucking, even when I know the sensation is too much, pushing him hard over the edge to a painful place.

"Ahh, ahh." He screams and pants.

Standing, I pull him off the table and force him to bend over its top. Jerking his sweats down to his knees, I push my face into his crack, rimming his anus with my tongue, while I jerk on his half-hard cock, encouraging it to stiffen.

He pants and begs, "Do it, do it."

I unbuckle my belt, open my pants, and thrust blindly at his hole. I hit my target, filling him in one hard, fast thrust. He curses, and moans. I jerk hard against him, taking what I want. His ass is tight around my big cock. Every thrust stretches him.

"Is this what you had in mind?"

"Yes, God, yes?"

"Is this what you crave?"

"More, I need more. I need you to lay my soul bare, take me to the edge, leave me shaking and screaming and puking."

I push into him—harder, deeper. Jerking his cock up and his balls down, I make him shriek. "Like the first time? At the cove?"

"Yes, yes!"

I spasm against him, filling him with my jism. I smack his ass as I pull out. "Stick around and I'll show you what I've really got. The cove was just a warm up."

"Dreams do come true, if only we wish hard enough. You can have anything in life if you will sacrifice everything else for it."

J.M. Barrie, *Peter Pan*

CHAPTER 24

GARRETT

I have no idea where we are going, I hope Thomas does. He seems to, I trust him. I guess I better—trust him—what else is left? In the blink of an eye I've made choices that will change the direction of my entire life.

At Salt Lake City he drives into a store-all compound.

The interior of his unit is like something out of a spy movie. Computers, satellite linkup, heavy artillery arsenal, enough clothes and disguises that he could change his identity a hundred times over. A truck. But not just any truck, a nineteen-sixty Ford in mint condition. When he unveils it, I am left awed, and antiques don't do it for me, but my God, what a beauty.

"I always hoped I'd need this one someday."

"We're taking the truck?"

"Yep. I'm a new man, a different man, gotta have a vehicle that represents the *new me*."

"This old truck represents the new you?" This worries me.

He explains as he loads the back with tool boxes and canvases. "This was always plan B, for when all else failed and I needed to hide away. It probably won't be a permanent gig, but for the next few weeks, while we figure out our future, I have to be the character people remember. Crazy guy, artist, drinks too much, smokes too much, doesn't talk hardly at all, and keeps to himself in the hills. The only snag in my plan is you, and of course Celia. Fitting you both into *my story*."

As I watch him become more laid-back artist, and less Thomas by the second, it becomes apparent how easy it is for him, and I realize if this is going to work for us, it has to become easy for me.

Over the next three hours we head west then south. The passing time means nothing as I dwell on who I can possibly be other than *me*.

"So, weird hippie artist dude, who do I become to fit in with that?"

"Think about it as a new chapter in your life. Who would you be if you weren't Lewd Larry?"

"Not a doctor."

"Okay, so where else can you go with the education you have?"

"You don't get it, I like being me!" *Has Thomas ever gotten to be himself?* After a moment I say, "I could be a college professor, I'm not sure how I'd pull it off without transcripts and recommendations, but as secondary career choice, I could see myself teaching."

"Awesome! See, now you're thinking. Documentation is easy. Validation, no problem. I can see you teaching, and college towns are easy to get lost in. My kooky artist scam wouldn't stand out at all." He smiles. "And there's always hot collegiate who want to get a little wild. We could host some *very private* parties."

Sharing a look, we laugh. I am encouraged we don't have to give up kink altogether. "What about Celia? How does she fit in? How do your children fit in?"

He lets out a heavy sigh. We must be getting close, because every mile we drive the tenser he becomes. I think he's worried she won't be there, wherever *there* is. "She has to create her own character and then we all work together, tweaking and defining our roles until our story works."

"What if she wants nothing to do with this?"

As soon as I ask the question, I regret it, realizing that he's probably been asking himself that since we left Washington DC.

"Throw your dreams into space like a kite, and you do not know what it will bring back, a new life, a new friend, a new love, a new country."

Anais Nin

CHAPTER 25

KITTEN

I am a mother.

I've counted fingers and toes, again and again. I stare at my babies, stripped down to their skin, memorizing every fold, every dimple, so important for keeping track of Boy Number One, and Boy Number Two, but more specifically so that they become real in my mind. I can't name them. I want Thomas here, and Garrett, to name them without their input would seem like I've given up on ever seeing them again.

I know Garrett must be worried sick after so many days of not hearing from me. He was busy with his mother, but he always called to tell me good night. Soon I will take the children into town, not Ely, we'll go to a different town, and I'll call him from a pay phone.

The last few days have seemed like such a dream. Did I really give birth?

I must have, because these two perfect angels are here.

I listen to their hearts, I listen to them breathe. They seem abnormally small and that scares me, but then I've never seen a newborn. I don't know if they are small, very small, or normal.

They're little piggies.

It seems I nurse them one by one, and no more than finish with the two of them until they want to eat again. They are so beautiful. I wish I had a camera so that I could photograph every angle of perfection, every second of their life.

If I am ga-ga over these babies, their brothers and sisters are even more over the moon in love. *Everyone* gets a turn holding them—even Atso—with close supervision and a pillow bolster.

It's been a long day, and I'm exhausted. I keep telling myself only another few hours until we can go back to bed—and I haven't *done* anything.

The courtyard is shaded in the evening, and so I move us all outside to enjoy the evening breeze. The twins fit perfectly inside a dresser drawer and it seems practical for transporting them around. I placed it near the chaise where they're sleeping contentedly.

"What's that?" Olympia asks and I listen, hearing a loud rumble. After days of desert silence it is jarring.

Heart pounding, I stand quickly, pulling the children back until I discover the source of the noise is dozens of horses' hooves pounding against the rocky terrain below us. *Wild mustangs.* We all creep closer to the low stone wall for a better view as the horses race through the valley. I lift Atso so that she can see, regretting the strain on my body, but when she points and claps, I tough out the discomfort. Hektor lifts Nikkos but has a hard time holding him because he is so excited.

"Listen," I say excitedly, "I think there are more coming."

But as I watch the break between the mountains the first group raced through, I realize the sound isn't coming from the canyon. It sounds like tires crunching gravel. "Inside! Inside! Hurry!"

I hand Atso to Olympia and grab the dresser drawer. We hurry inside, and I lock the doors. I push closed the heavy wood shutters and lock them from the inside before getting everyone locked in the bedroom.

Shaking, I pull the biggest gun from the closet I stashed it in. I don't know what it's called but it's some kind of automatic rifle and I find that knowing it fires a lot of rounds quickly is a comfort. I will shoot first and ask questions later.

A horn honks in a very distinctive pattern. *Honk. Honk-honk. Honk. Honk-honk-honk.*

Eyes wide, Hektor exclaims, "It's Papa!" and races out of the bedroom before I can stop him.

Stopping Olympia, I order, "Stay with the babies!" and chase after Hektor but he is already outside. I make myself slow down and ease through the courtyard with my back against the wall. It would be ridiculous for both of us to rush out willy-nilly. I edge out into the yard. It's rocky and full of sharp, weedy stubble, which is painful to my bare feet. I aim the rifle as I come around the corner.

"It's me! Celia! You're safe now!"

It takes a minute to register that it's Thomas. I'm not accustomed to seeing him with short hair. It doesn't help that he has on a ball cap and a dark, heavy stubble hides much of his face. He walks slowly toward me.

"Lower the rifle, Sophia. It's me."

I lower the weapon, and he takes it quickly before pulling me into his arms.

"It's you, it's really you!"

Garrett comes around the side of the house, carrying Hektor. Tears steak down the boy's face and Garrett is looking intently at the bottom of his foot. Glancing toward me, he explains, "Thorn."

Smiling, I want to rush to him as well but I can't make myself let go of Thomas. I'm overwhelmed and start sobbing. *They're finally here.*

Thomas picks me up and carries me toward the house. "The twins?"

I press my hands against the loose flow of the caftan I'm wearing. "They were born two days ago."

Garrett catches up and hears the conversation as we all enter the house. Thomas lowers me onto the sofa, kneeling as he lays me down. His eyes are full of concern as he asks, "Are you okay?"

It surprises me that he asks about my well-being instead of theirs. "We're *all* fine."

He lays his head against my chest, holding me close. "I wish I'd have been able to get here sooner. I'm so sorry."

Garrett sits in wooden rocker, looking pale, the thorn forgotten. Hektor stands on one foot. Hopping to the sofa, he climbs up and pushes his foot into my lap. "Auntie Ce?"

Thomas starts to reprimand him, but I stop him. "It's fine. Let me see your foot."

"Why are you out of the hospital?" Garrett demands. "They should have kept you two days at least."

"Got it!" I work the thorn free of Hektor's foot as the boy excited tells the story. "Auntie Ce had the babies in the bathtub. Did you know newborns can hold their breath underwater? They can swim!"

Olympia peeks out of the bedroom. "Can we come out now?"

"Oh God! Yes, sweetheart! Come, come," I call to her.

She holds Nikkos and Atso's hands, and seeing her father, beams. "I knew you'd come home!"

He rushes to them, hoisting up all three of them at the same time. Olympia and Nikkos giggle but Atso leans out of his arms, reaching for me. "Ommy, Ommy, Ommy."

I bite my lip as Thomas meets my gaze. "I'm sorry. I haven't encouraged it."

He walks forward and puts down Olympia and Nikkos. He seems robotic as he carries Atso to me, and I realize suddenly that Latisha isn't with them.

I take the little girl and she clings to me.

"It is good she has bonded with you," he tells me. He turns to his other children. "Let's take a walk."

"Shoes!" I say and all three children hurry to get their shoes on. Meeting Thomas's gaze I don't have the heart to ask. The truth is written all over his face. I start to cry, I can't help it. "I'm sorry, Thomas."

He nods, lifting Nikkos into his arms and taking Olympia's hand, before leading his children outside. Looking very solemn, Hektor glances over his shoulder at me and I try to force a smile through my tears. "It's okay, go with your father."

He nods, reaching out his arms for Atso. She shakes her head, holding on tight.

"The horses might come back," Hektor whispers.

With the promise of potentially seeing the mustangs, Atso goes to him and he takes her outside.

Alone, I ask Garrett, "Do you know what happened?"

"Not the details. Just that it was horrible." He comes over and kneels by the sofa. "Tell me you didn't really have the babies in a bathtub."

I shrug.

He presses on my stomach. It is tender, but not painful. "How's your bleeding?"

"Heavier than a period but not gushing—unless I pick up something too heavy. I'm learning my limits."

"No more lifting. You have us here to help you now." Shaking his head, he sighs with relief. "Was it a long labor?"

"A few hours. Stop worrying. If you want to do something, check out the babies. I think they're too small."

Hearing my concerns, he frowns and looks around the room. "Where are they?"

I tilt my head in the direction of the bedroom. "Far room. Tucked into a dresser drawer."

When he hurries to check on the twins, I race across the room to the window. I open the shutters and look outside, scanning the desert landscape for Thomas and the children. I can't see them and realize he must have walked with them down the rise. Creeping out into the courtyard, I don't have to walk too far before I catch sight of them sitting on the ground not far from the house. The sun is setting and it would make a beautiful photo, a father surrounded by his children, cast in a golden glow, except as I watch Olympia falls against him sobbing.

It seems so unfair that yesterday they were so excited, so happy following the births of the twins and today has to end on such sadness. I turn my back on their private moment and numbly walk back to the bedroom where I find Garrett has both babies stripped and laying in the center of the bed.

"Are they all right?"

"I think you're probably correct. They're a little small. I'd guess them at about five pounds each, but they were almost completely full term, so their lungs were well developed. They're pink. That tells me they're getting plenty of oxygen. They're not showing any signs of jaundice. All in all I think all three of you were damn lucky. Do you know how badly this could have gone?"

I press my fingers to his lips. "Sh-h. Just kiss me, tell me you love me, tell me we can go home and get our normal life back now."

My heart sinks when he pulls me into his arms and says, "I can kiss you."

It's a soft kiss, too gentle after our time apart, like he fears breaking me.

"And I do love you," he tells me as he lifts his lips from mine.

I seek his eyes for answers, worried he might have to leave and go back to Cincinnati, worried the danger I ran from may still be a threat in San Francisco even though Garrett and Thomas are now here to protect us.

He sits on the edge of the bed, pulling me down to sit beside him. "We can't go home."

"What does that mean?"

"It means just that. It would be too dangerous to resume our old lives. The people Thomas works for wanted me to go into some kind of protection program, new identity, new town, new job. Say goodbye to everything, including you and Thomas. I refused."

"And?"

"Now the three of us are starting over together. Actually, I guess the nine of us."

"Starting over?" I repeat dumbly. I know what he's saying, my brain just can't accept it. No more Lewd Larry's? No more Jackie or Enrique? "God. Who are we supposed to be? What do we tell our friends?"

"It's just us, Ce, our friends are part of the past we don't belong to any more."

No. I can't accept that. I won't accept it. It's too much. Just becoming the mother to six children overnight was insane—too much to get used to, but this—this is unthinkable.

Baby Boy Number Two starts to cry, which wakes up Baby Boy Number One. I unfasten the front of my caftan, and lifting each baby and tucking them under my arms like footballs, I manage to get them both attached to nipples simultaneously.

"That's amazing."

"No cow jokes," I warn.

He holds up his hands. "Never. I'm in awe of you. You seem *different*."

* * * *

After dinner, prepared by Thomas, with all of the older children tucked into the bunk bed room, Garrett, Thomas, and I, along with the twins, gather outside in the courtyard. The air is cool, the breeze promising rain. I lay on the chaise, covered by a blanket thoughtfully carried out by Garrett. The babies are bundled in their sleepers, hand socks, knit caps, and extra towels.

Sitting side by side on the stone wall, my men each hold one of the babies. The sight makes me tear up. I cover my mouth trying to push back the emotion, finally able to admit to myself, if not them, that I was terrified I'd never see either of them again.

"I'm so glad we're all here together," I say, and I realize I mean it. We haven't spoken any more about not going back to San Francisco, but I've dwelled on it, running the gamut of emotions. I've settled on acceptance. Whatever is, is. As long as we are together, as long as our ménage stays strong, I don't care where we live or what name I'm called by.

"What are their names?" Garrett asks.

I shrug. "Baby Boy One and Baby Boy Two. I wanted to wait until we were all together again before I named them."

"Seems like we have a lot of names to pick out," Garrett replies. Looking at Thomas he asks, "What's your alias this week?"

"Garrett!" I admonish, thinking he was being hateful but then he rubs shoulders with Thomas and I realize they seem different too. Closer. More relaxed together than I've ever seen them.

Thomas brings me the baby he's been holding, and I attach him to my nipple, even though it's only been about two hours. Better to feed him while his brother's sleeping than to get them both awake and worked up.

He sits down on the ground beside me and watches his son nurse. He says softly, "I take it Garrett told you?"

I nod. "Enough. I'll have questions later. Right now I'm just so glad you are both here, that we're all together. We can stay together, can't we?"

He and Garrett exchange a look before he answers, "Yes."

"Any idea where?" I ask, nervously, not wanting to stay in the wilderness forever. I need some noise, and the children need to make new friends. I see us all killing each other if we were forced to be holed up in this small adobe house for very long.

"Anywhere we want that people won't recognize us. Basically, that rules out California, Ohio, and Maryland for certain," Thomas answers.

"Probably Washington and Oregon as well, I've taught a lot of D/s classes in Seattle and Portland."

I detach the baby, feeling a little frustrated. It's all starting to sink in. "What about Lewd Larry's? What about *The Darkness*?"

Thomas takes the baby and tucks him into the dresser drawer. Another glance passes between he and Garrett and I have to admit, I'm starting to feel a little left out.

Garrett carries the other baby over and tucks him in beside his brother. "I'm going to take them inside. It seems a little chilly out here to me."

Subtle, real subtle.

Thomas takes my hands. "Garrett's had longer to get used to this than you have. I've already apologized to him—repeatedly—for fucking up his life. I just realized that you haven't had a chance to even process this. Everything has just *happened*."

"I blew up your house," I admit suddenly. "I'm sorry."

"I'm glad you blew up my house, that's how I knew where to look for you."

I hug him close. "I like our old life, even though it was going to have to change, because of the twins, and the children. I don't want to think it, but maybe this is for the best. We all have to redefine our relationships now."

"Meaning not just you?"

"That sounded mean and bitter. I didn't mean anything by it, but let's face it, if we went back to San Francisco and *our normal*, Garrett would be putting in fourteen hour days at Lewd Larry's, you would still be off trying to save the world, and I would be—"

"Stuck at home with six kids?"

"No! That isn't what I was going to say at all. I love your children! What I was going to say, before you interrupted—"

"Sorry."

"Was that if none of this had happened, I'd have a housekeeper, two nannies, and Enrique to make sure my life didn't change either. I'd be trying to divide my days and nights between The Oasis and *The Darkness*. I wouldn't have gotten a chance to bond with any of the children." I start to cry, hormones making me much too emotional. "I like nursing my babies, and rocking Atso and Nikkos asleep. I like discovering something different about Olympia and Hektor every day. I never thought I'd say it, but I like being a mommy, I don't think I need a nanny. That doesn't mean that I want to stop being Kitten completely, or that help with the housework wouldn't be appreciated, it just means that I want to find a balance and none of us had balanced lives in San Francisco."

"I did."

"That's because you're Superman, you have all those crazy special powers and you don't require sleep."

"So not true." He tickles me, making me laugh. "I *need* sleep."

I sigh heavily, snuggling against him.

"What's bothering you most?"

"Explaining us—three adults and six kids under one roof—we're gonna need a damn good cover story."

"It'll be easier than you think."

I push my nose into his chest, smelling him, and need rolls through me. "I wish I wasn't sore, I want you so bad."

"Did you tear?"

"I don't think so, just cramps, lots of blood."

"You like pain and blood isn't going to scare me." Thomas pushes open the front of my robe and lowers his mouth to my breast. "Besides, I want a share of my sons' bounty."

As his mouth closes over my nipple, I bite my lip and stare up at the stars. *God is watching.* "Doesn't this just seem obscenely wrong to you?"

He shakes his head, tugging my flesh with the movement.

I want him. Now. I arch my back, pressing my breasts up. He sucks on my nipples, drawing hard. Heat and a tingling sensation flushes down my breasts. Milk starts to flow freely from the breast he isn't sucking on. "Oh! Fuck."

"Relax." He keeps pulling, sucking on my nipple, and the gown on the other side soaks through. Pushing my breasts together. He sucks both nipples at the same time. My uterus starts to cramp, but it cramps in waves along with the sucking, and isn't a bad thing at all. It feels amazingly good. It happened earlier, when I was nursing the twins, but I couldn't admit I felt horny as a result of feeding my babies. That seemed *so wrong*. This doesn't seem any more right.

Thomas raises up and kisses me, filling my mouth with warm milk. I swallow, feeling disgusted, and turned on, and confused all at the same time. "Thomas!"

"Everything you're feeling is natural. Enjoy this. This is what it feels like to be a sensual woman. This is what it feels like to be a mother."

"Holy crap."

"Women should share these secrets. Pregnancy and childbirth and nursing are all wondrously erotic parts of being female. Don't fight the arousal flowing through your veins, embrace it."

I kiss him, sliding my tongue into his mouth, tasting my milk. My pussy tightens with need.

He tugs down the blanket and pushes up my caftan to massage my bare thighs. I'm wearing underwear and one of Atso's diapers to catch my flow since I didn't come prepared with any feminine products. *So not sexy.* I'm embarrassed. "Don't look."

"You're joking, right?"

He slides his hands up my thighs and over my pelvis, pushing down on my tender uterus. I cry out, I can't help it. "You like that? You like that pain?"

"Yes, fuck yes."

"We can't have sex, not for several weeks, risk of infection is too high, but we can *play* a little."

I push my pelvis up against his palms. "God, I *want* you."

"Sh-h, relax. Let's go inside, get you comfortable. Anything we do is going to be messy."

Thomas carries me inside. It's barely lighter in than out. A single kerosene lamp burns in the corner. We find Garrett stretched out on the couch. I blush, realizing the door and all the windows are open. I'm sure he's heard every word. I hold out my hand as Thomas carries me past the couch to the bedroom. Our fingertips barely contact but it seems electricity passes between us in that soft touch. Shaking his head, he stands up.

As Thomas lays me down on the bed and starts undressing, I hear Garrett locking up the house before following us down the hallway.

Once inside the bedroom, Garrett closes the door. He brought the lamp with him, and I see that the babies are already here, tucked into the drawer on top of a low table. Seeing them is like a cold shower. *What was I thinking?*

Garrett echoes my thought. "I don't know what you're thinking, but it will be weeks before you can safely have intercourse."

Thomas rolls his eyes. "You think I'm going to fuck her the day after giving birth? I might be a sadist, but I'm not an idiot."

"Then what?" Garrett demands.

"We're going to make love. You're welcome to join us. I need to reconnect to the both of you. This week has been emotionally devastating for all of us. Can you honestly say you don't want to blow off some steam?"

"I can't have sex in front of the babies," I say.

"They're asleep. They're safe. At two days old, they couldn't care less."

"I feel...*bad*...for even wanting to." I catch Thomas's face between my palms, making him meet my gaze as he sits down on the bed.

Leaning nearer, Thomas whispers against my face, "Embrace your emotions, sweetheart. Feel how high they can take you."

"I'm trying." I look at Garrett for censure, but as Thomas unhooks the front of my caftan, exposing my full breasts, it isn't judgment I see in his expression. He lowers the flame on the lamp so that only a soft glow lights the room and starts to undress.

Garrett lays down on the other side of me.

Thomas angles up on his elbow, so that he can look down at me. I feel like I still look pregnant even though my stomach has shrunk greatly. He rubs my stomach gently, with soft teasing strokes, meant to arouse. Garrett cups and strokes the breast nearest him. I know he wants to suck my nipple, but the last conversation we had on the subject was following Panda and Jako's performance and I was adamantly against any such *play*.

I really enjoyed Thomas sucking my breasts outside.

"You can suck my breast if you want to."

Garrett smiles and whispers, "Thank you," before lowering his mouth to my nipple. He sucks so softly, yet draws deeply. Need shoots down my spine to my core and I rock my hips. Thomas folds open the caftan the rest of the way. He slides down my panties, pulling the diaper away.

I panic, beseeching him with my eyes. Even though we've had messy sex before when I was on a period, this is different. "We can't. I'm bleeding. A lot."

In answer he holds up a folded towel and slides it under my hips as he promises, "No intercourse."

He lowers his mouth to my other nipple so that both men are nursing from my breasts. At the same time they slide their hands over my stomach, gently, teasing strokes meant to drive me mad. They both roam lower, finding my clit, massaging my slick labia lips. I try to not think about the blood, but neither one of them want me to ignore it. Thomas draws his wet fingers up my body, leading a dark trail. I'm happy for the soft lighting. I couldn't bare being under a spotlight.

Garrett too draws a path of blood between my thighs. He's the realist. "If your flow gets too heavy, we quit. Right now, your arousal is helping your uterus to clear and shrink, so the slightly heavier flow is acceptable. If you were in the hospital a nurse would come in about every hour and push on your uterus for the same affect, but it wouldn't be nearly as pleasurable."

Nice to have a doctor in the house to explain things. My joy diminishes greatly. I don't want to think! "Kiss each other."

The two men kiss each other directly over my face. I stretch my neck so that my lips graze over Thomas's stubble covered cheek, while they kiss. They turn their heads at the same time so that the three of us are kissing. Much better. This I like. I don't know whose tongue is in my mouth or who is biting my lip. I slide my tongue between both of them, tasting each one of them together, separately, again and again. "I want to suck on your cock."

"You need to be more specific, love. We both have cocks," Thomas answers sarcastically.

He's right. "I want to suck Garrett's cock while you fuck him from behind."

"That's very specific." Garrett chuckles and maneuvers into position straddling my shoulders and holding on to the headboard. He slides his dick into my mouth.

Thomas too maneuvers around and I know that he is taking a little extra time, massaging Garrett's anus with his fingers, stretching him, opening him.

The room smells musky.

I know when Thomas pushes his cock into Garrett's ass, Garrett's muscles tighten and his dick goes slightly softer. I bite down, pulling against his stiffness with my teeth, making him grow harder again with my roughness.

Between the three of us, we manage a rhythm and as Garrett's dick bumps against the back of my throat, it is pleasurable. Sometimes I think my uvula could orgasm if given half a chance. I don't want this to stop—ever. I love being here, with them.

Garrett comes first, pulling out so that his semen streams over my face. Thomas follows close behind, his last few strokes stronger, more forceful as he realizes Garrett has pulled out. Each thrust up Garrett's ass forces a little more cum out of his dick. I try to catch the sweet liquid with my tongue. *I love this. I love this.*

"Fear of danger is ten thousand times more terrifying than danger itself."

Daniel Defoe, *Robinson Crusoe*

CHAPTER 26

KITTEN

I awake alone in the bed and for a moment I can't breathe I am so afraid, but then I hear Thomas's older children playing outside and have to assume he is with them. They wouldn't be laughing and playing if he'd disappeared in the night. Or at least I believe they'd be clinging to me if anything was wrong. Strangely, I miss the weight of their bodies pressed around me and over me like a big puppy pile.

Atso's shrill squeal of delight comes through the open window and I am able to relax even more.

I wouldn't let them play outside the courtyard, even though I was fairly certain there wasn't another human being closer than a hundred miles. I wasn't so sure about scorpions, rattlesnakes, or God knew what other deadly varmint, that might lie beyond the walls.

A deeper voice comes through the window. Thomas. He doesn't sound happy.

Sitting on the edge of the bed, I push the wooden shutter closer to the wall and peek behind the white lace curtain. I can barely see Thomas, a shoulder. Leaning back against the stone wall enclosure, he is facing the other direction.

Garrett comes into view, and I see his is holding one of the twins. "Be reasonable. I am more than capable."

"It isn't your ability I question. There is no necessity."

"I believe there is."

Thomas pushes off the wall and as he walks he bounces. I stifle my laugh as I see his actions are keeping the other young son quiet. My breasts feel heavy already and just the thought of nursing the babies makes them tingle.

"You are not circumcising *our* sons."

Circumcision? I cringe just thinking about my sons' screams of pain.

"I forbid it."

I grimace. If this was just a power struggle over our babies' foreskins, that would be one thing, I really don't think flesh is what the argument's about. This is loss of power, pure and simple. Thomas holds all the cards—where we will live, who we will become—and in some ways it doesn't seem fair. I feel as lost and alone as Garrett. Well, maybe not as alone as Garrett, he is after all the consummate showman and playboy, but I'm feeling alienated too. I can sympathize.

Very softly I hear Garrett say, "I'm circumcising the twins, Thomas. Like it or not."

Pulling on a big, flowing caftan robe, I run for the door.

By the time I reach the courtyard, both twins have been deposited into the wooden drawer and my two men are squaring off. I clear my throat. With dark, angry expressions they turn and look at me. I scrunch my face into the tightest, sternest look I can give. "You will not quarrel in front of the children. If this is going to happen, take it into the desert."

Looking over the wall to where the children are playing in the sand, I plaster a huge smile on my face and call, "Breakfast!"

The children come running inside. By now they know the routine. Hektor gets the bowls down from the cabinet and the cereal out of the pantry, Olympia measures powdered milk and water then shakes the container to mix it, Nikkos and Atso both reach simultaneously to be picked up. I heft one toddler on each hip, thinking they both gained ten pounds each in the last few days. That or pushing two babies out of my body really did sap all my strength.

"Ommy, ommy." Atso presses her palms to my cheeks and pushes, making my lips pucker so that when she presses her mouth to mine it is a kiss.

"Mommy," I say. It seems important she learn to use English words since we don't know where we are going and Arabic may cause unwanted notice. The idea will be to blend in and not be noticed at all.

I don't miss the look that passes between Hektor and Olympia. For a moment I fear I've overstepped my bounds so soon after their mother's death. I feel horrible and fight emotion I hadn't realized was brimming under the surface. Feeling like I am in imminent threat of hyperventilating, I want to run into the bedroom and slam the door. I want to hide from this responsibility.

I can't.

I am the mommy now.

Moving slowly and purposefully, I put Nikkos into a highchair and watch Hektor and Olympia out of the corner of my eye. Hektor puts four bowls on the table and fills them with cereal. Olympia pours the milk, putting very little into the bowl intended for Nikkos and no milk in Atso's. When she is finished, I sit the bowl on Nikkos's highchair tray.

I sit in one of the chairs, holding Atso, and try to get her to take one of the banana flavored cornpuffs. She pats my cheeks. "Mommy."

Oh, shit. Now she says mommy.

I meet Hektor's gaze as he is pushing a spoonful of cereal into his mouth.

"Aunt Celia?"

I jerk and look at Olympia.

She is twirling her spoon in her bowl and not eating. She doesn't make eye contact even though she said my name. "Should we all call you mommy now, too? Instead of Aunt Celia?"

I don't know what to say.

I don't even know what to think. Aside from the tears they shared with their father, they haven't cried. I hated my father and almost had a nervous breakdown when he passed. How can they be so calm?

I watch her spoon swirling in the bowl and grab her hand to stop the motion. "Olympia?"

Her gaze meets mine, and I see her eyes are brimming with unshed tears.

"I am so sorry your mother is dead. I can never replace her in your heart."

She comes into my arms, sobbing, and I still don't know what to say. I've had years of experience working as a grief counselor in my father's parish, but nothing I experienced there prepared me for this.

"I want Mama."

"I know, baby, I know." I kiss her hair and she seems so very warm, not feverish, but warm. "I was only eight when my mother died."

God, did I just say that? Why did I tell her?

She pulls back, looking at me with wide, wet eyes. "Your mother died too?"

"Yes."

Hektor leaves his seat and joins his sister. He puts his hand on my arm. Sensing something is wrong, Atso squirms in my lap, fussing. I readjust her so that she can reach the cornpuffs in her bowl.

"Was your mother's death horribly gruesome?" Hektor asks.

What child asks that question? What did Thomas tell them?

I drop my face and nod. "I was with her when she died. She had hung herself with a rope around her neck, and I tried to hold up her weight."

Oh God. Why I am telling this?

The pain in my heart feels like I am there, like I am the young girl again, trying and failing to save my mother. Silent tears slide down my cheeks, but I don't wipe them away. "I tried to keep her alive."

Hektor and Olympia fall into my arms as I weep silently. Atso reacts with a sudden outburst of tears, frightened, and Hektor and Olympia are suddenly sobbing too. I am definitely not getting the mother of the year award here.

"I'm sorry, I'm so sorry," I tell them, hugging them, kissing them both. "It was a very sad day the day your mother left this world. She was a good woman, a strong woman, and I know she loved you."

Looking up I see both Thomas and Garrett standing in the doorway between rooms. Thomas is as pale as a ghost when he turns and walks away.

"I tell you the truth, whoever hears my word and believes him who sent me has eternal life and will not be condemned; he has crossed over from death to life."

John 5:24

CHAPTER 27

THOMAS

The desert is still and silent in the early morning heat. I ran as far as I dared, and I dare not be too far from my family. I needed to be alone.

Celia is bonding with my children and she makes it seem almost effortless, making it seem Latisha was expendable, replaceable, and I know my bitterness is unfair. This situation is not Celia's fault, and yet she is the only one of us behaving with any dignity.

Hearing Celia reveal the secrets of her soul, I know that she knows better than any of us what my children are feeling and she is willing to relive her pain to help them experience their own. I wish I could be as selfless.

Does pride makes me cling to the rules of manhood so that no one will see me express my sorrow? Or fear that my loved ones will not follow if they see anything less in me than strength?

Pulling off my shirt, I stand beneath the blazing sun. I need to feel the heat as a reminder I am alive. Stretching out my arms, I present myself to my God.

I want to share with him the ache ripping open my chest.

I know death intimately. I have caused a death wound and waited patiently for the last breathe. I have fought to keep a fallen comrade breathing and cursed the moment I knew they were gone. I have experienced the sense of a soul leaving a body, and so I believe there is *an after* beyond life.

I. Ache.

My heart, my mind. There is a heaviness in my gut that hurts as badly as a bullet.

I never thought I'd grieve Latisha so deeply.

I do not know if I am better off or worse for having seen the proof. Yes, I believe her death, but after seeing, I know she was executed, a single blow separating her head from her body.

No one held her as she died.

No one heard her last breathe or felt her soul fly.

I sob, thinking about that. She didn't deserve to die thusly. If it had to be so, her murderer shouldn't have been such a coward. He should have held her as closely as a lover. He should have experienced her death with her.

Standing, I scream. Raw. Primal. The valley echoes with my grief. I believe the ground beneath my feet rumbles. I scream until there is no more air in my lungs and I fall forward, oxygen deprived.

"Grief, grief, I suppose and sufficient
Grief makes us free
To be faithless and faithful together
As we have to be."

D.H. Lawrence, *Hymn to Priapus*

CHAPTER 28

GARRETT

Thomas is somewhere out in the desert, running, because Lord knows he needs to stay in shape. Heaven forbid the "secret-agent man" should get a little soft around his middle.

Celia. My *Kitten*. Covered in children, like a marsupial on the prowl, not just the twins, each attached to a nipple, but four more, surrounding her, touching her. Always touching her!

I am in a fucking desert! Surrounded by dirt! Dirt and rock *and more dirt.*

Life as I know it is over. Lewd Larry's. Home. My friends. *God. My friends.*

Jackie.

Morgana.

George.

Enrique.

What do I do now?

I walked away once before, away from my family, my fiancée, my future medical practice, with no more promise than the promise of love. *Tony*. Then, I think it was more hormones than true love, and the allure of living openly with my homosexuality and depravity.

Surely my ménage means more to me now than Tony ever did then, so why was it so easy to walk away from all I'd ever known and loved?

Why is it so hard now?

I want to sneak away and call Jackie. I need to hear her voice. I need to know that she is okay. I need to tell her once more that I love her. I always have, and I always will. I know I don't have to worry about Jackie. Jackie Sandburg always was and forever will be a survivor.

I want to call her!

Who will I ever be able to talk to that knows me half as well as she does? It is pure selfishness that would put her life at risk just to hear her voice again.

God.

Who will take care of Morgana now? Or Enrique?

Thomas assured me an agent, posing as an attorney, would travel to San Francisco with enough money to hide any trail we left and enough lies to trick our friends into not coming to look for us. He will get my affairs in order.

I have turned Lewd Larry's completely over to George.

By now it is probably a done deal, signed, sealed, delivered.

Lewd Larry's is mine! Damn it! It's mine!

I am tired…so fucking tired…and this insanity has only just begun. How will I ever survive an entire week? Months? Years?

"Can you watch the twins a second?"

"What?" I look up at Celia, knowing she asked a question, but not having a clue what she said.

"The babies. Keep an eye on them while I take Atso to the potty. Thomas said every hour so there's no accidents."

I nod robotically and watch her lead Atso away by the hand. The other three children follow her.

I sit in the chair she vacated and look down at the sleeping twins. It would be so easy to circumcise them right this second. *Snip. Snip.* Foreskin gone. Bending over I push up a sleeper, push down a diaper. So easy—if I had a scalpel.

"What are you doing?"

"Nothing," I say too quickly and my voice comes out too high pitched and sounding guilty. "I was seeing if he was wet."

I can see it in her eyes that she doesn't believe me and without a word she picks up the drawer and carries it outside to a shady corner of the courtyard. I follow her, but am stopped dead in my tracks, hearing a scream.

Celia and the children are just as alarmed.

The scream seems to go on forever.

The children hug Celia's legs and she looks at me, fear and questions she's afraid to ask out loud filling her eyes.

"It's okay," I assure her, praying that it is. I look at my watch, knowing Thomas took off half an hour ago. If he isn't back in thirty minutes I'll follow the animal trail he took even though I have no idea how to track him if he went off trail.

* * * *

She sees him before I do and commands the children to stay with me as she takes off down the steep trail leading from the house.

"We want to go with her," Olympia demands.

"Not this time. Celia needs to talk to your daddy."

Crossing her arms, she stomps her small foot and gives me a look that is terrifying. I try to cajole her, "You used to like staying with Uncle Gar."

Her bottom lip pouts out, and her eyes fill with tears. "I want my Mommy."

Beside her Atso and Hektor turn on the waterworks, both of them wailing. "Mommmeee."

Oh God.

I have truly been transported to hell.

And then the twins wake up and start to cry.

"I have found the paradox, that if you love until it hurts, there can be no more hurt, only more love."

Mother Teresa

CHAPTER 29

CELIA

The trail is steep and rocky, too much for the flip-flops I left the house in. I yank them off and step carefully with bare feet. I'm so relieved when I find Thomas; I throw myself into his arms. "Are you all right?"

"I'm fine."

"We heard a scream."

Thomas pulls me into his arms. His skin has been warmed by the sun and his shirt is soaked through with perspiration, but I am so relieved he is not injured I don't care. I hold him tight. He kisses the top of my head. "I'm sorry I scared you. I needed to vent."

I look up into his face and his body shadows me from the sun so that I can see his features. "I thought as much. I'm so sorry. I should have never allowed the baby to call me mommy and then the older ones would have never—"

His mouth closing over my lips stops me from saying anything else.

I'm an idiot.

His pain has nothing to do with what I said. My words might have triggered the reaction but the ache was already there.

Pulling away, I cup his jaw. He is growing a full beard and his stubble is still stiff. I will be glad when it softens. I rub my hands back and forth, enjoying the prickle. I think he enjoys it too, because he closes his eyes.

Wrapping my hand around his neck, I pull his face down to kiss me again. "I don't think I'll be able to wait six weeks."

"Is that what Garrett told you?"

I nod.

"It's safe once you have stopped bleeding for a few days."

"He is a doctor. He should know what he's talking about."

"What he is is a pain in my ass."

I rub my hands down his back and reaching his buttocks, squeeze tight through his shorts. "Pain in your ass, huh?"

"Yesss," he hisses.

I bite his cheek. "I think I'll be more agreeable to your time table."

He moans when I bite harder.

I want to cause him pain.

I push his shirt up, baring his chest, and bite, sinking my teeth deep into his pecs. He grabs the back of my head and forces my face tight against his chest, making it impossible to bite or even breathe.

"You know I have something you can chew on if you need to use that mouth of yours."

Still can't breathe.

He releases me, and I suck in air. "Please, Lord Fyre. I need *you*."

He unbuttons and unzips. I gladly drop to my knees, needing to service him, wanting to heal him. I want to make him forget Latisha ever existed even though I know he will think of her each time he looks in his children's faces. But not every child. Two of his children will remind him of me.

His erection springs forward, hard and ready. Before I even push his head into my mouth, I can taste him—the taste I've memorized as him—and salivate. I feel like an addict denied, I've never wanted anything as badly as I want his cock in my mouth.

His palm in the center of my forehead holds me back. "Why, *Sophia*, why do you want to suck on my cock?"

"I adore your cock."

"Why?"

I reach with my lips and teeth, trying so hard to gain access, but he holds me back, damn, strong, man. "I need to taste you, I need you to come in my mouth."

"Tell me why."

"Isn't it enough that I have missed you for months? Isn't it enough that I need you like I need air to breathe and food to eat?"

"That isn't the reason."

"Please," I beg, refusing to tell him the truth, and too overcome to think of a lie. "Let me comfort you. I am yours to use. Use me."

He releases my forehead only to grab me by the hair on top of my head. It hurts, but I don't care. He pulls me into him, insistently, and I gladly open my mouth to take him, but he pushes in too hard, too fast, too deep, making me gag and choke. My eyes water. He pushes deeper, and I gag and choke again. Tears slide over my cheeks. He pushes harder, deeper, and his length goes deeper into my throat, leaving me gagging around it. I'm past choking now, I can't breathe.

He uses my throat, deep, deep, deeper.

Vomit forces its way from my gut, and he pulls out only long enough for me to spit.

Catching his gaze, holding it, I watch his face darken with lust as I take his cock back into my mouth. This time it isn't him forcing himself deep, it is me taking him deep, swallowing him, milking him with the muscles in my throat.

"God, my love."

My love.

The emotion that's been riding me hard all morning strips me raw, and I give all of it to him in my gaze. *I love you, I love you, I love you. Please let me heal you.*

Thomas's eyes close, and his head drops forward. His lips move, I know he is saying something, but I can't understand the words, and then I *understand*. He is praying.

I release him only long enough to lick his shaft once, down and back, letting my saliva drip out of my mouth to make him slick. Wetter, I slide his shaft into my mouth, and he hisses with pleasure.

"Sophia." He growls my name softly, but it's a warning growl. He is coming—hard and fast and thick and creamy. I swallow and keep swallowing.

Holding onto his thighs, I pull him deeper into my throat as he jerks with a finality.

* * * *

Hearing the twins' screams, my mind goes straight to a bloody circumcision and I run the rest of the trail, Thomas close behind. When we reach the courtyard, all the children are crying but it is the twins I go to first, checking their diapers to make certain they are intact.

Standing, shaking from head to toe, I face Garrett and slap him as hard as I can. "How dare you!"

He backs way from me. "I didn't do anything."

"You put doubt in my mind, you mother fucking bastard!"

* * * *

The children are easier to console than I am. An hour later I am still shaking, and Thomas insists that I go to bed and rest. I don't want to rest. I want to hurt someone. Really hurt someone and Garrett seems like the most worthy target of my anger. Facing Thomas, I command, "Keep him away from my children."

I guess I sleep, I don't remember my mind ever shutting down to sleep. I kept arguing. Arguing with everyone, Thomas and Garrett, telling them that I didn't want to sleep, didn't need to sleep, but then I wake up realizing I did.

I lie still on the sofa, listening intently, and hear thunder in the distance. It is a low rumble, and I don't fear it because it seems far, far, away. Rain would be wonderful. The cool breeze coming through the windows is very nice.

I realize that the darkness isn't just due to the approaching storm. It is dusk, and I've slept away the entire day.

I think the babies must be hungry, but feeling my breasts, they aren't full.

I almost feel like I recently nursed them, but I couldn't have because I was sleeping.

I slapped Garrett.

Master.

I wonder what the punishment is for slapping Master?

I don't know if I want to find out, but two soft male voices draw me out of bed like a magnet. Passing the children's room, I peek in and see four sleeping children. The sight makes me smile, and I wonder to myself how it was so easy for them to steal my heart.

Garrett sees me first and stands quickly. He starts toward me, not waiting for me to come to him, and my heart races. I expect now I will find out the exact punishment for being the worst slave ever.

I am surprised when he wraps me in his arms and pulls me into a hug. He holds me. He holds me so long it becomes awkward, and I have to force myself to relax in his embrace and not struggle. He keeps holding me and after awhile our breath matches, and I feel that I am sliding into and out of him. I think I am still dreaming.

Master says, "I'm sorry."

Definitely dreaming.

I try to wiggle out of Master's dream arms, but they hold me tighter.

"Relax."

My dream Master is definitely making me uncomfortable.

"I haven't been here for you."

No, no, no.

"If you ask me for your freedom, I will give it to you."

"That isn't what I want."

"Really?"

"I'm sorry I slapped you." I try to pull away, to look into his eyes, to make him understand, but he holds me tighter than a vise.

"I deserved it."

I go completely limp in his arms, and it seems to be what he was waiting for because he lifts me and carries me to the couch. Sitting, he positions me on his lap. I look toward Thomas for help, but he is sitting cross-legged in a thickly upholstered chair and one baby is propped into the bend of each knee. Either he is ignoring me and Garrett completely or he is completely enraptured by his sons.

"Look at me."

I do, meeting his gaze.

"There is no room in our relationship for lack of trust...or doubt. I've caused both."

I take a deep breath and hold his gaze, forcing myself to, because this isn't easy. *Spank me, beat me, but please don't bare your soul to me—that would hurt too much.* I know I'm not going to like the direction of this conversation. I feel it. Deep in my guts. I dread his next words.

"As your Masters, we've made some decisions regarding your future."

Oh, fuck. No, no, no!

"You, Thomas, and the children will leave as a family."

What about you?

"And I will be *your* brother."

"No!"

"Listen! This is the cover story we have decided on, and this is the way it is going to be."

I turn my head to look at Thomas, but he isn't looking at us. Garrett grabs my chin and jerks my head around. "I. Am. Your. Master. You will call me Lord Ice or Master in private."

I shudder, frightened, realizing I don't trust him and I do have doubts.

He strokes my shoulder, teasing his fingertips over my gooseflesh. "It's okay if you fear me while you learn to trust me again."

I can't breathe around the lump in my throat.

Lord Ice kisses my shoulder. "I like *your fear.*"

"Today I begin to understand what love must be, if it exists. When we are parted, we each feel the lack of the other half of ourselves. We are incomplete like a book in two volumes of which the first has been lost. That is what I imagine love to be: incompleteness in absence."

Edmond de Goncourt (1822-96) and Jules de Goncourt (1830-70), *The Goncourt Journals entry for 15 Nov. 1859*

CHAPTER 30

THOMAS

Celia is naked and sitting on Garrett's lap. He has been torturing her for over an hour with caresses and pinches meant to tease and titillate—meant to mind-fuck—meant to regain control, and as much as I'm enjoying the show, I'm exhausted. The twins sleep beside me in their makeshift bed. My only decision is whether I really want to walk to the bedroom or sleep in the chair.

My cell ringing is a jolt.

"Get out. Now!" Hearing Pepé's command over my cell, I react.

Standing, I command, "Get out of the house!"

I assume they will both obey as I run back toward the bedrooms. I grab Atso and Nikkos and hold them tight as I shout for the other two children to get out of bed. I am surprised when Celia jerks the now terrified and screaming Atso from my arms. She holds out her hand to Nikkos and he goes to her. His eyes are wide and he is obviously terrified, but he is silent. Without a word, she turns and runs. The exchange takes seconds we didn't have, but with six children to get out of the house I also know it will take all three of us.

Hector and Olympia have grabbed their Go Bags and I usher them out at a dead run.

We gather beside the house, Celia and Garrett are already buckling the two youngest kids into car seats in the back of the car she drove here. We don't have infant seats for the twins but I see they are still tucked into the dresser and it is wedged in the back on the floor. The car isn't safe, there has no doubt been reports to both sides concerning its make and model. Fleeing on foot isn't safe. *Fuck!* "Out of the car, into the truck. Now!"

"That isn't safe!" Celia argues, and I wonder if she even realizes she is naked. She's right though. We can't escape in the truck. She slides into the backseat, putting Olympia on her lap.

"Garrett? Where's Garrett?" she asks, sounding terrified.

He answers the question, climbing in the front. He went back for the diaper bag and Celia's caftan. Starting the engine, I shout, "You never go back!"

"She's naked!"

"Better her naked than you dead." I don't turn on the lights and drive off-road as fast as I can, following the wild mustang trail and staying close to the canyon walls. It is only fifteen minutes later that there is an explosion behind us. A fireball lights the sky. *Someone breeched the adobe's perimeter.* Between Halleck and Deeth I get us on a main road and second guess myself before turning and heading north on State Route 225.

I had no doubt we were in danger but having not stuck around long enough to find out who was searching for us, I now have no idea who *found* us.

I'd hoped we could stay there for several more weeks, because we are unprepared for a move and now we're on the run with no money, no food, and no clothing in an easily identifiable vehicle. I take a deep breath, forcing myself to remain calm and hoping no one asks what the plan is. We don't have one.

"Daddy, should you turn on the GPS now?"

I look in the rearview mirror, meeting Hektor's gaze. Why didn't I think of that? I have so many contingency plans to keep my children safe, but I didn't think about falling back on any of those plans. I smile at him, trying to appear reassuring. "What month is it?"

"June." He smiles back at me in, our gazes locked in the mirror. I wink at him and am relieved when he looks out his window, an expression of contentment on his face. Level headed, calm, he trusts *the plan.*

A quick glance at Garrett and Celia proves they don't. Pale, tight lipped, neither one of them signed up for this.

"Where are we going?" Garrett asks.

"The Twin Cities."

"Minneapolis-St. Paul?" he asks.

"Yes."

I look at him. He's staring through the window at the passing night. He's shaking his head, clearly not happy, but he doesn't say anything, and I don't say anything else. Eventually, everyone except the two of us fall asleep, and the tension bouncing between us is most unbearable. I decide it's going to be a long night.

"Are you up for this?"

He meets my gaze, and I seek answers in his face before returning my gaze to the road. After a long moment he gives me his answer, "Before you left, we were a ménage with problems, and now, for better or worse, we're a family. I can't be her husband wherever we end up, but you can be and I expect you to place her above all others. Your children. Me. And I'll do my part by being there for both of you."

"It is not wise to neglect the present for the future, for who knows what the future will be...?"

H. Rider Haggard, *Allan Quatermain*

Epilogue

Celia

Five months later

St. Paul, Minnesota

I settle the twins into a tandem stroller for an afternoon walk. I love walking around the neighborhood when the sun is high in the sky and the air has a crispness to it. Sweater weather. The leaves are changing color, making me realize how much I've missed seasons living out west. We have a large maple tree in the front yard, and it is a brilliant shade of orange. The falling leaves have been raked into piles for jumping into. The children are adjusting to our new home. Our new life. At the moment the oldest two are in school, both a grade lower than my husband would have liked, but after placement tests, the best place for them to start. The school's academic counselor assured us it was because their standards were so much higher than the norm, and we didn't volunteer that they hadn't had formalized schooling for over a year.

We have a three story brick English Tudor with nine bedrooms, seven bathrooms, and a full, finished attic, which we turned into a delightful playroom. The house is as old as the town, constructed in the eighteen thirties when houses were designed with parlors instead of great rooms and real wood was used everywhere. It has *history*. It seems ironic that we are creating a future here based on falsehoods and doing everything in our power to hide our pasts.

"Hello, Mrs. Xanthis!" My widowed neighbor across the road calls out to me and waves. She is ancient, her face wrinkled and her hair snow white. She keeps her hair pulled up into a tight bun, and she is so thin a strong wind would blow her away. I push the stroller across the street. "Good afternoon, Mrs. Karasavas."

I wasn't surprised when I learned our quiet neighborhood was predominantly Greek. My husband seems to have a knack for finding places where he unobtrusively fits in. Though he was disappointed there wasn't a private Greek school for our children nearby, there is an orthodox church and an independent private school not too far away. I'm sure we seem very ordinary.

The widow bends over and touches her arthritic, deformed finger to my youngest son's cheek. "He is so innocent. So precious. How many children do you have?"

I've told her several times already over the months we've lived across the road from her. "We have six children, Giorgios, Ourania, Dionissis. We call him Nissos. Anthanasia, Stavros and Thanos."

She nods and smiles. "Strong names."

"Yes, my husband named them."

"Your husband."

"Yes, my husband, the artist, Kyriakos, remember? He showed you his studio just last week."

She smiled, her eyes twinkling. "Oh yes, the handsome artist. He's your husband, you say?"

I stifle a laugh. "Yes, he's my husband."

"There's another handsome fellow I see going in and out. Is he married?"

"No, that's my brother, Gregar Leschova. He lives with us. I told you that. He teaches at the university." I smile secretively. It is still very hard to call him my *brother*. He is my lover, my Master, but this sweet old woman wouldn't understand our lifestyle, our life.

"Oh! A professor. My husband was an educated man. Poor thing died five winters ago. You say your brother's *single*?"

"Sophia?" Thankfully, my brother calls my name from the front porch. "Lunch is ready."

I turn and wave at him. "Coming!"

Excusing myself from Mrs. Karasavas is never easy, but I manage to get back across the road. *Eventually.* Hurrying inside, I am grabbed and pulled against a solid body with enough force to knock the wind out of me. The foyer is dark, and although I might have screamed given the last few months, I don't. A rough hand covers my mouth, but I remain calm. My pussy tightens, knowing.

"The boys are asleep," Master whispers against my ear. "Nissos and Atso are out in the studio with their daddy."

Even though the hold he has on me is painful, his voice holds promise of fun to come. "I'll take the twins to him. Go to the basement."

He releases me and I fall backward a step. He is already pushing the stroller toward the studio at the back of the house. I think I hear him humming. Our life is so very different here than what we had before, and I worried that of all of us Master would have the hardest time adjusting. He has, and hasn't. It was strange at first, a foreign world, with new rules of behavior, but once he started teaching at the university things *improved.* He seems happier and more relaxed than he's been in years.

I don't dawdle, knowing what is expected of me, and hurry through a small door and down a dark stairwell. I hate the dark, but don't dare turn on a light. I tread carefully, not risking falling, and when I reach level ground I feel my way to the center of the room.

It is pitch black and chilly.

I shiver, both cold and afraid of what hides in the darkness. Silly. Childish. As I undress, letting the damp underground air caress my skin, I imagine eyes watching me.

I. Hate. The. Dark.

I drop my sweater and undershirt on the ground. I unbutton and unzip my pants, hearing every sound. Creaking floorboards above, hissing and pinging pipes below. I pull my pants down as I step out of my shoes, then hop on one foot to remove my socks. I hear a tiny squeak. *No, no, no.* I know we have mice, I hope we don't have rats. What is taking Master so long?

Squeak.

My ass clenches in fear, and it is all I can do to pull down my panties and kneel on the cold, damp concrete floor. I lean forward, presenting myself in complete obeisance. *Hurry, Master.*

My ass is in the air and I feel horribly exposed as a cool breeze teases over my labia. I'm wet, ready, growing wetter with every passing apprehensive second.

Drip, drip, drip. The sound is from a leaking water pipe. Old house. Old problems. The dripping doesn't make me fret. The scurry of little mice size toenails on cement does. I whimper, I can't help it.

I jerk at the sound of a striking match, not realizing Master has joined me. I was too focused on my fear. He lights a small glass domed oil lantern and brings it near, casting a circle of light over my naked body. Squatting, he draws his finger down my bare arm. The touch makes me realize I am shaking. Cold? Fear? I think he guesses fear because he says, "I like it when you tremble."

"Master?"

"Sh-h, relax." He sits the flickering lamp on a low table and walks a slow circle around me. "Whatever should I do to amuse myself this afternoon?"

I let out a slow breath, only slightly less nervous now that he is here. I could think of a few things we could do, but he doesn't ask my opinion.

"Stand up."

I obey, moving quickly, glad to be off the cool concrete. He takes hold of my elbow and leads me to one of the floor beam supports. "Lay, with your head next to the beam."

Great, on the floor again. I lie down on my back.

"Pull your knees up."

I do, tucking so that my knees are close to my shoulders.

He produces a length of rope and, working by the light of the single flame, ties my ankles high and tight, pulling them toward the beam. My knees are pressed to my shoulders.

"Hands."

I stretch toward him, and he wraps my wrists similarly and ties them to the beam as well. I feel like a crab stuck on my back, opened, exposed. I watch as he gathers four sections of metal wire grid and attaches the sections around me on the floor, boxing me in. The hair stands up on the nape of my neck. I don't like where this scene is going at all.

He disappears into the shadows and returns with a small cage that holds four white mice. *Oh no. No, no, no!*

He lifts one of the mice out of the cage by its tail and dangles it over my stomach, letting me see it up close and personal as it struggles for freedom. "Isn't it lovely?"

"No."

"You don't think its little, red beady eyes are cute?" He brings the mouse close to my face so that I can get a good look at the mouse's eyes.

I shriek a little. "I don't like this."

"You will," he promises and lowers the mouse onto my bare stomach.

"Ahhh! No. P-please. D-don't do this." I am verging on totally freaking out. I try to relax and rationally tell myself it's only a single mouse. It isn't going to bite me. I am so close to safe wording right now—but I won't—and Master is counting on me not. We agreed, Lord Ice would only come out to play if I didn't safe-word and if I do…

"Oh God, oh God. Oh God!"

Master lowers the three remaining mice onto my chest and stomach. One of them sits between my breasts, looking at me, stroking his whiskers with his paw. The other three scurry around, running back and forth on my stomach. I am not sure who is more afraid—them or me.

Chuckling, Master blows out the flame.

I'm good for two minutes, maybe two minutes, it seems like hours. I cry out each time they move…and they move around a lot, running on and off my stomach, running around and under my ass. One falls and rolls off my stomach, its warm fur a caress I don't enjoy. Another runs over my exposed genitals, its small toenails feeling like a Wartenberg wheel. I shriek, scream, cry, beg. I don't safeword. I do piss myself, not even realizing I've pissed myself until I feel the warm liquid pool under my ass.

"Please! Lord Ice. Stop this. Please?"

An eternity later, the flickering flame returns and I realize he has been sitting beside me the entire time. He didn't leave. I look down, looking for the mice and find them huddled in a corner. Master collects them one at a time and puts them back in their cage though the last one he dangles over my face. "Kiss it on the nose."

I shake my head.

"Kiss the little mouse goodbye and thank him for playing with you today, or we'll start this game all over again."

He lowers the mouse until its face is almost touching my mouth. As soon as I pucker, I feel it bob against my lips. *Oh God.* "T-thank you f-for p-playing, Mr. Mouse."

Lord Ice takes the mice away in their cage, disappearing into the shadows. I try to pull myself together. I shudder and shake in my bonds.

Master returns and folds away the metal pen.

He steps closer, kneeling. He brushes his fingers over my mouth. "Did you like kissing the mouse?"

"Yes, Master," I lie.

He presses his lips to mine, a soft kiss, a chaste kiss. From his pocket he retrieves two small mousetraps. "I found these. Barbaric. I think we can put them to a better use than killing those adorable creatures, don't you agree?"

"Yes, Master."

He pinches my left nipple out and traps it between the wood and metal of the trap.

"Ahhh!" It hurts, radiating pain all the way back to my spine. Nursing has desensitized them some, but not enough.

He traps the other nipple.

"Oh God!" My pussy contracts with the pain, and suddenly my breasts are filling with milk from the stimulation. Within seconds I feel full, and want relief, then immediately think of my sweet, beautiful babies latching onto a nipple that was tread over by a mouse. *Ewww.*

Master rubs his hands over my skin and cups the underside of my breasts without disturbing the mouse traps. "How beautiful."

"I feel, dirty and disgusting."

He taps the trap, making the metal bite tighter. "I didn't ask."

Standing, he walks to a cabinet and takes out a thin birch cane. I know what's coming and brace for it as much as I can in my tied position. Returning, he doesn't announce that he is going to punish me. He just does. Striking the back of my thighs, my ass, the sweet spot that makes me scream because it hurts so badly it feels amazing. I want him to hit me there again and again, even though I know it will hurt to sit for a week.

* * * * *

There is a small shower stall in the basement, and I am more grateful than words can express when I am finally allowed to wash. I hated the mice, I loved the caning. As soon as the warm water hits my breasts my milk lets down and pours over my stomach. I bathe quickly, dry, wrap in a terry cloth robe and race up the stairs. Master preceded me and I meet him in the parlor, where he has the twins waiting.

If I said it wasn't strange going from scene to mommy, I'd be lying.

I sit carefully, my welted bottom yet another reminder of just how odd my life has become, not because I have the welts, but because I am nursing a child *and* I have welts.

With Master's help I attach each of my babies to a nipple and enjoy the sheer bliss of having them drain me. He leaves me with my sons, disappearing into the kitchen where there are shouts of, "Uncle Gar!"

Some things have changed. Some have stayed the same.

I hear the clang of pans and know that Gregar has started dinner. Most nights his nieces and nephews help—it's becoming a *family* tradition. That is a change I like very, very much.

I sigh contentedly when Kyriakos joins me, sitting at my feet and watching the babies nurse. I smile at him gently when he lays his head on my knees and stares up at me.

"What?" I ask softly, watching his face.

His hair is finally growing out. I like it long. He promises that this time he is going to let it grow so long he can sit on it, his beard too. The thought makes me smile, because he is my eccentric artist husband and that allows me to be a little odd too.

Where my robe fell open, he kisses my bare knee and then the inside of my thigh. "I was just thinking I'd really like to make love to my wife tonight."

I blush, I can't help it. My Lord Fyre in husband and father mode is quite adorable. I bite my bottom lip more than anything because Lord Ice didn't fuck me in the basement, he only built my need to a point of agonizing ache—and then set me free. "I'd like that too."

"I think it's Uncle Gar's turn to tuck all the munchkins in bed and read bedtime stories."

"Oh, I quite agree. It's the least he can do."

Kyriakos smiles wickedly, making me wonder if he was aware of Master's plans for the mice. I ask, "Did you know?"

He only smiles evilly and takes Thanos to burp. I lift Stavros to my shoulder and pat his back. I accuse, "You did."

He laughs openly.

"I hate you both!"

He shakes his head. "No, you don't. You love us."

I don't admit anything.

An hour later we are sitting at dinner and Giorgios can't sit still because he is so excited about his science project and his father told him he must wait until after we eat to tell me about it. The moment is finally at hand and he enthusiastically leaves the room…and returns with a small cage, holding four white mice. He brings them near, so I can get a *very close* look at them. It is all I can do to not scream.

"I'm going to teach them to run a maze!"

I gulp. "That sounds very exciting."

He nods and over his head I see both his father and his uncle turning purple with held in laughter. *Oh, the sadists I love.*

About Roxy Harte

Roxy lives in southwestern Ohio in a small town bordered by fields and railroad tracks with her husband and teenage daughter, two boisterous dogs, Petey and Jazzi, and two independent cats, Miss Kitty and Blackie. She can be found penning her next novel almost any day of the week. Writing for her is like breathing and sex, it is requirement for survival. However, she does have a few hobbies for when she is suffering from writer's block including gardening, hiking, and rock climbing. She loves microbreweries, Renaissance festivals, and hearing from her readers.

Roxy's Website:

http://www.roxyharte.com/

Reader eMail:

roxyharte@gmail.com

ABOUT THE CHRONICLES OF SURRENDER SERIES

Book 1: *Sacred Secrets*
Available in ebook from Lyrical Press

Book 2: *Sacred Revelation*
Available in ebook from Lyrical Press

Book 3: *Unholy Promises*
Available in ebook from Lyrical Press

Book 4: *Echo of Redemption*
Available in ebook from Lyrical Press

Book 5: *Cries of Penance*
Available in ebook from Lyrical Press

Book 6: *Vow of Silence*
Coming soon from Lyrical Press

WHERE REALITY AND FANTASY COLLIDE

Discover the convenience of Ebooks
Just click, buy and download - it's that easy!

From PDF to ePub, Lyrical offers
the latest formats in digital reading.

YOUR NEW FAVORITE AUTHOR
IS ONLY A CLICK AWAY!

LYRICAL PRESS INCORPORATED
WWW.LYRICALPRESS.COM

Shop securely at www.onceuponabookstore.com

GO GREEN!

Save a tree read an Ebook.

Don't know what an Ebook is? You're not alone.
Visit www.lyricalpress.com and discover
the wonders of digital reading.

YOUR NEW FAVORITE AUTHOR
IS ONLY A CLICK AWAY!

LYRICAL PRESS
INCORPORATED
WWW.LYRICALPRESS.COM

Shop securely at www.onceuponabookstore.com

LaVergne, TN USA
28 December 2010
210369LV00002B/61/P